Roger led her to the edge of the bed and she sat down. He slipped to his knees and kissed her. Her dark brown eyes were closed and she was smiling.

She held out a foot and he took her shoe off. It was black patent leather and extremely chic. He took off the other shoe. Her toenails were painted a delicate shade of rose pink.

She eased her skirt up. He had a perfect view of her thighs, a flash of smooth flesh and shiny black underwear. He was going to kiss the insides of those thighs very soon ...

Amour Secret

Marie-Claire Villefranche

HEADLINE DELTA

First published in 1996
by HEADLINE BOOK PUBLISHING

A HEADLINE DELTA paperback

10 9 8 7 6 5 4 3 2 1

ISBN 0 7472 5067 7

Typeset by Keyboard Services, Luton, Beds

Printed and bound in Great Britain by
Cox & Wyman Ltd, Reading, Berks

HEADLINE BOOK PUBLISHING
A division of Hodder Headline PLC
338 Euston Road
London NW1 3BH

Amour Secret

Shopping

It was the end of May, the best time of year in Paris, warm and sunny for sitting over a drink at a café table on the pavement, or strolling through broad streets, enjoying the day, ready for adventure if it should present itself.

What better time than three in the afternoon, when what needs to be done that day such as work, has been done, and a pleasant lunch has brought a feeling of well-being? Mid-afternoon, before the day sets into a pattern, is the right time for new vistas to open before curious eyes, for new friendships to commence.

Roger Chavelle was walking alone along the Avenue de l'Opera, no particular destination in mind, when he saw ahead of him and threading her way through the throngs of people hurrying to and fro a woman who enchanted him at the very first glance, even though he saw only her back and her face in profile.

He stepped out faster to catch up with her – he wanted to see her full-face, to observe the colour of her eyes, a dark velvet brown, was his guess. And to define the shapeliness of her bosom under her clothes. It was important to him to know about her.

He drew alongside just at the moment she halted in front of a shop window. The brief glimpse he snatched was enough to inform him she was in her mid-twenties, his own age. She was stylishly dressed in a tailored two-piece costume of steel-grey. She wore no hat, and her glossy hair was such a dark brown it was nearly black. Cut short like a man's and parted on the right, it swept back over her ears to a smooth fullness at her neck.

Roger drifted to the shop window and stood a metre away from her, pretending an interest in the display. To his astonishment it was a bookshop. He did not trouble himself with the titles of books on display, he was too occupied with his surreptitious study of the woman beside him – wondering what it was about her that attracted him so fiercely.

Her skin was clear and pale, her eyebrows were plucked thinly and tinted black. Her nose was long and straight, her lips dark red and full. Lipstick was the only make-up he discerned – but experience suggested a touch of powder on those smooth cheeks.

And her perfume, it was delicious – he beat his brains trying to recognize it. Not Chanel, that would present no difficulty. Givenchy perhaps; Balmain? In her ears were pendant tear-drop pearls. They were pretty ears – Roger felt a great need to kiss them and put the tip of his tongue into them. To make her sigh, to open her legs. She was very beautiful, he decided. More than beauty, she had an appeal that was ambiguously sexual.

A small red flower was pinned to her jacket lapel. A dark red little flower, picked to match the colour of her lipstick. She wore no blouse under her double-breasted jacket – delicate skin was exposed down to where the lapels crossed. How easy it would be to slip a hand inside and fondle a breast through her bra – which would be an elegant one, he decided.

They were not large, her breasts; he saw that from the fit of the jacket. But it would be tremendously exciting to hold them, to play with them – he was in no doubt of that. And through her close-fitting skirt he was able to make out the neat and round cheeks of her bottom. His fingers were trembling to stroke them and squeeze them.

Standing there on the avenue in the afternoon sun, pretending an interest in new books in a shop window, he was stripping her totally naked in the secrecy of his thoughts. Her body was long and slender and would be high-waisted, he could see that. Long-thighed too. Slender thighs. She would have a darling *lapin*, he decided – a thick triangle of very dark brown curls between her legs. He had a most powerful longing to slide her knickers down and see those curls, feel them and part them and touch the soft lips beneath.

Evidently she had seen all she wanted to see of books for the present – she turned away from the window and set off at a pace that was neither hurrying nor dawdling. Five metres behind came Roger, following her delicious perfume. But a certain confusion had entered his mind. A double-breasted jacket, short hair like a man – he found it impossible to ignore a possible implication of these outward signs.

Perhaps this beautiful stranger had no interest at all in men – their attentions, their bodies, their abilities – even men as fascinating as himself. Her interest might be in other women.

He followed her till they came level with the grandiose opera house – all columns and balustrades and bronze statues – keeping five metres behind. He was watching the immensely attractive up-and-down slide of the cheeks of her bottom under her grey skirt as she walked. He was lost in admiration of that suave rhythm.

But if she was left-handed and kept men away from her

... what atrocious irony that would be. He could visualize her naked, on her back on a bed, with her legs spread wide, while another naked woman lay between them with her tongue probing that dark-haired *lapin* and sending flickers of ecstasy through her, and making her moan *je t'adore* to the woman who was pleasuring her.

How beautiful a picture it was in Roger's mind. This charming stranger naked on her back, eyes closed and her body shaking as the other woman's tongue lapped over her secret little bud, her thighs pressed apart by delicate hands, a smooth cheek pressing against the inside of her thigh.

There was an empty tour-bus parked outside the opera, though it seemed to Roger a little early in the year for tourists. But foreigners were unpredictable. Twenty or thirty of them dressed in unsuitable clothes were down below in the cellars, hoping to see a masked and caped phantom. In truth all they would see for their money was a collection of fake jewels, musical scores and photographs of over-weight, dead singers.

Roger had no interest in the doings of tourists, his mind was engaged with an image of the dark-haired woman in the grey suit naked and on her back. And logic suggested that it would be the other way about. She had a strong and intelligent face – surely she would be the one to take the initiative. Her composure told the truth – she would make love to the other woman. It would be her tongue touching a soft and open *joujou*.

Not hers, but the other woman's legs would stretch wide apart to the little spasms in her belly. And moan in orgasm, writhing and arching her back off the bed. Roger saw the entire scenario in his mind, the enchanting stranger dominating the other woman with fingers and tongue. And he wanted frantically to touch her hand and stroke those fingers of hers. And touch her tongue and caress it with his own tongue.

They were past the opera house and she waited on the pavement in the Boulevard Haussmann to cross when the lights changed. He was near enough to reach out to touch her neatly rounded bottom – but he restrained his natural impulse. His desire to meet her was too urgent to run the risk of being dismissed as a bottom-pincher. The traffic roared past; cars, buses, vans, endlessly circulating. He wondered if she was aware of his presence just behind her or the force of his stare on her delicious cheeks.

The lights changed and there was a rush of pedestrians across the road from both sides – confusion, side-stepping and pushing where the two hordes met in the middle. Roger lost sight of her in the crush and stood aghast on the far side pavement glancing left and right in dismay. The crowd was even thicker here than it had been on the Avenue de l'Opera.

His heart skipped a beat when he caught a glimpse of her back twenty metres away and receding. He dodged through the press of people until he had almost caught up – then she turned into the Printemps department store. It would be very crowded in there – it always was. It would be all too easy to lose her completely on any of the ten sales floors.

She could vanish through any of the six or eight doors to the street. Boldness was called for. *L'audace, toujours l'audace*, as Georges Danton urged the revolutionaries in 1793. After that they guillotined him. She was waiting by the lift. When it came he followed her in. The doors closed and the lift was so crowded he was pushed close against her. He breathed in and out softly, his mouth open, letting himself be held against the woman he was pursuing.

His thighs were touching her neatly curved little bottom.

And in his trousers his stiff part was caught between his hot belly and the pressure from outside. So delightful was this sensation that Roger prayed she was going all the way up to the top floor and that more people would get into the lift and force her even closer to him.

She was half a head shorter than he, this desirable stranger, her back was to him and he could see the top of her glossy head and the parting of her hair and inhale her perfume. If he knew what it was he'd rush to the store's cosmetic department to buy her a bottle. But as things were, if he dared stick his neck out and glance over her shoulder, he just might be able to look down the front of her double-breasted jacket.

She got out of the lift at the fourth floor – it was a moment of complete desolation when she moved and the delightful pressure against his loins and belly disappeared. In the scramble around the lift doors of people getting in and people getting out, and nobody waiting a second for anybody, he was trapped and held as the doors closed and the lift rose again.

He'd lost her! She was gone, vanished somewhere in the store. He pushed his way out vigorously when the lift stopped at the fifth, using his elbows and muttering apologies that sounded more like curses. He dashed for the escalator, it was useless to wait for a lift going down. In his fevered imagination it seemed like an eternity before he was back on the fourth floor.

He ranged across the sales floor from wall to wall, from left to right between counters and displays. A sign informed him the beauty and hairdressing salon was on this floor and he made his way in that direction. But he saw her standing by a display of swimwear and breathed a sigh of relief.

He decided not to take the risk of losing her again. It

might be final next time. He walked right up to her with his charming smile on his face and spoke to her. *L'audace, toujours l'audace*, was what he said. Then he introduced himself and suggested they went to the café upstairs to talk a little.

She smiled and accepted without hesitation. She'd understood what he'd meant by the quoted words; that he was so eager to make her acquaintance he was ready to take any chance.

They sat at a little table under the huge multicoloured glass dome of the store's top-floor café and sipped little glasses of Pernod with ice. That was her suggestion – Roger found it quite enchanting as a drink for mid-afternoon. There seemed to be the slightest touch of decadence in the idea – the subtlest hint of perversity. It was how a little love affair should begin. Or so it seemed to him.

Her name was Marie, she said, Marie Brantome. She removed her thin grey suede gloves and laid them on the table and Roger saw the wedding-ring on her finger. His heart plunged steeply. She shook her head and told him he shouldn't believe all he saw.

That encouraged him. As did her next words.

'As for audacity,' she said, lowering her eyelids, 'it took you so long to approach me I thought you'd lost your courage.'

'You knew I was interested in you before I spoke to you?'

'You followed me all the way along the Avenue de l'Opera and into the store. In the lift I thought you were going to rape me in front of twenty people. It would have been amusing to scream and accuse you of molesting me and see how you got out of that. But then you stayed in the lift when I got out. I concluded you had lost your nerve and gone home. It was a surprise when you found me again.'

They chatted for half an hour without really saying anything. Marie offered no information about herself apart from her name, and Roger wasn't certain it was her real name. He too said very little about himself. He wanted to know a great deal more about this enchanting stranger before he opened his heart to her. His suspicion that she had lesbian preferences slowly faded when he saw that she welcomed his attentions. And found him attractive.

On the other hand, it might be a sham. She might harbour secret intentions of her own. There was only one sure way to find out, and that was to see if she would permit him to undress her. He stroked the back of her hand across the table and told her that he adored her and he knew a discreet and pleasant little hotel, not five minutes' walk away.

She looked thoughtfully for a moment at his handsome face and his ready smile. Roger held his breath – everything hung in the balance. Then she smiled and nodded and turned her hand palm up and clasped his fore-finger tightly.

The St Lazare railway station is just around the corner from the Printemps store. And as everyone knows, wherever there is a station there are always small hotels nearby. Ten minutes after Marie had agreed to accompany him Roger led her by the arm into the foyer of a small hotel he had visited previously. In truth, he'd been there several times before – the department stores of the Boulevard Haussmann were useful for picking up women.

He knew the man on duty behind the reception desk – there was an old arrangement between them. Roger passed a folded banknote over the counter into the man's out-stretched, ready hand and in return received a key. Brief smiles were exchanged, but no word was spoken – there was no need.

The man behind the counter looked oddly at Marie's back when Roger led her to the lift. Perhaps he was asking himself if she dressed in a severe suit because her preferences were for other women? Then why had Monsieur Chavelle brought her to the hotel and taken her up? If he'd made a big mistake he'd be in for a surprise when he tried to slip his hand between her thighs.

The lift was small and slow and creaking – it might well have been installed at the same time the Eiffel tower was built. The cage was open and decorative wrought-iron, suspended by a thick black cable from a great iron wheel up at the top of the shaft. Hardy passengers could look up and see the wheel turning slowly to haul them up to their floor.

Roger stood beside his new friend, facing forwards, ignoring the stare of the man on the counter below, who was hoping for a glimpse up her skirt as the lift rose creakily. They were hip to hip, seemingly paying no attention to each other. But one of Roger's hands was behind her back and he was stroking the round cheeks of her bottom through her skirt. She said nothing – only wriggled her bottom a little against his palm.

Then they rose through the ceiling and were out of sight from below. Roger lifted her steel-grey skirt at the back, to caress her bare thighs above her stockings. He slid his hand up to her cheeks, feeling them appreciatively through her thin knickers.

'I'm half in love with you already,' he murmured, mouth close to her ear and the sweet perfume of her glossy dark hair in his nostrils.

The lift clanked to a jerky halt. The corridor was too narrow for them to walk side by side and Roger led the way to room 236 and unlocked the door. She entered and looked around curiously while she removed her thin suede gloves and dropped them on the dressing table with her shoulder bag. Roger locked the door and crossed the room to draw the long curtains over the window.

They stood facing each other and close together near the bed, without speaking. Roger kissed her and passed his hands up and down the curves of her body like a blind man trying to learn them by heart. She unbuttoned his jacket and put her hands inside to stroke his chest. Her dark brown eyes were closed and she was smiling faintly while he kissed her.

He led her to the edge of the double bed and she sat down. He slipped to his knees and kissed her, his hands on her shoulders lightly. *The moment of truth*, he said to himself. She held out a foot and he took her shoe off. It was black patent leather and extremely chic. She stretched out her other leg and he repeated the process. The bulge in his trousers was impressive and most insistent.

He held her feet in his hands, noting how cool they were. Her toenails were painted a delicate shade of rose-pink.

'Take my stockings off,' she suggested.

She eased her skirt up. He had a perfect view of her thighs, a flash of smooth flesh and shiny black satin underwear. He was going to kiss the insides of those thighs soon.

'You have beautiful legs,' he murmured, a truism hardly worth mentioning, but what else can a man say at these so intimate moments with a woman?

He reached under the skirt to undo a stocking from her garter belt and slipped it down her long, perfect leg and off. Then the other one. Her skirt had lifted a little higher during the slow and delicate process of taking her stockings off and he now had a clear view of her underwear – that strip of shiny black satin between slightly parted thighs.

She smiled at him. He kissed her bare feet and slid his hands up her skirt and her thighs. Her legs moved further apart – his fingers touched the smooth satin that concealed her mound, that strip of shiny material between her legs, warm from lying close to her body.

'Show me your breasts, Marie,' he murmured, his hand pausing. She bent forward to kiss his eyes before unbuttoning her jacket and taking it off. Roger smiled in pleasure to view her rounded breasts contained in the cups of her bra. It was as black and shiny as her knickers. He wanted to kiss her breasts and lick them, suck their buds till she moaned in ecstasy. And he wanted to rub his stiff male part against them.

His hand dropped to his trousers as if he meant to unzip them and bring out his hard-standing part and put his urgent desire into action. Marie smiled to observe the move and reached round behind her to unfasten her bra. She let it fall on the bed and showed him her bare, high-set breasts.

'Do you like them?' she asked.

'They are exquisite – let me see you hold them.'

She cupped them in her hands and stared into his face as she played with them, lifting them, stroking them, jiggling them – and then plucking at their tips. Her buds were pink rather than red, resembling more those of a young girl than a grown woman. Roger put his tongue out a little, an unconscious gesture that showed her what he wished to do. His male pride jerked strongly inside his trousers and he laid his hand over the long bulge to calm it.

'Can you kiss them?' he asked.

She bent her long neck and forced her left breast

11

upwards as far as it would stretch and stuck her tongue right out. But the tip of her tongue came nowhere near her bud.

'Have you ever known anyone who could?' she asked curiously.

'Yes, once,' he sighed, 'try the other one.'

She pushed her right breast upward towards her mouth, but with no more success.

'You must kiss them for me,' she said, her eyes shifting from his hand as it moved slowly over his bulge up to his flushed face. Her tongue flickered in her open mouth.

She reached over to take his head between her hands and pull him towards her, until his face lay against the soft flesh of a breast. The skin under his cheek was smooth as satin – the warm smell of her skin was delicious, her perfume was breathtaking. He turned his head to kiss the pink bud of a breast, his folded legs were trembling beneath him. He drew the bud into his mouth and sucked it, as a small child would.

'Ah yes,' Marie sighed.

She undid the side of her skirt and raised herself so that he could pull it down and off. His fingers roamed over black satin knickers, feeling the smooth slippery texture. He slipped them under her bottom and down the length of her legs, and took them off and dropped them on the bedside table by the lamp.

Her thighs moved apart and he slid between her knees, sitting back on his heels to admire her dark curls. He touched them, he stroked the soft lips, he opened her with two agile fingers. He was enchanted by her *joujou* – he had seen very many of them and knew that no two were ever the same. Some had a loose, well-used appearance. Some had a girlish look even after being penetrated and ravaged. Others had a tight-closed and unwelcoming look, they required patience to make them blossom into ecstasy – and then sometimes became insatiable. Some had a plump and comfortable appearance, they were easily pleased and very grateful. Without being able to explain to himself why, Roger was convinced that Marie's was the sexiest he'd ever seen in his life.

Within the dark brown curls the protruding lips were long and thin. Roger was irresistibly reminded of a mouth pouting a little and demanding to be kissed. He'd never be able to think of Marie again without growing instantly stiff and wanting furiously to get inside her.

When he glanced up from her entrancing *joujou* to her face, he thought he saw a peculiar look in her velvet-brown eyes. A look of ambiguity was it, a trace of doubt, a feeling of uncertainty – something like that. *Oh la la*, he said to himself, perhaps we have at last reached the real moment of truth.

Getting her into a hotel bedroom was not the barrier. Now was the moment she would decide if male fingers feeling her between the legs were to her liking or not.

'*Cherie*?' he said, raising his eyebrows.

'Oh yes,' she answered and let herself fall backward onto the bed, her arms spread wide as if she were crucified – a position that indicated more clearly than any words that she was totally his to do as he pleased with. She still had her wristwatch on, a thin gold case on a mottled snakeskin strap – the effect was to make her look even more naked than naked.

Roger stripped his clothes off in five seconds. His long hard part stuck out and throbbed – but she didn't even glance at it. That puzzled him; in his experience women wanted a look at the length of stiff flesh that was about to penetrate them. Long or short, thick or slender – they

13

wanted to know what was going to slide up between their legs. Not this woman, it seemed.

Better not to advance too quickly. He went down on his knees again to stroke her thighs and belly with passionate hands. She sighed and trembled, her legs moved further apart, but to Roger the way she was lying with her arms outflung suggested a victim more than an eager lover.

He knew what to do about that – it was necessary to show her he adored her. He put his handsome face between her warm thighs and adored her with his lips – with his wet tongue and with his fingers. He adored her sexy, dark-curled *joujou* for so long and with such intensity that after a while she cried out shrilly as her back arched off the bed and she shook in ecstatic throes.

The instant she lay quiet again, Roger mounted her hot belly. He steered his distended pride into the wet and pouting lips he had been adoring – a long push sank him deep into her.

'*Ah mon Dieu,*' she moaned as he rode her with long, strong and rhythmic thrusts, '*ah mon Dieu . . .*'

She didn't lock her long legs over his back to hold him – she spread them as far apart as possible and lay wide open for him, passive under his urgent desire. Roger panted and thrust with a will until he spurted into her heaving belly – she screamed and bucked under him at his climactic moment.

Did her little scream arise from a second orgasm of her own? Or could it be a protest against what he was doing to her – who could tell? Perhaps she believed men expected to hear cries of pleasure from the women whose bellies they lay on. But that, he told himself, was too cynical – she had seemed to enjoy herself as much as he. And when he slid out of her slippery wetness and lay beside her on the bed

14

she turned towards him to put her arms around him. He kissed her and she kissed him.

Five minutes later she sat up and said she really must go. It sounded final to Roger, her announcement; it was as if she had satisfied her curiosity about him and that was it – goodbye and good luck. The thought was irritating – he'd never been treated like that by a woman. After he pleasured them they wanted more, it was for him to decide when the *affaire* was ended, not them.

There were folding doors at one end of the room. Marie opened them, standing naked with her back to him, to reveal washbasin, shower, bidet and toilet side by side. She glanced over her shoulder at him, her expression blank, then folded the door half-across to screen herself from his sight while she made use of the bidet.

Roger stayed on the bed, naked and thoughtful. He knew he was good-looking, women fell for him easily. He had a handsome face and a strong, graceful body. Women wanted to stroke him and kiss him. Most women, that was – but Marie had hardly looked at him when she'd slid off the bed and gone to the folding doors.

Roger was certain her preference was for women, not men. That belief posed an unanswerable question – why had she come to the hotel with him? Why had she let him undress her and caress her naked body? Why had she opened her legs for him?

She was out of sight behind the folding doors but he knew she was sitting astride the bidet washing her *lapin* with warm water and soap, removing the traces of his passion from her body. She would put her clothes on in another minute and comb her hair at the dressing table and leave. And he'd never see her again.

There wasn't enough room behind the half-closed doors

for her to stand up and dry herself properly. She pushed the doors back and advanced a step into the room, patting herself with a thin hotel towel. A sense of modesty may have impelled her to screen herself behind the doors while she sat with legs open to wash, but that no longer applied, it seemed.

She was standing sideways on to him, leaning forward slightly with legs parted, drying down between her thighs – a pose that showed the beauties of her breasts in profile. And the rounded cheeks of her bottom.

Roger lay on his side on the bed and watched her in delight – he was growing long and hard again. Her breasts were even more exciting now because he knew what they felt like. And what they tasted like when he licked them. He stared in admiration at her belly with its deep-set button. And he stared enchanted at her fleece of dark brown, nearly black, curls.

It was impossible to let her walk out of his life and vanish. He slid off the bed and stepped towards her. She turned to face him in surprise, caught sight of his stiff swollen part swaying in front of him and gave a little gasp. He pulled the towel out of her hand and dropped it to the floor, he was down on his knees to grasp the cheeks of her bottom and kiss her *joujou*.

'But I have to leave,' she murmured, 'I mustn't be late.'

Roger ignored what she said. When his tongue lapped over the soft lips between her thighs she sighed again and put her hands on his shoulders for support. He opened her with gentle fingers and flicked the tip of his tongue over her exposed bud. It made her gasp and tremble and say his name for the first time.

'Roger,' she sighed, 'yes, Roger...'

It was absurdly flattering to hear her speak his name at

such a moment – and immensely exciting. His stiff part was twitching wildly, he wanted to rub it against her thigh and her belly and slide it into her *joujou*, wet and moist from his tongueing. But in his mind her reaction had firmly established the belief that she preferred a pliable tongue to a stiff shaft in her.

In another moment she shrieked and gripped his hair and held his head close to her. Her body writhed to the movement of his wet tongue on her bud.

'*Ah Dieu*!' she moaned – the sudden orgasm turned her legs to rubber. She sank down quivering to her knees, hanging on to his shoulders to stop herself falling flat. Roger's tongue trailed up her belly and up the valley between her breasts, up her neck and into her mouth. He held her tight against himself, his arms round her waist, while he kissed her until she was calm again.

Her eyelids were lightly closed, her mouth slightly open. She put her arms around Roger and pressed her warm body against him in a gesture more affectionate than any he'd seen from her yet. But though she was tranquil, he was far from it. He was rubbing his hard-standing part on her bare belly, feeling that in a few seconds he would spurt furiously on it.

They were on their knees on the thin carpet, belly to belly – locked in each other's arms. Marie slipped a hand between their bodies and held his male pride for the first time. Roger's hand was behind her back, squeezing the cheeks of her bottom. It was complicated, kneeling like that, but he turned her around until she was in front of him and poised on her hands and knees.

In a moment his lips touched the smooth flesh. He was kissing her bare bottom fervently.

'I shall be late,' she murmured, 'I must go, Roger.'

'Not yet,' he pleaded, 'stay a little while, I adore you.'

The sight of her down on all fours with her bare rump at his disposal was extremely arousing. Her perfect breasts hung under her, waiting for his hands to take charge of them. But first he knelt close and slid his hands up and down inside her thighs to persuade her to part her knees wider.

Her dark-furred *lapin* was a joy to see – that soft mound with the long fleshy split, the lips moist and shiny from his tongue and from her own climax. He fingered it to make it wetter still – so wet and open he could slip two fingers inside easily.

Marie said nothing while he was so pleasingly engaged – not a word, not a sigh, her only move a quiver of sensation from time to time through her long beautiful body. She stayed firmly put, on all fours, letting him do what he wished, patiently awaiting his pleasure.

Which seemed to him strange. But this was hardly the time for the complexities of female psychology, he was much too aroused, his favourite part was clamouring urgently for attention. Hands on her hips to keep her steady, he set the red-purple head of his eager part to the loose wet lips between her thighs.

He stared down fascinated at his long length of stiff flesh poised to plunge into her. The sight was utterly entrancing – he knew if he delayed another minute he would fountain his delight on to her thick black curls. He'd adore watching himself do it, but not just now – he wanted to do it inside her, to assert his male right to penetrate her. He grasped her slender waist between his trembling hands while he pushed slowly into her.

'Oh,' she said faintly – the only word she had spoken for the past five minutes, if *oh* counted as a word.

18

To decide the exact meaning of it was beyond him – perhaps it meant, *Oh what a big hard lovely thing you've put inside me*. But on the other hand, if he was correct about her preferences, it might mean, *Oh what a nuisance men are when they push that thick ugly thing of theirs into a woman*!

Not that it mattered to Roger at that moment – he was mounted firmly on her rump, his precious part deep inside her. He swung his loins back and forth in a strong masterful rhythm that made her whole body shake. He lay forward over her back to grasp her hanging breasts and roll them in his hands.

He heard himself panting to the thrills that ran through him, he felt his critical moment approaching fast. He thrust harder into her wetness and she wriggled her smooth-skinned bottom against him to speed up his pleasure.

'Marie,' he gasped, *'je t'adore, je t'adore...'*

At once she rammed her bottom at his belly to trigger off his crisis. He gave a long cry as his climax flooded into her – she shook and panted as if she'd just run a marathon. *Marie, Marie*, he was murmuring, but she didn't answer.

He lay on the bed to rest while she washed herself behind the folding doors again. She dressed quickly, he watching the whole time. Her black satin knickers were on the bedside table where he'd dropped them when she let him take them off. She was close to the bed when she picked them up and put them on, so close he could have stretched out and kissed her smooth belly.

He didn't. He knew she didn't want him to. She'd set her mind on leaving and wanted no more of his fingers or tongue touching that darling patch of dark curls. He lay and watched her put on her shiny black knickers and her bra, her stockings – more and more of her long, slender body was concealed from his sight.

By the time she put on her beautifully tailored skirt and her double-breasted jacket, he was stiff again, from staring at her while she dressed. She pretended not to notice his condition as she bent over him and kissed his cheek. But for just an instant he felt her thin-gloved fingertips trail along his hardness.

'Where can I phone you?' he said. 'I must see you tomorrow.'

'You can't phone me,' she said, holding out the hand with the gold wedding-ring to make her meaning clear. 'I'll phone you if I can get away. Tell me your number.'

He recited it twice to make sure she'd remember. She touched him lightly on the lips and she was gone. Only the fragrance of her perfume lingered on the pillow to assure him it hadn't been a dream – she really had been there with him.

To understand her was impossible. She wore a wedding-ring but Roger didn't really believe she was married. She dressed like a lesbian, she almost behaved like one when he had her on the bed – and yet she had come to the hotel with him and had let him do all he wanted to her.

Evidently Marie Brantome was a woman of many secrets. So much so that she wouldn't tell him how to get in touch with her. And it seemed to him doubtful whether she would phone him. But when he went into the shower before dressing and leaving, he saw she had left her thin gold wristwatch with the snakeskin strap on the shelf over the washbasin.

He picked it up and kissed the glass as if were her hand – he breathed in the faintest trace of her perfume that clung to the strap. He fastened the watch around his sturdily standing part, the buckle underneath his pompoms, the dial lying on his shaft. It would stay there while he was hard, when he drooped it would slip off. The little watch said twenty minutes to five – he was sure now that Marie would come back to him.

Working

Roger Chavelle knew for a certain fact he was good-looking. Not because of what he saw every day in his mirror when he shaved, but because it was how he made his living. He was a male model.

On the morning after the encounter with Marie Brantome in the department store, he made his way to the Agence Drouet to check if there were any assignments for him. He was reluctant to go, in case Marie phoned. He'd expected her to call and ask if he'd found her wristwatch an hour or two after she left the hotel – but she didn't.

If she was married, which he doubted, she might not have been able to get in touch while this hypothetical husband was about. It was more likely she'd phone in the daytime. Roger wanted her to phone him so he could persuade her to meet him. He'd dreamed of her that night.

It was a vivid dream – though less a dream than a remembrance of a moment in the hotel room. Marie naked, pale skin and black hair – Marie letting herself fall backward on the bed, her arms spread as if she were on a cross. That watch on her wrist, thin gold case on the snakeskin strap. He was on his knees between her parted thighs, his hand on her patch of very dark curls.

He woke wet with perspiration, his stiff part standing out of his pyjama trousers. As full consciousness returned he found an uncomfortable and inconvenient thought in his mind. *I'm half in love with her*, he realized, *this is absurd – I don't know her*. He reached out for her little watch lying on his bedside table. It was almost eight o'clock.

Love or not, he couldn't stay in all day waiting for her call – if she ever did call. He knew so little about her he couldn't with any assurance guess what she might do. But he had to work. If he didn't work he'd go hungry. He'd be unable to pay the rent. Or buy clothes. He certainly wouldn't be able to afford to take Marie to cafés and restaurants and small hotels.

The Agence Drouet was to be found up three flights of stairs, in an old building on a busy street. The receptionist looked up from her typewriter when he entered and she greeted him warmly. She was a thin woman in her early twenties, with long arms and large round spectacles. She adored Roger, naturally.

'*Bonjour* Monsieur Chavelle,' she said affectionately. 'Please have a chair. Madame Drouet has someone with her but she won't be long. Would you like the new *Paris-Match* to read?'

Roger said pleasant things in return. He sat down to wait and glanced around the walls of this outer office. Everywhere there were large photographs, most of them of women – Madame Drouet's models were nearly all female, that's where the demand was. But she had a few men on her books. Roger's picture was up there by the window, a head-and-shoulders of him in an expensive hacking jacket of fine tweed and a dark blue knitted silk tie.

After he'd satisfied himself that his picture was present and correct in the display, Roger's attention turned very naturally to the pictures of pretty young women. The photos were fashion shots, the models were variously

shown in sleek evening frocks, chic daywear, short silk
nighties, underwear so fine you could almost see through it.
Whatever the makers had to advertise.

Roger particularly liked underwear shots that showed a
lot of smooth young skin. Lacy bras and smooth-fitting
knickers. If he was kept waiting long enough he'd go stiff
inside his trousers, just looking at these photos while his
imagination roamed free. It was not all imagination. He'd
made the personal acquaintance of several of these pretty
models and entertained them.

The entertainment continued after dinner in bed, that
went without saying. In the past two years he'd undressed
and kissed and caressed and made love to eight or nine of
the best-looking women in modelling. He'd never fallen in
love with any of them. They were friends. Even when they
closed their legs again.

One of them came out of Madame Drouet's office at that
moment – a tall blonde with a sleek figure and a graceful
walk; Nadine Bernier. Roger stood up to greet her, took
both her hands while he kissed her on both cheeks.

'Roger, *cheri*, I haven't seen you for months,' she said
with a devastating smile.

Nadine had long and beautifully-shaped legs, as he well
knew. He knew what it felt like to have those legs entwined
about his waist. What was also endearing about Nadine was
that she always smiled when she was being ravaged. She
didn't do it consciously – he'd asked her. It was a sort of
half-smile brought on by the strength of her emotions when
she lay on her back and a man she liked was on her belly.

'Nadine – you are more beautiful every time I see you,'
Roger declared. 'We must get together soon – I will ring
you to fix a date for lunch or dinner.'

'Yes,' she said, 'make it soon, *cheri*.'

He wouldn't phone and she didn't expect him to. They both had other interests, but they were being polite to each other. Then off she went, and the receptionist said Madame Drouet would see him now. He nodded and smiled while he lowered his eyelids for a heartbeat in a manner he knew was fatal to unattached women. She sighed and stared at him as he went into the inner office.

The owner of the business, Madame Drouet, reached across her desk to offer him her hand. He took it lightly and kissed it, a little courtesy never went amiss.

Madame Drouet was wearing a black Chanel two-piece today with a plain white blouse. She was middle-aged and elegant, friendly but shrewd. The colour of her hair changed at least once a year – at present it was a striking black and silver mixture and cut short, like an upturned basin on her head. She had diamond rings on her hands and a lot of make-up on her face – Roger guessed it took her an hour and more to prepare for the day when she got out of bed in the morning.

There was a Monsieur Drouet somewhere in Paris. But he'd been long since kicked out of the business and out of Madame's life because of his infidelities. Like Roger, the absent Drouet was very fond of young women in skimpy silk underwear that showed a lot of smooth bare skin and uptilted breasts. But his wife took strong objection to his excessive handling of the firm's stock-in-trade and the parting had been an acrimonious one.

The first time Roger went to Madame Drouet's office to see if she'd take him on as a male model, she seduced him with all the ease of long experience. If *seduction* is a possible word to use of a droll little episode involving a man of twenty-something who'd chased girls since his four-teenth birthday and an attractive woman in her mid-forties.

Seduction was the word Roger himself used later on his way home, grinning about this sudden and unexpected event.

He introduced himself, she smiled approval of his looks and his clothes. She looked at the pictures of himself he'd brought with him, she asked about his experience – as a model, that is. She stood up and came from behind her desk and walked round him slowly, studying him from each side. She put her hand under his chin and tilted his head upward.

She asked him to take off his jacket. She ran her hands along his arms, over his biceps and down to his wrists. She held them for a moment or two, his arms down and a little out before him. She was wearing an elegant white roll-top pullover that day and a black skirt. She was a good head shorter than he and into his thoughts came the realization that, because she was holding his arms out, his hands were close to her breasts.

He suppressed the thought. He was here to advance his career, it would be folly to annoy Madame Drouet, although he could not deny to himself, her costume jacket being open, that her breasts had an interesting appearance. Interesting, that is, for a woman of her age. His girlfriends had always been about his own age. His impression was that breasts lost some of their youthful spring and started to droop a little when thirty approached. And sag sadly at forty.

The pair under Madame Drouet's thin and close-fitting sweater were pointed and firm – perhaps a bra alone achieved that look. In other circumstances it might be interesting to find out – on the other hand why bother when so very many young and beautiful women were to be met on the streets of Paris every day?

Madame Drouet continued her close inspection of the new candidate for her agency to represent. She slid a hand over Roger's chest and belly — the ideal male figure was broad above and flat below, she told him — and the bottom should be not too large, but have neat round cheeks.

'Do I embarrass you?' she asked. 'It is very necessary to be honest and open about these things. To live by your appearance, you must be ready to let your appearance be judged critically.'

'Of course,' he said, 'I understand perfectly.'

He was struck silent to feel her hands on his bottom, feeling the cheeks briskly. Not just a casual touch to check their size and shape through his trousers — but a long and thorough feel.

'You've a good bottom,' she said, 'a pity your thighs are not a few centimetres longer, the distance from knee to groin is of some importance.'

That made no sense to him. He was about to ask her why when she reached down and ran her hand up between his thighs. Up from mid-thigh to groin — then down and then up again until she was gripping his thigh so high her thumb was pressing under his pompoms. Pressing tightly.

'You have good strong thighs,' she said in a husky voice, 'an excellent start, Roger. I hope I may call you Roger. My name is Gilberte.'

'A charming name,' he said, wondering if this could really be happening to him.

She was shameless. She stroked his half-hard part through his trousers with her whole hand. She explained to him that coyness was completely out of place in the world of modelling — male or female.

'Think of me as an expert,' she told him. 'Remember that I've seen more handsome young men naked than you can imagine. I'm an expert in lithe young bodies.'

Roger stared straight ahead, his mouth open and his

mind in a whirl as Gilberte unzipped his trousers. She had his stiff part out and clasped it with her diamond-ringed hand – it gave three or four quick jerks and she held it tighter.

'Be calm, Roger,' she said softly, 'leave everything to me.'

Her hand slid up and down; he was at full stretch and knew he was impressive. He stared down at the pointed breasts under her pullover and they weren't jiggling to the movements of her arm. This suggested they were tightly confined in a bra. To stop any sag, he thought, she is of that certain age when gravity causes even the firmest of breasts to droop sadly. But her hand on him was moving with the familiarity of long and frequent experience.

'Ah Madame...' he sighed. He wondered if this was a test that would-be models had to pass satisfactorily.

'Gilberte,' she reminded him.

'Gilberte, Gilberte,' he sighed, the sensations made him sure he would pass any test she set him. Should he put a hand up her pullover and fondle her breasts, did she expect that of him?

While he was trying to resolve that question, Gilberte pushed him backward until his legs met her desk. She suggested that he sat down – not so much a suggestion as a command that nobody in so intriguing a situation could possibly disregard. He perched on the edge with his feet on the floor and his legs splayed.

'I can see you and I will get on well together,' she told him while she undid her skirt and let it slide down her legs to her ankles. She was wearing scarlet knickers, bright scarlet with a fringe of black lace. A surprising choice – an unusual choice – for one of her mature years and standing, he considered.

'To become a successful model it is necessary to be adaptable – and I'm sure you can be adaptable, Roger,' she said.

He watched while she slipped the scarlet knickers right down. She bent over to take them off, stood up dangling them from two fingers and trailed them over his face for a moment or two. She dropped them on the desk beside him, and took hold of the stiff and throbbing shaft standing up from his open trousers.

'So far you measure up well to the preferred specifications,' she murmured, stroking his pride with one hand while she cupped his pompoms in the other.

Her bare belly was slightly plump, her thighs were short, but smooth and strong – they'd grip a man between them very firmly. The curls at the meeting of these useful thighs were dark brown and thick.

'Fifteen centimetres and a bit,' Roger murmured, thinking she was asking him the size of his most cherished part, 'and twelve centimetres in circumference.'

'Long and thick,' she said, 'that's good, Roger.'

She pressed close in between his splayed thighs, a finger in herself to open the way, her other hand steering his hard shaft to where she intended to have it. He sighed and pushed a little as he felt her warm flesh taking in the head of his prize part. She gripped him by the hips with both hands and impaled herself on him with a fast lunge.

'Yes, very satisfactory so far,' she murmured, 'now we'll see what you can do.'

She was bouncing her belly vigorously against him, a rhythmic dance that sent spasms of pleasure racing through his body. And evidently through hers too – her face assumed an expression of urgent yearning, eyes closed and painted mouth open. Roger slid his hands up under her thin white pullover to reach her breasts – he wanted to bare them and handle them.

Whether they were soft-sagging or firm-pointing didn't matter in the state of sexual excitement he was in – he felt the usual urge to get his hands on female flesh. He pulled the sweater up under her armpits and revealed a bra the same bright scarlet as her knickers, and also with a lace fringe in black.

He needed to get both his hands round behind her, to find the fastening and get the bra off. Before he could accomplish that, Gilberte speeded up her assault on his deep-embedded stiff part and he shook and moaned in pleasurable sensation. He was only a second or two away from spurting his desire into her, his hands lay over the bra cups, squeezing her breasts through them.

'Ah Gilberte,' he sighed, as his belly clenched in the first spasm of ecstasy.

'Ah yes,' she gasped, thrusting herself fast and hard against him. Her eyes were open now – they were a dark and opaque brown with shiny black centres. She stared into Roger's face, waiting to see the overwhelming sensation when it struck him.

He jerked inside her warm wetness and fountained his passion, crushing her breasts in his hands. *Ah, ah, ah, ah*, she moaned as her body shuddered in orgasmic spasms.

For his first five or six visits to her office he was content to participate in her expert little game of seduction. She knew how to touch him and stroke him almost to the shuddering pinnacle of sensation, but never let him quite reach it. Her diamond-ringed fingers would unbutton his shirt to slip inside and tickle his flat nipples with a skill that made him arch his back and sigh continuously.

By their second meeting he had become her virtual slave.

When she unzipped his trousers and put her hand inside, his emotions were so intense he was on the very edge of spurting his passion into her hand. She never permitted him – everything she did was for her own pleasure, his was incidental.

Her fingers would stroke his stiff and twitching flesh with a light and sure touch. She would make him perch on the desk with his trousers down to his knees while she did things to him that gave him devastating sensations, until he reached the point where she knew he could bear no more. Then she would open her legs and welcome him in – whisper in his ear while he thrust frantically, *You are beautiful, Roger, I adore you, cheri.*

Of course, thinking about it afterwards, he realized that she had been auditioning him, so to speak. When he came to know her better and understand her way of business it became apparent to him that male models had to be able to pleasure her as and when she required them to – or she wouldn't have them at her agency.

He passed her test satisfactorily – he was taken on, she found work for him; well-paid modelling jobs. This had been going on for two years since their first meeting. Nowadays when he went to her office he knew exactly what was expected of him.

The receptionist ushered him in. Gilberte reached her hand to him across the desk and he kissed it. The desk was nondescript, an ordinary polished piece of brown wood – but it had some interesting memories for Roger. By his reckoning he had in the past two years obliged Gilberte Drouet 217 times, in various postures, on that desk.

He perching on the edge with her standing between his thighs, she perching with her legs open while he stood between them. On her back on the blotter with her legs hooked over his shoulders while he stood close. She face-down on the desk and her feet on the floor, he lying over her back. And so on – this office desk required imagination and ingenuity – Gilberte demanded full use was made of it.

It would have been many more than 217 if he'd been to call on her every day. It would have been every working day of the week – Saturday mornings included. But to tell the truth, he was not overly pleased to pleasure Gilberte every time he saw her. That first time, long ago, it was amusing because it was unexpected. She had *seduced* him.

It was not until she'd pulled away from him, bare-bellied and making little sighing sounds of contentment, leaving his sticky part standing up out of his trousers – only then did he realize completely what had happened to him. He chuckled to think he'd been manipulated as if he were a girl on a casting couch.

After that, the weeks passed, and he was expected to pleasure her every time he went to the office. But he ceased to think it amusing. He did it, of course – he was by nature unable to say no to any good-looking woman who offered her body to him. But in his thoughts it was now like a husband climbing onto his wife's belly every night at bedtime. Not because he greatly wanted to, but because it had become a routine expected of him.

After the courtesies of kissing her hand across the desk – the scene of more urgent activity than Roger knew about – and after he'd said the appropriate things, he went around to her side of it. She was wearing a grey Chanel two-piece today, with a plain white blouse. He perched on the edge of her desk, legs spread – she unzipped his trousers with a casual flick of her hand.

'My favourite man,' she said, easing out the part of him

that pleased her most. 'Why don't you come to see me more often?'

Her fingertips were playing up and down to make him grow long and thick – a process which never took more than a few seconds.

'So big, so hard,' she murmured appreciatively.

Roger closed his eyes and let himself be played with. He soon became very aroused, Gilberte had an expert way of handling him – he began to murmur and sigh and shake. She knew how far to go with him – at the right moment her tantalizing fingers released his throbbing flesh. She stood up quickly to slip her skirt off her knickers.

They were pale blue today, he much preferred it when she wore bright, bold colours. Scarlet, azure, crimson, tangerine. She'd been wearing scarlet knickers the first time he met her and was introduced to her unusual way of doing business. His hands were trembling now, as she stood very close and he felt down between her thighs to her bare brown-curled delight.

'Now, Roger,' she said softly, her feet well apart.

After so sustained a degree of stimulation it required little more to take him over the edge. She had his throbbing shaft in her hand and guided it to where she wanted it to be.

'Very slowly,' she sighed as he tried to ram up into her.

She gripped him tightly between her fingers, controlling his penetration. But it was not a question of fast or slow, and she knew that. The sensation of sliding into her slippiness brought on his climax instantly. His hands grasped her shoulders and he wailed ecstatically as he began to spurt into her at the moment of entry. And all she had done to him led up to this – this was what she wanted to happen, to demonstrate to him and to her who was in control.

Five minutes later, when he had recovered a little and could be coaxed back to a useful hardness, she once more demonstrated her power over him – but in another way. She pulled him down off the desk and turned her back to him. She bent over and put her hands flat on the blotter. Without skirt or knickers, bare-bottomed, her cheeks were round and smooth to his hands.

From this angle of view her *joujou* was plump and fleshy – the lips were wet from what he'd done to her. He stroked it slowly, he parted the lips, he rubbed a fingertip lightly over her bud. She shivered in pleasure and said, *Yes, Roger, now* ... He pressed the swollen head of his male pride to that slippery slit and he pushed firmly into her.

'Ah, you do it so well,' she murmured.

His hands were on her hips, holding her tight, while he swung back and forth in a masterful rhythm. This second time it would take him longer, of course – Gilberte would receive a strenuous ravaging before he spurted into her again. Which was precisely how she intended it to happen – she would reach orgasm three or four times while Roger was labouring at her body.

'*Ah Dieu!*' she suddenly exclaimed.

Her first time had arrived and her body was responding to his strong strokes – she was gasping and pushing her bare bottom at him, driving him in deeper.

'Yes Gilberte,' he sighed, 'do it for me.'

He didn't stop when he felt the ecstatic tenseness ebb out of her body. He felt her parted legs shaking under her and put his hands under her belly to help support her. Her arms bent out at the elbows a little, but she didn't collapse on the desktop.

He maintained his rhythm, sliding in and out of her wet, warm flesh. She would never forgive him if he pulled out and stopped – she wanted much more from him than one quick orgasm. Gilberte was a woman of strong emotions and determination – she made her wishes clearly understood.

Inside his belly he felt tiny spasms of pleasure, warning him he was close to spurting. That would displease her, she was not ready for the final ecstatic detonation, not for some time yet. He slowed down his thrusts and willed himself to hold back his natural reaction. Not let it happen. Not yet, not till Gilberte was ready for it.

A quarter of an hour later she had reached orgasm four times. Roger was only hanging on by his fingertips, so to speak – his embedded part was jerking to a nervous rhythm of its own beyond his control – and his gasps were loud enough to be heard in the outer office. Gilberte too was in a state of frenzy, she rammed her bare bottom against his thrusts. But she was in control of what was being done to her.

'Now Roger!' she said sharply.

He stabbed furiously into her and she convulsed under him and squealed to the spurting of his ecstasy into her. It was a long hard climax for them both, noisy and convulsive.

When at last she was tranquil again and pulled away from him, Roger took a step back and sat down in her swivel chair. He was temporarily winded – his proudest part was drained of its pride and dangled out of his trousers, small, wet and limp. Gilberte pushed herself up from the desk on straight arms and she turned to look at him.

'That was marvellous, Roger,' she said. He could see drops of perspiration on her forehead. And on her bare plump belly below her white blouse. Her *joujou* was very wet – but not bedraggled. Roger was pleased and proud to see what he'd done to it – that wet and slippery and now loose-lipped *joujou* – dearest Gilberte might be a demanding monster, but there was enormous delight to be gained from satisfying her.

'I must tidy myself up,' she said. 'I won't be long, and then we can talk. I'll tell Celeste to bring you strong black coffee with a dash of cognac in it – you look as if you need it.'

She straightened her stockings and hitched up her garter belt and slipped her skirt on. But not her pale blue knickers, those she tucked in her handbag. With a little kissing gesture of her mouth at Roger, she went off to the toilet.

He sat slumped in the chair, gathering his strength after the vigorous exercise of the past twenty minutes. There were women, he said to himself, that you undressed and caressed and laid on their backs and played with till you were ready to slide on top and slip it up them and have a pleasing ride. With these women there was no strain, no effort, no compulsion, just pleasure.

When you were ready, you did it a second time and they adored you for it. If they stayed all night, you did it to them again. Then there were other women – Marie Brantome was one – who made you so furiously excited that you wanted to do it to them again and again and again until you collapsed senseless on the bed.

Then there was Gilberte. You didn't do it to her at all – you thought you did but you didn't. She did it to you. She knew how to excite you – she understood how to make you desperate to do what she wanted you to do. At the time you believed it was your own excitement driving you. Only afterwards you realized it was hers. That she'd had her way with you. By then you didn't care.

Roger was so engrossed in these considerations that he

forgot his trousers were gaping wide and his shrivelled stump lay soft and pathetic and exposed – forgot until the door swung open and in came the thin receptionist Celeste carrying a tray.

A moment of shock – it was too late to snatch his zip up! An idea came to him and he ran the swivel chair he sat in rapidly forward until his belly was jammed against the edge of the desk and his lower half was out of sight.

Celeste gave him a curious look but made no comment about his sudden movement. She was not stupid, she must have guessed what the reason was for his brief despairing activity. She must know that underneath the desktop his trousers were unzipped and his ruined pride completely exposed.

She gave him a cup of black coffee and left the other one for Madame Drouet when she returned. She stood back a step from the desk and folded her arms over her narrow chest. She had breasts so small they hardly showed through her clothes, Roger noticed, but she had a friendly smile on her long, thin face.

It was evident that she knew what went on when handsome young men came to the Agence Drouet to talk to Madame. Here upon this very desk. The thought came into Roger's mind that perhaps this Celeste even spied through the keyhole. If she did then she had seen his beloved part in full and energetic action, sliding up into Madame Drouet and ravishing her to squealing ecstasy.

He returned Celeste's smile warily.

'Is there something else you would like, Monsieur Chavelle?' she asked. He wasn't sure how to take it. Did she mean sugar in the coffee or did she mean something else? Was she offering to take her knickers down for him?

She was so thin and tall, this Celeste, she seemed to have

no hips or breasts or bottom worth the name. On the other
hand, it might be interesting to strip her naked and to
inspect her body and see how strongly or weakly she
responded to fingers between her thin thighs. Down in his
lap Roger felt a brief stir as his resting part twitched a little.

'Thank you, Celeste,' he said, his smile charming. But
before he had time to say more, Gilberte returned, looking
very spruce and businesslike.

She waited for Roger to get out of her chair so she could
sit down and he tried to convey to her by meaningful looks
it would be embarrassing to stand up while Celeste was
there. She didn't understand what he was getting at and she
began to look annoyed at his impoliteness in keeping his
seat.

Gilberte was angry, Roger was mortified – the only
person who was smiling was thin Celeste. Gilberte noticed
it and sent her back to her typewriter with sharp words.
When the door was shut behind her Roger pushed the chair
back and stood up to show his plight, apologising profusely.

'I fail to understand,' Gilberte said coldly, 'why you
should sit here with your trousers open after I left you.'

Roger said he'd been so completely overwhelmed by
making love to her that he'd sunk into a reverie and
forgotten his condition – he adored her to a point where all
other considerations slipped out of his thoughts.

By then she was sitting behind her desk, back in control.
And Roger, with trousers zipped up properly, was sitting
on another chair. She stared at him thoughtfully, hardly
listening to his unconvincing explanation.

'Where were you yesterday?' she asked, 'I expected you
here, after lunch.'

Yesterday! He was in a hotel bedroom with Marie
Brantome and she let herself fall backward on the bed – her

arms spread wide and her thighs open. Offering him her round perfect breasts and her dark-haired *joujou*. Making him fall in love with her. But he couldn't tell Gilberte that!

Exploring

Three days went by, three days which seemed to Roger
like three weeks. It was three days since his unforgettable
encounter with Marie Brantome in the hotel near the
Gare St Lazare. Three days of thinking about her and
wanting her – and being anxious about her because she
might phone while he was out. He played with the idea
of staying in his apartment all day long, but that was
impossible.

He fretted to think that if she called two or three times
and got no answer, she might conclude that he had given
her a false number because he didn't want to see her again.
But in truth it was a matter of life and death to him to be
with her to explain how he felt about her. And to undress
her and kiss her all over and make her lie on her back with
her legs apart.

She wore a wedding-ring – it didn't necessarily mean that
she was married. She didn't give the impression of a woman
who went to bed with a husband every night. Roger
doubted if there was a husband – he thought it much more
likely she lived with another woman. But if that was true,
then why had she agreed to go with Roger to a hotel? And
let him undress her and do so very many delicious things to
her?

Husband or female lover, the presence of either would

41

explain why she couldn't phone at some times of the day. If he'd given her his address, she could have sent him a letter – or a postcard. A meeting could be arranged. If she'd trusted him enough to give him her address – useless regrets; more than two million people lived in Paris. How could he hope to find her?

The telephone directory was of no help to him. It listed five by the name of Brantome. On the second day after their meeting, Roger had phoned them all. Three men and two women answered the phone and all disclaimed any knowledge of a Marie Brantome.

Roger almost persuaded himself that she didn't want to meet him again – she'd had second thoughts about him, she'd realized that she didn't really like what he'd done to her at the hotel. Her true preference was love with other women, he felt certain. Her visit to the hotel with him was an experiment she wanted to make – but it was not a success. He'd never see her again.

She rang in the early morning, before eight. Roger was in bed alone. He'd woken early to find that the pride of his life was awake before him and was very hard and thick in his pyjamas. He woke up thinking about Marie – perhaps he'd been dreaming about her again, he wasn't sure of that, but his mind was filled with an image of her.

She was standing naked in the hotel room, drying herself – he took the towel from her and knelt at her feet, his face pressed to her warm smooth belly. His hands were clasping the cheeks of her bottom – he wanted her to stay with him and she was getting ready to go. Then as if his prayer had been answered Marie sank to her knees and his tongue trailed up her belly and up between her breasts, up her neck to her mouth. They were on their knees on the carpet, belly to belly, locked in each other's arms.

Lying in his bed in the early morning, Roger was clasping his stiff part, thinking of Marie, wishing she were there. And then the phone rang. He looked at his bedside clock – it said twenty minutes to eight. No one rang him that early in the day. He was out of bed in an instant, rushing for the phone, convinced that it could only be her.

And he was right. He heard her never-to-be-forgotten voice in the earpiece saying his name. He sighed in delight and without waiting for further conversation he told her that he adored her and needed to see her. She ignored his passionate declaration.

'I rang to ask if you have seen my wristwatch,' she said. 'I lost it somewhere that day we met. I can't think where – in the café perhaps. Or the strap may have broken in the street.'

'Or you may have left it in a hotel room,' said Roger.

He was certain she knew exactly where she'd left it. She said nothing to his suggestion and he went on quickly – he wanted to impress on her his urgent need to see her.

'I found it after you'd gone and I've been taking care of it, waiting for you to ring me.'

That little watch was all he had of her, a precious souvenir, a keepsake of incalculable worth. He'd taken it everywhere with him, he slipped a hand into his pocket and touched it often, to remind himself how ardently he adored its missing owner. It was in his trouser pocket wrapped in a handkerchief when he ravaged Gilberte Drouet so lengthily against her office desk.

'Meet me this morning,' he said persuasively into the phone.

'You promise to bring it with you, Roger?'

A thrill ran through him to hear her speak his name. At least she remembered it! And his telephone number – that

43

must surely mean that she had a certain degree of interest in
him.

'But of course,' he said. 'Where are you now – at home?'

'Why do you ask?'

'So we can decide on a convenient café halfway between
us. No other reason. Can't you trust me a little?'

'There are complications,' she said vaguely, 'I can't
discuss them. Where are you?'

'On the Left Bank – near the Place Denfert.'

'I'm on the Right Bank,' Marie said. 'I'll meet you at
eleven on your side of the river. At the Café Flore – you
know it?'

'Of course,' Roger said, not pleased that she should even
ask him – not to know the Flore would be like not knowing
where the Arc de Triomphe was.

'At eleven,' she repeated, and rang off.

Naturally, he was there fifteen minutes early. A few stops
on the Metro and a walk along the Boulevard St-Germaine
– it was a fine sunny morning, perfect for the time of year.
He felt happy and optimistic – he was going to see Marie
again. He selected a table with care, out on the pavement
but close to the window of the Flore to be away from the
traffic.

He had also chosen his clothes carefully – he was out to
give an impression of casual elegance. He had noted when
he was with Marie in the hotel that her underwear and
shoes and her handbag came from expensive shops. The
couturier label in the jacket of her stylish suit impressed
him. She was a woman of considerable means – or lived
with someone who was.

She arrived ten minutes late. She was more beautiful
than he remembered her. Again she wore a tailored two-
piece costume and this time it was charcoal-grey with a faint

chalk-stripe. Black glossy hair cut short as a man's and parted on the right. Ruby studs in her ears and a little matching flower on her lapel.

'*Bonjour* Roger. I can't stay long,' she said breathlessly as he rose to kiss her hand, 'I'm pleased you found my watch.'

The elusive perfume that had attracted him the day they first met, he scented it on the inside of her wrist. His heart gave a bound and he experienced a happy little twitch in his trousers. Without doubt she also sprayed this alluring perfume behind her ears and between her breasts.

It was by Lanvin, her perfume, he was reasonably sure of that because he'd been back to the cosmetics department of Printemps and sniffed at every perfume they had on sale in order to trace the one that lingered in his memory. Marie wore no blouse under her jacket and he could see down to the divide of her breasts – if he dared lean over her, he would be able to catch a trace of that expensive fragrance ascending from between them.

Beyond that, as he recalled vividly from the encounter in the hotel room, she also dabbed the perfume in her groin.

His attention being drawn to her groin in this way, what was more natural than that he should think of that warm and pretty *lapin* between her beautiful legs. She'd allowed him to touch her dark curls, to feel the soft lips there, to open them and kiss them. And to slip his stiffness up into that pouting *joujou*!

These memories served to make him very hard indeed inside his underwear. He glanced down at Marie's lap – she had crossed her legs under her charcoal-grey skirt. He thought of silk knickers inside the skirt, and of the long soft lips pressed gently shut by her crossed thighs.

More than anything in the whole world, he wanted to

pull that skirt down and slip her knickers off. To uncross those thighs – to rain kisses between them ... and so on and so on ... he turned his attention with some difficulty back to what she was saying.

She sat down next to him. The waiter hovered, she asked for a small black coffee. Roger had already finished one – he ordered a glass of cognac.

'My watch,' she said again, 'may I have it?'

'It's a beautiful wristwatch,' he said, 'it suits you well – was it a present?'

She shrugged and pouted, not answering his question, and held her hand out for it. Roger had other thoughts. That watch was a symbol of what had happened between them in the hotel room – an afternoon he would remember all his life. He refused to hand it over without sentiment and see Marie put it on and forget about their fantastic afternoon. Or drop it in her handbag, as if the matter were closed and finished and forgotten.

He smiled his charming smile and put it on her slender wrist, fastening the snakeskin strap neatly. That done, he kissed her wrist on the inside and looked up into her face with admiration and urgent desire in his eyes. Her complexion was so clear, her eyebrows black and fine-plucked, her nose so straight and thin. He wanted desperately to kiss her, to have his arms around her.

'I am half in love with you, Marie,' he told her, 'it started as soon as I saw you in the Avenue de l'Opera. I knew instantly that I had to speak to you and find out your name.'

He tried hard not to sound heavy or boring. He didn't want to scare her away, now that she'd agreed to meet him.

She shrugged and smiled and said nothing. There was no

reason why she should believe him. He set out to charm her, to enchant her, to make her take him seriously. Without being too serious, that would never do. She was a woman of many secrets, he wanted to gain her confidence, to know those secrets, to understand her.

She had started by saying she couldn't stay long, but she was still there at the café-table with him after half an hour. This gave him to think he was succeeding in winning her confidence – or at least her interest.

'I want you to come with me to my apartment,' he said, taking the risk of rejection.

'But why?' she asked, her dark brown eyes calm as she stared at him unblinking. 'What is it you want?'

'I want you to know where I live – so you won't have to rely on the telephone if you want to meet me.'

He could see the hesitation in her eyes. The lost wristwatch had brought her to him – but when there was no question of that would she think it worthwhile to meet him? Because meeting him implied letting him make love to her – had she made up her mind whether her experience in the hotel room was amusing enough to repeat? Did she like the feel of his arms round her naked body and his stiff fifteen centimetres up inside her?

'You told me on the phone where you live but I've forgotten,' she said casually. He told her again.

'Oh yes, I know where it is,' she said, 'there's that Lion of Belfort statue standing in the middle.'

'And are there statues where you live?' he asked, hoping she would tell him her address.

'I think so,' she said vaguely, 'yes, I suppose there must be – but I've never really noticed.'

'And where do you live?' he asked, hoping not to sound as if he was pressing.

'In the eighth,' she answered.

It didn't help Roger at all. The eighth arrondissement stretched from the Arc de Triomphe almost to the Opera. It contained the most elegant and therefore the most expensive parts of Paris to live in. It was as he thought when he saw her underwear – Marie had a lot of money to spend. Or she was a woman on whom someone spent a lot of money.

Another five minutes' conversation of this and that and to his delight she agreed to go with him and see where he lived. There was not a moment to lose, she must not be allowed to change her mind. He pushed money under his empty glass for the waiter and walked her to the taxi-rank near the traffic lights, hand under her elbow – and all this inside two minutes!

He lived in the fourteenth arrondissement, in a street just off the Place Denfert-Rochereau – one of the busiest crossroads in all of Paris. His tiny apartment was on the topmost floor of an old building with no lift – he consoled himself with the idea that climbing up and down flights and flights of stairs was exercise that kept his figure trim.

Truth to tell, Roger's apartment was not impressive. A greedy landlord had remodelled the building to accommodate more people than the original architect had planned. As a result one of Roger's rooms served as sitting-room and bedroom – by day the bed was a divan to sit on. His other room served as kitchen and bathroom at different times of day – though the bath was only a shower.

But he had a balcony, just large enough to hold a long row of earthenware pots with bright red geraniums growing in them. And he tended them lovingly, he watered them and nourished them and persuaded them to blossom from late spring well into autumn.

Marie glanced round his small sitting-room. She said nothing, but she took in the divan under its sunflower-pattern cover – she had accepted Roger's invitation knowing what that involved. Her presence signified consent – while he proceeded with tact.

She took the only armchair. Her skirt was above her knees and at once Roger leaned over her and kissed her mouth, forcing her head back and her chin up. She put both her hands on his chest, perhaps to push him off, but perhaps not – he smiled at her and slipped his hand up her charcoal-grey skirt to stroke her above her stockings, where her thighs were bare and smooth.

'Now I'm here I don't know why I agreed,' she said. Her hands were warm on his chest through his shirt.

'Because I am falling in love with you,' Roger told her, 'and you know it.'

'What nonsense!' but she wasn't trying to push him away from her now. If she ever was.

His hand was moving softly between her thighs, his fingertips brushed over her *joujou* through her thin knickers. Her head was a little to one side – as if she was waiting for what he would say or do next. But Roger had said all he wanted to say to her. If she made a joke of it, that was her loss.

He kissed her again, a lingering kiss, and her mouth opened a little. The wet tip of his tongue slipped in – below, under her skirt, his hand felt its way down the top of her knickers until his fingertips touched the soft lips of her *joujou*. Now she was breathing faster – under her clothes his fingers had opened the dark-haired lips and were touching her bud.

'Ah Roger,' she murmured. He felt her little bud swell under his fingertip and he felt the moistness he was causing.

Surely if she responded so quickly to his touch she must feel something for him – some affection, some regard? But there was so much he didn't know about her that it was impossible to guess what her emotional reaction was.

'You know I am in love with you,' he said, his eyes gazing at close quarters into hers, his finger caressing her bud in a way that sent tremors of delight through her belly. He was standing half in front of the armchair, awkwardly bent over her, hand up her skirt. In a sudden surge of strength and desire he slid one arm under her knees, the other about her shoulders – and lifted her off the chair.

She was not very heavy – he was grateful for that. Four steps across the room to the divan, with her arms around his neck and her mouth clinging to his mouth in a blind kiss. He sat down on the edge of the divan, she held his mouth to hers for a long minute before releasing him.

They were beyond the point of needing words. She took off her jacket – Roger sighed when he saw the white lace bra that held her elegant breasts. She took that off, she slid her skirt down her legs. And her white lace knickers, showing the tuft of dark curls where her thighs met. She took off her stockings.

By this time Roger had shed his clothes too. He knelt to part her legs with his hands on her knees. He stroked the dark brown curls between her thighs, he opened the long warm lips with two fingers and was lost in admiration – another minute and he was going to slide into it and die of ecstatic sensations.

'Perhaps you love me a little,' she said, with a sighing note in her voice, 'more absurd things have happened.'

With all his heart Roger wanted to recreate a certain scene – it had haunted his waking dreams and his sleeping dreams – that moment in the hotel room when Marie fell backward onto the bed. With her arms spread wide as if crucified, that thin gold watch on her wrist, making her look more naked than naked.

He put his hands on her bare shoulders and pressed gently, to let her know what he wanted her to do. His mouth was on hers in a long kiss – but the past is not so easily restaged and dreams are not so readily turned into actuality. Marie had a different thought. She held Roger firmly by his stiff part while she drew her legs up on to the divan and stretched herself.

Whatever might be in his mind, he went along with her, willy-nilly, it would have been too painful to do otherwise. He found himself lying on his back on his own divan, Marie propped up on an elbow, staring down at the fifteen centimetres of hard flesh that she held in her scarlet-nailed hand.

'So much talk about falling in love,' she said, 'but in truth what you want is to push this stiff thing up between my legs.'

'Oh, yes,' he agreed, 'it is a most important aspect of being in love with you.'

'Is it?' she asked, her clasped hand sliding up and down his hot and solid shaft. 'I don't think I've ever been in love.'

'But you have a wedding-ring on your finger,' he replied, 'it must signify something.'

'Yes, but what?' she said softly. It was clear she wanted no answer to her question – perhaps there wasn't one.

And in any case, Roger was enchanted by then by the rhythm of her hand moving on his cherished part. She was leaning over him to stare in fascination at the leap and twitch of the length of flesh she was stroking. He watched her face. Her cheeks were a pretty shade of pink, her mouth was slightly open. He wondered what emotion was causing this – he didn't believe it was simple sexual arousal. She was complicated and mysterious, she lived in a universe he didn't understand.

'How lucky you are to be a man,' she said, 'all that you need to make you happy is to get *this* inside a woman. Twenty thrusts and you feel happy.'

'Not any woman,' he murmured, 'you, Marie, between your legs, that's what makes me happy.'

'So you say now,' she retorted, her hand flicking up and down in short and fast strokes that set off spasm after spasm in his belly. 'I am not a complete fool about men – anyone will do for you when this stands up long and stiff.'

She was studying the straining shaft in her hand intently. So much so that Roger wondered how much she really knew about men. He was convinced now that her sexual experience was with women, or with one other woman. It had been an experiment for her, the visit to the little hotel near the Gare St Lazare – he was sure of it.

It followed therefore that this visit to his apartment was an experiment also – to check whether she was right the first time or not. At least she was interested enough in him to experiment once more – which meant there was a chance for him.

He reached up to touch her mouth with his fingertips and then to stroke her glossy black hair. She looked so serious, leaning over him to watch the effect on him of her intimate attentions. To her this must seem very strange, he thought, because usually she is the one naked on her back with her legs apart. A woman's hands on her thighs, a woman's head between them, a woman's wet tongue on her exposed bud.

'You say you love me,' she sighed, 'then you must feel happy, now I am with you and naked. Are you happy, Roger?'

Her hand raced up and down – Roger's response to her question was a long gasp of delight as he gushed like a fountain.

'*Je t'adore*, Marie,' he gasped, '*je t'adore* . . .'

She waited for him to become calm again, his pride clasped in her hand. She was watching how it lost its stiffness and shrank after its sticky little moments of glory. She had made all that happen – Roger could discern the close interest in her eyes. He wondered what she was thinking, what her conclusions were. Was she impressed by what she saw or indifferent? When she spoke, he was astonished by what she said.

'Do you feel your body is your own?' she asked. 'You told me that you model for a living – that is to say you put on clothes chosen by other people and they take pictures of you. They tell you to smile or to look thoughtful, to stand here or sit there. They have mastery over you. Your body belongs to them.'

'No, I never felt like that,' he said. 'It is only a question of putting on suits or jackets or hats for an hour while photos are taken for advertisements. These people pay for my time, but they do not buy me or control me. What a strange idea!'

All the same, a trace of doubt crept into his tone because he suddenly thought of Gilberte Drouet; in her office, her back to him, bending forward with her hands flat on the desk, her skirt up round her waist to expose her bare bottom. His hands holding her hips while he slid in and out of her wet warmth. And he had to keep going until Gilberte was satisfied – four or five times to orgasm, never less for her.

You thought you were doing it to Gilberte, but in reality you were the one it was being done to. She made you want to do what she wanted to do. You loved it at the time – even if your body was not your own.

Marie heard the faint doubt in his voice and stared down into his eyes. She smiled briefly – not a smile of amusement but one that recognized he knew what she was talking about. Not that he was going to admit it.

She is talking about herself, he thought. She knows very well how it feels to be controlled by another. She has been naked on her back many, many times, with hands forcing her thighs apart. Another woman's hands. Expensive rings and painted fingernails.

What can it mean, he asked himself, this curious situation of hers, these ambiguous feelings? He had the intelligence not to ask. If she ever wanted to tell him about herself – her life or her feelings – she would do so when she was ready. To trust him with her secrets was a decision of importance – not one to make because he'd twice undressed her and seen her naked.

Marie lay down beside him, her long slender body close to him. She smiled while his hands moved over her, around her breasts and in the hollows of her armpits, the narrowness of her waist, under her to stroke the cheeks of her bottom. That smile wasn't for Roger, it arose from secrets in her mind, a memory of other times and other hands across her belly.

And yet her flesh responded to his caress. Her thighs opened, she sighed, her breasts rose and fell to her faster breathing. Roger's luminous brown eyes seemed to devour the body stretched out naked for his adoration. His sensitive fingers were gliding across her soft flesh, between her legs, over the secret bud he had exposed. He brought her to a delicate orgasm before he knew it and stared at her in sudden delight as she gasped and shook.

When it was over and she opened her eyes he was caressing her entire body with his eyes, from her face down to her knees. She gave a little sigh – whether contentment or exasperation, Roger couldn't decide.

'Do you want me to do it to you?' he asked.

'Yes, of course,' but she said it softly and he wasn't at all sure if she really meant it. He refused to let that trouble him – it was just one more mystery. She'd presented him with enough mysteries to keep him guessing forever. One more didn't matter. She was here with him, lying naked on his divan bed, that's all that mattered.

He slid down to the bottom of the divan – trailing his tongue down her belly so that she squirmed in surprise. He grasped her slim ankles and arranged her legs the way he wanted them to be. He knelt on the floor, his bare chest on the sunflower-patterned cover between her legs. His thumbs were in her groin, his head poised above her dark-haired *joujou*. She felt his tongue touch her firm little bud.

'Ah yes,' she murmured.

Yes, Roger thought, this is how you are used every night, the way that is familiar to you, Marie. On your back naked and your thighs wide open, a woman's tongue compelling you to experience pleasure again and again, making you shriek and cry *je t'aime*! She pays for your expensive and mannish suits, she insists your beautiful glossy hair is cut short and parted.

While Roger paraded these male fantasies in his mind, his hot tongue lapped over her little bud expertly – as expertly as any lesbian lover could do it, he told himself with pride. Marie's loins jerked up in near-ecstasy.

'*Ah mon Dieu!*' she sighed, her bottom squirming on the divan in her anticipation. Quicker and quicker his tongue-tip licked, and her breath came in short gasps.

'*Ah Dieu – oui* Roger!'

Her eyes were closed and she was lost in whirling sensation – but she knew who was giving her this delight. She'd spoken his name, not a woman's name, not Gaby or Michelle or Simone or any other female name – she'd cried out *Roger*!

In an instant his belly was flat on hers, his thighs pressing her thighs apart. He gripped his beloved fifteen centimetres of hard flesh and steered its head into her wetness. She shrieked as he pushed it into her to the limit.

'*Je t'aime, Marie!*' he said. 'You must believe me!'

With her hands grasping his shoulders, she jerked and panted in a flurry of fast hard movement, wriggling hips and quivering thighs. Roger held her face between his palms and kissed her as if he'd never let go. He felt the jolting of her orgasm through her body – and a moment later, he spurted forcefully into her.

When he could speak again he demanded, *Now do you believe me?*

Her fingernails moved slowly down the length of his spine.

'Does it matter?' she asked, with a little shrug under him.

Earning

On Thursday Roger met his friend Edmond Planchon at a café near Les Invalides. They were not greatly interested in memorials of old military triumphs – they liked the open expanse of greenery and the impression of space and tranquillity. It was not real, this impression. Only a few steps away traffic crawled noisily along congested streets.

Edmond was a male model too – this was how he and Roger had first come to know each other. Both of them were on the books of the Agence Drouet – it was of Madame Drouet they were chatting over a glass of red wine.

'She is a monster,' Roger said, but with a certain affection.

'Not the least doubt of it,' Edmond said. He was the same age as Roger, within a few months, and he had a thin black moustache.

'Her demands are outrageous,' said Roger.

'Completely,' Edmond agreed.

'When I am in her office I feel my body is not my own,' Roger continued, using Marie's words. 'Do you feel the same?'

'Do I feel that my body belongs to her? Of course not – what a ridiculous idea. You are too fanciful, Roger.'

'Perhaps. But all the same, you must admit that when Gilberte unzips your trousers and slips her hand inside, she's in charge of events. There is no point in arguing with her if you want to stay with the agency. She owns your body.'

'You have the right to say no,' Edmond reminded him.

'Ha! I bet you've never said no, any more than I have.'

'But why should I? It is easy enough to understand her. When she kicked Drouet out years ago she promised herself no man was going to get the better of her again.'

'Therefore she must get the better of them?'

'She believes she can control events because she can push you and me and others down on her desk and straddle whoever she has with her that day. She bounces up and down on him – she decides how fast, how hard – and how long the pleasure is to last.'

'You've proved my point,' said Roger, 'though your experience of her is not the same as mine. Once or twice she's made me lie on her desk while she rides me – but usually she bends over the desk with her clothes up round her waist and her knickers off.'

Edmond shrugged and grinned.

'She likes my face better than yours,' he said. 'She wants to see me when I'm doing it to her. She prefers not to see you.'

'Not true,' Roger retorted, 'I'm better looking than you. She makes you lie on your back because you're shorter than I am and you'd never get it into her, standing behind her.'

'Standing up or lying down,' said Edmond, 'the most important thing is to get up her and stay hard while she has four or five orgasms in a row. I made the mistake once of letting myself get carried away and doing it before she was ready. She went into a tremendous fit of the sulks. Has it happened to you?'

'I'm careful not to let it – but this only goes to prove what I said: your body isn't your own when you're with Gilberte. It is hers to use for her pleasure.'

'You take these things too seriously,' Edmond said. 'What are we talking about, after all? This is no affair of trumpets and drums – it is just a question of slipping it up the middle-aged lady who provides us with a better living than we could earn if we had to work in a shoe-shop. Why all this psychologizing? Do you feel ill or have you become religious or are you in love?'

Naturally, it was impossible for Roger to explain about Marie Brantome and his fiery passion for her. In his turn he shrugged and waved at the waiter for two more glasses of Beaujolais. And to stop Edmond from pursuing his question, he put a question of his own.

'Have you ever seen Gilberte's *nichons* bare?'

'Why no,' his friend said, 'there's never time for it – or so it seems. I have a good feel when she's kneeling over me on the desk. I've even had my hands up her sweater, but I've never got her bra undone. They feel a bit soft perhaps, but not bad for a woman over forty. Have you had a look?'

'No,' Roger admitted, 'I give them a squeeze when I'm up her from behind. She's got a firm and pointed pair when her clothes are on – but I think it's her bra does that. They'd flop if you had them out bare.'

'As neither of us is ever likely to see her stripped bare, it makes no difference.'

'Let's have a little bet between us,' Roger suggested, 'which of us can see Gilberte's *nichons* bare first. Not a quick flash, mind you – a good long look and feel. What do you say?'

'You're on. How much do you want to lose?'

'You're going to lose, *mon ami*, not me. Let's say a dinner at the Brasserie Lipp. Agreed?'

'Agreed. I shall enjoy eating at your expense. Shall we have a time limit on the bet? A month, say, starting from now?'

'When are you due to see her?' Roger asked suspiciously.

'Tomorrow morning at eleven. Are you afraid – do you want to call the bet off?'

'Certainly not,' Roger said firmly. 'We'll have a time limit, of thirty days, starting today. If neither of us manages it in that time, it's a lost cause. And if you can persuade her to let you have them out and bare in your hands tomorrow morning, I'll buy a bottle of best champagne to go with the dinner.'

'Done!' said Edmond. 'I shall phone you to tell you about it and you will have the priceless benefit of hearing how a master goes to work.'

'Advice on women from you is worth three times nothing,' said Roger, 'but I'll take a chance – I have an appointment later on today. A Madame Larose. I don't know her but Gilberte says she is a sympathetic person. God knows what that means. Do you know her?'

'Larose?' Edmond said thoughtfully, 'let me think. Where does she live?'

'Rue Laugier, up by the Etoile somewhere, very *chic*.'

'No, I don't know her. You must improvize, as we all do.'

Punctually at five o'clock, Roger presented himself to Madame Larose at her large and elegant apartment. He was newly bathed, his brown hair washed and shining, his face smooth and smiling. He smelled discreetly of expensive cologne and he was wearing a mid-blue suit expertly cut.

Beatrice Larose was a plump and shortish woman of
perhaps forty, her fair hair expertly arranged in long waves,
her broad mouth painted dark red. She wore a little black
dress and a strand of pearls. The bodice of her dress was cut
in the cross-over style and low enough for Roger to see the
deep cleavage between ample breasts.

She smiled at him – it was a cheerful smile and his guess
was that she was a good-natured person. She took the five
roses he had bought for her from a pavement flower-seller
he'd passed as he walked from the nearest Metro station.
To present flowers to unknown ladies was an idea of his
own – he hoped that it helped to create an atmosphere of
friendliness and cautious trust. But Edmond had found it
amusing when Roger told him about it.

'It's not flowers they expect from you,' he'd said with a
sly grin, 'it's a different sort of stem, thicker, if not so long.'

Edmond could say what he liked – Roger continued to
buy a few flowers when he went calling. Madame Larose,
for one, found his offering charming. When he kissed her
hand, she found that too was charming. In truth, as he soon
realized, she was determined to find everything about him
charming.

The sitting-room she took him into was furnished in
excellent and expensive taste. In Roger's experience, this
was the moment when women were inclined to go into a
panic, not knowing how to proceed. It was for him to help
overcome these temporary little problems and set the right
mood.

Before Beatrice Larose could sit down on any one of her
silk-covered sofas or chairs he took her hand in his,
standing close to her, and complimented her on her
costume. On her perfume and her pearls, on her complexion, on everything he could think of. Her pale blue

eyes stared at him a little myopically, her mouth was slightly open, but no words emerged.

None of what he said made much sense, it wasn't necessary. He rambled on amiably, putting her at her ease, giving her time to persuade herself that he was a friend – someone she knew in the past and had half-forgotten but was happy to see again. After all, he wasn't a plumber sent for to mend a water-pipe – he was there to make love to her, to give her complete satisfaction.

While he was chatting to her in this purposeful manner he was weighing her up in his mind. In his experience plump women were slower to reach an orgasm than the average – if there was such a thing as an average woman, but he was profoundly distrustful of that concept.

His assumption was that plump women had so much more flesh to stimulate. It took longer for the sensations to build up inside their tubby bodies to climactic release – there was further for the little spasms of pleasure to travel, through their big soft breasts and round-domed bellies. Therefore it took them longer. It made no difference to him, he was not paid by the hour.

As if it were his own home, he led her to the nearest white silk sofa. They sank down, sitting so close together his thigh pressed against her thigh. The trick was to convince these rich ladies they were being courted by a true admirer – that enabled them to appease their conscience.

Women needed the romantic touch. They became uneasy when they recalled they were paying a charming young man to make love to them. Much better for him to play the role of seducer – so then they easily convinced themselves that they were compelled to do what they wanted to do all along. Against their better judgment of course, this business of having their knickers taken down.

'Beatrice,' said Roger, 'I am so happy you invited me to come here today. You are delightful, truly delightful.'

While he was speaking he slipped his hand into the cross-over bodice of her stylish dress and clasped her left breast. It was the size of a small Charentais melon, he thought, his favourite summer fruit. His palm lay over the smooth material of her bra.

Ah, what a pair of nichons she has, he said to himself. He was astonished and aroused by the weight of soft flesh in his hand.

'It was kind of you to call,' she said a little breathlessly. She sounded very formal, considering the circumstances. But few women are able to maintain any degree of formality with a man's hand deep inside their dress and stroking their breasts.

Roger found a concealed zip above her shoulder-blades and ran it down. He eased the dress off her fleshy shoulders and let it slide down to her waist – so much smooth pale skin, so huge the mountains of her breasts inside a capacious black bra! He felt for the fastening and freed it – her breasts fell forward as if to overwhelm him. They were massive, they hung down under their own weightiness.

'What a pity we have not been able to meet before,' he said in a very sincere tone, 'we really must make up for lost time.'

He had seized her breasts with both hands for a very thorough feel. He wanted to get his stiff shaft between them and rootle till he spurted, but he didn't believe for one moment she'd let him. Ladies who paid for the services of charming young men had a way of insisting that things were done the conventional way – otherwise they didn't think they'd had their money's worth.

For Beatrice Larose it would surely be flat on her back, with her plump legs wide open and he lying on her fat belly.

'Delicious,' he said, 'utterly delicious,' his hands stroking and tugging and squeezing and rolling her mountainous breasts.

'Madame Drouet confided in me that you almost raped her,' she said, her head turned to stare at Roger. He noted that her fine porcelain cheeks were flushed pink, 'in her office – and in the middle of the day! In broad daylight!'

Roger couldn't decide if this statement was an accusation or a statement of approval. He knew it was untrue. Any raping that took place between him and Gilberte was by her, not by him. But he presumed she had invented this fiction to interest Beatrice.

To arouse her curiosity, as it evidently had. To increase the fee for his services. Gilberte Drouet was a keen businesswoman, everyone knew that.

'I may have been carried away by my emotions,' he said, going along with Gilberte's tale, 'it was a very exciting situation.'

'What situation, what do you mean – tell me what happened!'

'Madame Drouet was dressed provocatively that day – in a thin silk blouse that was almost transparent. Looking at her made me desperate to kiss her body from her eyes to her toes – my blood was on fire to rip her clothes off.'

'*Mon Dieu*!' Beatrice sighed. 'And all this in an office!'

'I almost succeeded in having my way with her,' Roger went on with a chuckle. 'I had my hand inside her knickers – in another two minutes she'd have been on her back with her legs apart and I would have been on top of her.'

'On her own desk!' Beatrice exclaimed.

'Yes, on the desktop, with her silk blouse wide open to show her breasts! But her receptionist came into the room just then – naturally I had to stop what I was doing to her.'

Beatrice sighed and moved her feet apart on the carpet.

'What a dangerous man you are,' she murmured. 'Gilberte warned me I'd be taking a fearful risk by inviting you here – you have a reputation for using women for your pleasure whether they want to or not. She made it very clear to me. But in spite of that I felt I had to meet you.'

'Ah yes?' Roger said, an eyebrow raised, his hands busy with her roly-poly breasts.

'I told Gilberte I was certain you would not molest me,' said Beatrice, her voice faint.

So that's how we are to play out this little game, Roger said to himself. Madame Larose is the gracious hostess receiving her visitor for polite conversation. I am the guest who exceeds the bounds of courtesy by unexpected advances in the sitting-room.

The scenario was one he had encountered more than once before with married women. It was expected of him to take advantage of her good nature by molesting her. Good, he thought, now we both understand how the comedy is to be played, it is simple enough to make her fantasy come true.

'You are an elegant and very desirable lady,' he said, 'it is impossible for me to keep control of my emotions when I am with you. You are truly running a risk, as you were warned.'

There was a pause while Beatrice registered his words and considered them. He was pleased she didn't want him to play the rough street type – the most unlikely women sometimes wanted to be smacked about and knocked down and brutalized, knickers torn and thighs bruised – lightly, of course. Middle-aged women most usually, he'd found. Especially the religious ones – a crucifix around the neck was almost a guarantee that sexual violence was required.

He did the semi-rape when requested, but for his taste it was unnecessarily exhausting. While Beatrice was still engaged with her thoughts he pulled her dress up to see her thighs, from her knees up to nearly her underwear.

He slid his palm over bare flesh above her stocking-tops – at his first touch on her skin she started and gasped loudly. Then she sat still again, staring down at his hand as if mesmerized.

'You are charming,' he said, giving her an amiable smile, 'no other words can better describe you, Beatrice.'

His hand was between her thighs, stroking her expanse of warm soft flesh – she found her voice at last.

'Do you mean that?' she asked doubtfully.

'Every word – I admire you, as an elegant and desirable woman ought to be admired.'

'We'd better go into the bedroom,' she said.

'Certainly,' he agreed, 'but do not be too hasty to end these wonderful moments – when we go to the bedroom we both know what will happen. It will be marvellous, it will be exquisite, mind-bending and soul-shaking. This I can assure you now, because it is clear in my mind. Your sumptuously generous body naked upon the bed, while I lean over you to kiss your breasts . . .'

Beatrice was staring eagerly into his face, her cheeks a rose pink from emotion. Her hand lay on his thigh – he felt its heat through the cloth of his trousers.

'Roger, yes . . .' she moaned, 'I shall be naked for you and you will kiss my body all over . . .'

'But before then,' he said – knowing that he'd captivated her and it would be easy enough to bring her to satisfaction

– 'let us abandon ourselves to little surprises. Are we alone in the apartment?'

'Yes, alone,' she murmured, 'no one will disturb us.'

Roger's hand was caressing between her thighs, feeling thick curls through her knickers. The knickers were black – it seemed to him sometimes that well-to-do women wore black all the time. Like village widows! Personally he liked women in bright, vivid colours – the day Gilberte Drouet had worn scarlet knickers had captured his imagination forever.

But his own preferences were of no importance in this sort of intimate situation. The lady who paid the fee had the right to wear whatever she liked – old turnip sacks if that pleased her. It was his job to strip her naked and give her what she wanted. He pressed a finger along the split of Beatrice's *joujou*.

'Have you ever sat naked here in your sitting-room, Beatrice, here on this sofa?'

'No, never, of course not,' she said, sounding almost alarmed by the suggestion, 'what a very strange idea!'

Roger's hand was in her black knickers, his fingertips on the thick, soft lips between her legs, stroking them slowly.

'But I want to see you naked here,' he murmured to her, 'then I shall remember you like that forever – bold, lovely and naked on your white sofa.'

'No ...' she sighed, 'no, no ...'

Whether her sense of propriety was outraged or not, there was no show of resistance from her when he pulled her dress up over her head and draped it over the sofa arm. True, she stared open eyed at him – evidently no one had ever undressed her before on her sitting-room sofa – but she was happy to let Roger do these amazing things to her.

He slipped her stockings down her chubby legs and off.

At the moment of truth, when both his hands were at her waist to slide her knickers down, she seemed almost to panic briefly.

Her hands seized his hands – there was a doubtful look in her pale eyes. And then she surrendered and went so far as to help him take her knickers off. She sat naked on the elegant sofa, a big fleshy woman, pink and smooth, massive breasts that gravity was pulling down towards her plump belly.

She sat with her fair head tilted to one side, as if she were waiting for some comment from Roger. He knew a better ploy than words – he slid off the sofa and down on his knees between her feet, his hands pushing her pudgy knees apart. He bent down and planted a score of ardent kisses on her soft belly.

'But in the sitting-room!' she sighed, 'I don't believe this is happening to me, it is impossible!'

'Lean back,' said Roger, 'close your eyes, breathe slowly and lose yourself in pleasure.'

She did – her head on the sofa back, her short-fingered hands resting on her fleshy thighs.

He had them well apart, those mighty thighs, exposing a thick thatch of light brown hair between them. He ran his fingertips through it, he prised the lips open and heard her gasp. He took her heavy breasts in both hands and sucked at the dark-red buds until they were standing hard.

'This is how I shall remember you, Beatrice,' he said, 'naked and lovely in your sitting-room – a memory to cherish forever.'

Beatrice seemed to have lost the faculty of articulate speech – she made a throaty sound while her hands scrabbled at the zip of his trousers. Then she had his stiffness in her hand and was tugging at it. He slid nearer to her on his knees until the tip of his hard length touched her bare belly.

With expert hands he turned her and lifted her legs until she lay full-length on the sofa, her knees drawn up and her head on the arm where her little black dress lay. There was no time to take off more than his jacket, she was already moaning lightly. He arranged himself rapidly on her. Lying on her fat belly and breasts was like being face-down on a soft feather-bolster.

She reached blindly for the stiff fifteen centimetres sticking out of his undone trousers. He heard her sighing as she steered him where she wanted him to be – she pressed the purple head of his length into the thick soft lips of her *joujou*.

'So strong, so very strong!' she sighed, almost sobbing. 'I can't help myself. I should never have allowed this to happen – but I am too weak to say no to you, Roger.'

With a strong push he was inside. He lay forward on her, they were belly to belly, her head lolled on the sofa-arm, her eyes staring at nothing, her mouth slackly open. Roger held on tight to her big floppy breasts as he thrust rapidly in and out.

'*Ah cheri . . .*' she moaned, '*ah cheri . . .*'

He was doing it to her so briskly that her body jerked to the rhythm of his thrusts. A feeling of power gripped Roger – as it always did when he penetrated a client and gave her the benefit of his abilities to thrill her and send her spinning head-over-heels into orgasm.

He stabbed harder, his hands clenched on her breasts, holding back the wonderful sensations that threatened to explode inside his belly. His professionalism insisted that the woman must be satisfied before he let himself attain his own supreme moment. At times this was difficult. Some women needed a very long time to climb the slope of ecstasy and hurl themselves over the high cliff at the top.

In particular plump women with big bellies and bigger breasts – but not Beatrice! At least, not on this occasion. She'd been aroused by his words and his approach – above all by being made to strip naked in her own elegant sitting-room. She responded with a shrill climactic wail after only a minute or so of thrusting, smacking her bare belly up at him in fast little spasms. He grinned fiercely as he spurted into her. Things had gone well.

It wasn't always so. There had been disappointments and there had been near-disasters. The first time with some clients could be awkward because their expectations were not clear. And their reactions could be bizarre at times. The lady he had visited in Clichy – she had fainted dead away during her second orgasm.

Or that one with the appendix scar who asked him to kneel and pray for forgiveness with her – naked and side by side in front of a religious picture on her bedroom wall. And she holding his drooping part in her hand – he'd just used it vigorously to give her a shattering orgasm. With her *Ave-Maria* hardly finished she dragged him down on the floor and begged him to do it to her once more.

Francoise was her name, Francoise Lenoir, late thirties, darkly good-looking, living apart from her husband. And absurdly religious. Never without a gold crucifix dangling between her breasts. Painted statuettes of saints stood in every room, there were pictures on the walls, and she went to Mass every morning. She went on a lot about sin and wrong-doing, especially when she was committing the carnal.

The second time Roger was requested to visit her he'd thought of the ideal way to satisfy her opposed aspirations.

He fondled her breasts and between her legs, he went into the bedroom with her, stripped her naked and asked her to kneel down and say her prayers. Instantly she was on her knees at the bedside – elbows resting on it and hands pressed together in pious supplication.

Roger knelt behind her and opened the lips of her hairy split with his thumbs. She cried out to St Antoine to save her when he pushed his stiffness into her. Her eyes were closed, of that he was sure, and she continued to pray aloud for forgiveness while he gripped her by the hips and rammed into her warm moistness.

Her orgasm was silent, but profound. Her body shook to rapid little spasms, she gasped and stammered as she went on praying, and Roger pressed close against her and slammed into her – till she fell forward on her face and lay twitching.

All this was a great success – since that day she'd insisted on having two prayer meetings a week. Saints' days were important to her, feast days and fast days. She had become one of Roger's regulars, and to show his respect he mailed religious postcards to her whenever he passed a shop that sold them.

Although Beatrice had been taken aback by the suggestion that she should allow herself to be undressed in her sitting-room, a different mood had taken over since her orgasm on the sofa. She lay at ease on her back, contented and limp-limbed, Roger fully dressed on top of her – almost fully dressed, that is, only his jacket off.

He pulled out of her, his cherished part dwindling. He sat on the edge of the sofa, looking at her face while he analyzed his performance in his mind and recorded details in his memory that would be useful to him in future. As for Beatrice, it took some time before her thoughts were sufficiently collected for her to comment on what had happened.

When she spoke, it was to ask him to go into the bedroom with her. He smiled his charming smile and said, *But of course, cherie*, and reached out his hand to her. She grasped it to pull herself to a sitting position – then she was on her feet beside him and her vast breasts wobbled as she pulled at him to make him stand up and take him into her bedroom.

That wobbling of soft dangling breasts made Roger's male part twitch. He had seen many bedrooms and he had lain on many beds. He knew how it would go in there. Beatrice would spread herself on her back and open her legs and wait for him to commence what he had been paid a fee to do. That gave him no problems, he was able to climb on to any naked woman and perform satisfactorily. But sometimes it was tedious, this climbing on top.

As Beatrice tried to pull him to his feet he pulled back hard and brought her down to sit on his lap. She was heavy, no doubt of it, but he was braced for that. She looked surprised to find herself sitting naked on his lap, but she pressed her warm body against him and nuzzled his cheek.

'If my husband came home and saw me like this,' she said with a smile to reassure him it wasn't going to happen.

Roger smiled back while he felt her heavy breasts. He kneaded them and squeezed them, he played with the red-brown buds until she was sighing in pleasure and her eyes were half-closed.

'Let's go to the bedroom,' she murmured, 'something you don't expect will happen to me if you keep on doing that.'

'I know exactly what will happen to you,' he informed her, 'I fully intend it to happen.'

His hand slipped down to her plump thighs, they opened – his finger found the moist way in between them and played over her little bud. He put his other arm underneath her to feel between the big round cheeks of her bottom. This would be an experience totally new to her, he was convinced, as he pressed a fingertip to the little knot of muscle in the crease between the cheeks.

'Ah no – no perversions!' she exclaimed, her body shaking so hard her breasts wobbled again.

Roger grinned and didn't answer. He was using both fingers to good advantage, one at the front and one at the back.

'No perversions!' she gasped again, red-faced and squirming.

'I'm a dangerous man,' he said, 'Gilberte warned you about me before you invited me to your home. I use women's bodies for my amusement, whether they want me to or not.'

Beatrice's orgasm came very quickly – she writhed on his lap, her round belly bulging as she pushed herself against his hand. When her throes of pleasure seemed to slow, he pushed his other finger into the tight little opening hidden between her massive cheeks. She shrieked and jerked about as if an electric current was being passed through her.

Her new spasms went on longer than he expected, the intensity decreasing only very slowly. Then with a final sighing gasp she subsided. She lifted her chin from his shoulder and leaned back a little to stare into Roger's eyes.

'Why did you do that to me?' she asked, her voice tremulous, 'it's not normal, that sort of thing.'

'I am a sensual man,' he said, trying to sound assertive, 'my passions are unusually strong. I need no permission to caress a woman's body as I think best.'

He was sure now that Beatrice would become a regular. She was the typical neglected wife of means, that was his assessment, a woman wanting to experience the pleasures she'd heard about and never known.

'I should have listened to Gilberte's warning,' she said, her voice shaking, 'you mean to rape me and deprave me!'

'Resign yourself to it,' he advised her.

'You have degenerate morals!' said she, pleasantly alarmed.

'You have the most exciting body I've seen for some time,' he told her.

While she was pondering this untruth he struggled to his feet with her in his arms. And though he was fit, it was a struggle. He thought ruefully that she weighed a lot more than the last woman he had picked up and carried, beautiful Marie. But with Marie it was pleasure, this was business.

He had frequently wondered why women surrender sexually when they are picked up and carried. He had discussed it with Edmond more than once, but they had never agreed on the answer. It was a useful thing for a man in Roger's profession to know.

He carried Beatrice across the drawing-room, his knees just a little shaky beneath him. She guided him to her bedroom, he set her down on her back on a large comfortable-looking bed.

During these exertions his prize part was sticking boldly out of his open trousers, swaying up and down. He began to undress. As he unbuckled his belt Beatrice reached up, her eyes shining with expectation, and she took hold of his stiff length.

'So strong,' she sighed, the very same words she had used when she'd held it before.

Roger was certain now that he'd acquired another regular. And that was a pleasant thought – it was an indication of progress in his career. He flung his clothes off and was on the bed with her in a moment, her legs opened to let him kneel between them. He fingered her thick pelt of light-brown curls, he stroked the wet lips that were loosely open now.

'The moment you knew must eventually arrive,' he said slowly, knowing the words women like her wanted to hear, the words that aroused them with thrilling hints of danger and fleshly desire, 'the moment is here. Prepare yourself – I'm going to penetrate deep into your belly. I shall push all the way in and fill you full with my hard strong flesh.'

'Strong hard flesh,' she sighed, 'all the way inside me . . .'

He had already been inside her once, of course, but his guess was that she didn't count that because it was on the sofa – not on her bed. Ladies like her were slaves to a certain propriety.

'*Ah mon Dieu*,' she whimpered softly, 'you mean to ravish me! I cannot find the words to stop you – you will deprave me!'

Her thighs strained wider apart. Roger lay forward on her fat belly and stabbed straight and sure into her slippery depths.

Compensating

Roger was leaving his apartment on Saturday morning, soon after eleven, when Marie Brantome arrived. There wasn't even time for her to ring or knock – he opened the door to go out and she was there. Her gloved hand was raised, a startled expression spread over her face.

'Roger!' she said breathlessly, 'I shan't keep you a minute, but there's something I have to tell you.'

'Come in,' he said, his heart beating faster. He reached out to take her hand and raise it to his lips. He pulled her firmly over the threshold.

His own conclusion slipped into his mind – that the woman who is picked up and carried by a man has surrendered herself. With an ardent smile he stooped to get hold of her and take her to the divan. Whatever it was she had come here to tell him could be deferred until after he had undressed her and made love to her.

Marie thought otherwise. She took a step to the side and back to evade his grasp. He straightened up, feeling mildly foolish.

'Come and sit down,' he said, 'I'm so pleased to see you.'

If she sat on the sofa with him he'd have an arm round her in no time and a hand in her jacket to stroke her breasts – it was a foregone conclusion.

'No,' she said, 'what I came to tell you can be said in a few words – there is no point in spinning it out. And there will be no discussion.'

She was wearing the stylish steel-grey two-piece costume that she had worn the first time he had seen her, strolling after lunch along the Avenue de l'Opera in the sunshine. Her black hair, parted on the right, shone glossily. Roger's heart was melting to see how beautiful she was. But her long intelligent face was stern.

Her little manoeuvre to avoid being swept up off her feet had put her back against the wall beside the door. Roger stood less than an arm's length away from her, but he respected her wish to deliver her message. As long as it wasn't going take more than a few moments – he doubted his ability to be near enough to her to smell that enticing perfume she used and keep his hands off.

'Well?' he said with an encouraging smile.

'I've tried to phone you for two days,' she said, 'but you're never in. That's why I came today to tell you.'

'Tell me what?'

'That it's finished and we won't see each other again. That's what I came here to tell you, Roger.'

'But this is unreasonable,' he said, reaching out to take her wrist, the one with the thin gold watch on the snakeskin strap, 'you can't just arrive and say goodbye and disappear forever.'

'Yes, I can,' she said, 'goodbye, Roger.'

Her wrists were very fine – Roger's fingers met around the one he was holding. He glanced down, this was the hand with the wedding-ring, but she was wearing white suede gloves and he couldn't see her ring. Not that he believed she was married, of course.

'Why?' he asked – as disappointed lovers have since love was first invented.

'No discussion,' Marie told him, 'no excuses, no reasons. Let me go now, Roger.'

'But I love you,' he said, 'I refuse to be rejected.'

'Ah yes, love,' she said. 'You are Roger Chavelle and you love me. We met in the Printemps department store and I thought that we could be lovers. But now we can't.'

Roger wondered what secrets and what mysteries lay behind her words. She was a very strange woman, Marie Brantome, impossible to understand – but that didn't change his feelings towards her. And at present his emotions were in turmoil, the fear of losing her was making him frantic. Not that he'd ever possessed her in any significant way, he understood that. He had been allowed to kiss her belly and lie between her legs for unguessable reasons of her own. That was all.

He hardly knew what he was doing when he reached down to slip both his hands under her skirt and up her thighs, the soft kiss of silk stockings on his fingertips. The skirt rode up – and he moved in closer, until they stood belly to belly, face to face, toe to toe. His arms were around her, he was holding the cheeks of her bottom through her thin knickers.

His motives were confused and futile, and only partly sexual. His most urgent desire was to hold her close to him, to prevent her from going away. He wanted to cling to her, to possess her, to hold her forever. This same desire could have been expressed adequately by putting his arms about her waist – but he was too muddled to fully appreciate what he was doing.

Marie turned her head to stop him kissing her. He kissed her cheek instead of her mouth, and then her elegant little ear. He kissed her nose, her eyebrows. Through swirling painful emotion he realized he wanted to kiss her *joujou* – but that was out of the question in the circumstances.

'Let me go now, Roger,' she said softly.

The cheeks of her bottom were round and taut, ideally shaped, in Roger's opinion. And he had seen many, many women's bottoms. His fingertips caressed warm flesh through thin silk and inside his trousers his unruly part was standing boldly upright.

'No reasons, no excuses,' he said, using her words and trying to sound in control of himself, 'but tell me one last thing. Do you find me unacceptable as a lover – or would the same be true of any other man?'

In Roger's unhappy thoughts there was no doubt concerning her motives for breaking off with him. Her preference was for other women – he'd been sure about that since he first undressed her in the little hotel near the St Lazare railway station. She had tried him out, let him kiss her and lie on her belly, to see if she could accept male caresses.

But the truth as he saw it was that Marie's nature compelled her to need love of a different sort. On her back on a bed with her legs spread wide, yes, but with another woman to crouch between them and probe her dark-haired *lapin* with a wet tongue.

That was the image in Roger's mind that had tormented and excited him since he first made love to her – Marie getting dressed and leaving him to go home to another woman, her body still shaking from the ecstasy he'd given her – but naked again with her eyes closed as a woman's tongue explored her secret bud and her legs were pressed apart by another woman's hands.

In his imagination he could hear Marie's little gasping

cries and sobs as she was swept into shuddering orgasms – by someone who had breasts of her own and a *joujou* of her own!

But Marie was becoming dissatisfied with this other someone – on a whim she'd tried out Roger, that was his interpretation of her surrender to him in the hotel. She was still undecided – so she tried a second time in his apartment. Now she'd made up her mind, she knew what she wanted, and it was, *Goodbye, Roger.*

'No discussion,' she repeated, 'but an answer for you – it is impossible for me to have a lover.'

Roger's fingers were stroking her in the cleft between the cheeks of her bottom while he considered the implication of her words. He'd been right all along. He slid a hand around her hip to her belly under the skirt and to the join of her thighs, he touched her soft curls through the silk.

'I feel I've never really known you,' he said.

His upstanding part was throbbing – something had to be done about it. He slid his hand down the front of her knickers, down her warm belly, until he touched warm lips. With his other hand he opened his trousers and pulled out his hard-straining part.

'You knew from the beginning that I am married,' she said, 'I never concealed that. Why are you doing this to me now, are you trying to prove something?'

He didn't trouble to answer her question – he had never for a moment believed in the authenticity of the gold wedding ring on her hand. Its purpose was to mislead. He pressed the tip of his middle finger into her *joujou* to find her sensitive bud.

'This is absurd,' she said. 'I came here on a serious matter, but all you can think about is sex. I could have sent a picture postcard and saved myself the journey!'

'I have never felt this way about any other woman,' he said.

Marie waited for no further explanation, she took hold of his stiff part with her gloved hand. What she intended was unclear, to herself as much as to him. Perhaps she was going to put this stiff hugeness back inside his trousers, to make him understand all was finished between them.

Or perhaps she wanted one more feel of its strength and size, to remember him by. Whatever the half-formed intention may have been, the reality was dramatic – the sudden touch of soft suede produced sensations so strong that Roger's knees felt shaky and he knew with clarity that he was going to spurt into her hand. All emotions that were raging through him – his disappointment, his dismay, his despair – all were transformed by that touch to sexual and released like a detonation.

'Then this is goodbye,' he gasped, pushing his belly forward, ecstasy throbbing through him.

He crushed himself against Marie, attempting blindly to push into her – he clutched her by the waist while his legs trembled and his hot passion spurted on her knickers.

'Roger!' she exclaimed – she tried to push him away from her as she felt the wet surge.

He held her tightly, forcing her back against the wall. After her first exclamation she resigned herself to being used by him so abruptly and waited until he was calm again. Then she pushed him away and held her skirt up about her waist while she looked down to inspect the damage.

Only now did Roger take note that she was wearing orchid-pink knickers – small and very chic, with a trim of black lace round the legs. The front was darkly wet from waist-band to seam with his outpouring of desire.

'You've soaked them,' she said. 'I can't wear them like this, what on earth am I to do!'

'Take them off,' he suggested. 'You can rinse them – they'll dry in twenty minutes and we can talk while you are waiting.'

She had no intention of letting him inveigle her into sitting on the divan-bed with him – she knew what that led to. He would have her naked and on her back inside five minutes. She slipped the knickers down her legs and off.

'You rinse them,' she said, handing them to Roger.

He stood with the sodden little item of pink silk in his hand and stared at her while she smoothed down her skirt. She looked at her glove – there was a wet spot on the thumb. She shook her head at Roger, turned to open the apartment door and left.

Not a good start to anyone's day, to be told by the beauty he adores that he will never see her again. Roger was left aghast, leaning against the wall, staring wildly at the door Marie had shut behind her when she walked out. Her orchid-pink knickers were dangling from his fingers, the long wet stain on the silk was a reproach to him – she'd taken the trouble to visit him when she needn't. She could simply have vanished from his life without a word of goodbye, he wouldn't have known where to find her.

This meant she had a certain affection and regard for him, it was obvious. Instead of recognizing this when she was with him, all he had been able to think of was getting his hands into her knickers. He was ashamed – for him that was an unusual emotion, one he hadn't felt for years. He must apologize to her, explain how desperately he loved her – he must find out why she wanted to end their *affaire* and persuade her not to!

Action, not regrets! He sprang to life and dashed out of

the apartment to catch up with her, stuffing her knickers into his jacket pocket. He was halfway down the stairs, taking them two at a time, when he realized his trousers were undone and open and his dangler was hanging out and flopping about. A pause for him to flip it in and zip up, then he was racing down again.

Marie had a long start on him, he couldn't say how long he'd been drooping disconsolately against the wall. She was nowhere to be seen in the street, left or right. Logic suggested to him that she'd be making for the Metro – he ran in the direction of the Place Denfert-Rochereau.

He caught a glimpse of glossy black hair and a steel-grey suit, far ahead of him. He dodged round people walking sedately along the pavement, he called her name. She didn't hear him – and she didn't go down the steps into the Metro station, she got into a taxi waiting on the rank on the Boulevard Raspail. He waved, he shouted, all to no avail. By the time he got there the taxi had pulled away.

There was nothing else for it – Roger jumped into the back of the next taxi in line and said, knowing how idiotic it sounded, 'Follow that cab!' The driver turned to stare at him balefully – he was an unshaven type in a tatty pullover with a strong smell of yesterday's garlic about him.

'You a cop?' he asked, ignoring his passenger's command.

'No – the woman I love is running away and I must catch her.'

Even while he was saying it Roger knew how totally ridiculous it must seem. The taxi driver didn't burst into laughter but he shrugged in a manner that conveyed more clearly than words what he thought about his passenger. But a fare was a fare.

'Where's she going?' he asked, switching on his engine.

'If I knew that I wouldn't have to follow her,' Roger said in a tone that indicated his displeasure at these delays and questions.

The driver shrugged again and pulled out into the fast-moving stream of traffic without warning. Marie's taxi was well out of sight by then, heading north up the Boulevard Raspail. But this is a long straight road, and if the taxi carrying her stayed on it there would be no great problem in catching up – especially when Roger's driver displayed his murderous ability to hurl his machine around and past other vehicles. Poor Roger gripped the seat and shut his eyes in dread of violent and messy death.

It proved to be a long chase, along the Boulevard all the way to the ornate National Assembly building, then across the Seine to the Place de la Concorde, up the Rue Royale to the Madeleine church. 'Are you sure we're following the right cab?' Roger kept asking, to which the only reply he got was a grunt. And now and then the driver would ask, 'Is that the right taxi in front?' And all Roger could say was, 'I hope so!'

The absurd pursuit ended near the Parc Monceau; the taxi they were following turned up ahead and lost itself in the traffic. Roger's driver made a tour of the streets around the park, slow and thorough – but it was futile. Roger stared at the large old mansion blocks, built a hundred years before for the rich, now expensive apartments.

The right sort of area for Marie – he was sure she lived with someone with money to spend on her. If he knew her real name he could question every concierge within half a kilometre until he found her. But she'd never told him the truth.

He walked through the park, feeling devastated, past the lake where children were sailing little boats, past a statue of some forgotten worthy. Marie hadn't been sure if there were statues in the neighbourhood where she lived. But of course there were, everywhere in Paris there were statues.

He walked down the Boulevard Malesherbes, taking in nothing, to the Boulevard Haussmann. Then along it until he came to the Printemps department store.

This was where it began. He took the lift up to the café with the stained-glass dome and ordered a glass of wine while he sat and tried to recover from the shock he'd sustained. He wondered if Marie bought her underwear in this store – her knickers were in his jacket pocket, orchid-pink silk, soaked with his desire.

Perhaps if he hung about the lingerie department for a few days she would eventually turn up. But to what end? She'd told him clearly enough that it was over. Chasing her in a taxi had been a stupid idea, born of despair. The best thing to do was forget her. He felt a little better after deciding that and moved on.

About five he phoned his friend Edmond Planchon. The prospect of being alone on a Saturday evening was too much to bear. But there was no answer. Edmond was out. Roger drifted on, he was a long way from the Parc Monceau, but he paid no attention to his surroundings.

A voice greeted him, hauling him out of his introspection. It was Nadine Bernier, sitting alone outside a café, shopping bags under the little table at her feet. The last time he'd seen her was in Madame Drouet's outer office. He'd promised to phone her – naturally he hadn't done so. He'd been engrossed heart and soul in thoughts of Marie ever since.

Nadine was tall and beautiful and blonde – a model who made a living by slinking up and down designers' catwalks. Roger liked her, though he had to admit to himself that her talents were in her face and her figure. She was not the cleverest of women. In fact, she was only interesting in bed, with her long sleek legs wrapped around his waist. With all her clothes on she could be perfectly boring.

But she was someone to talk to. So he sat down and talked to her about nothing. It was better than talking to himself in his head. Anything was preferable to that, after hours and hours of it. She wasn't going anywhere special, Nadine said. And nor was Roger. For once their interests matched – or more exactly their lack of immediate interests and purpose.

She'd been drinking *fine a l'eau*, he saw – cognac with water. He ordered the same for himself and more for her. Nadine was in a mood of depression, that very soon became evident.

'Nothing ever works out as it should for me,' she said with a sulky pout. 'I work and work, I break my head to earn a living. And that's all. I meet a man I find fascinating and he takes me to dinner. And then we go to bed. Inside a week I adore him and want to be with him all the time.'

'He's a lucky man,' said Roger, not meaning it but wishing to say something to comfort her.

'He says he adores me,' she went on, with an angry grimace on her beautiful face, 'then in another week he is tired of me. He goes to another woman. Nothing lasts. Nothing.'

'Ah, it is the same story for me,' said Roger, the corners of his mouth turning down. 'I meet a woman who enchants me – we go to bed and it is incredible. I am happier than ever in my life. But I am a fool, because suddenly she decides she does not like me as much as she thought. She says goodbye and I am desolate.'

'Once I could understand,' said Nadine, 'but when every

man I am attracted to inflicts the same misery on me by the same lies and the same desertion, I am bewildered.'

'Every one?' Roger said, an eyebrow raised.

'Life – a nightmare!' said Nadine. 'We love for three weeks, we quarrel for three days, we part forever.'

An hour later, after two or three drinks, it was settled that they would go out together that evening – not for amusement, of course – there could be no question of that for two who were as disenchanted as they were, Roger and Nadine. But they agreed it was not good to be alone on a Saturday evening – what depths of depression they might plunge into on their own! Being together would not make either of them happier, but it was reasonable to be miserable in each other's company.

They decided to go to a little nightclub they both knew – for dinner and to dance. But not before nine – and first Nadine had to change and make up. Roger didn't want to ride the Metro to the Place Denfert and then back to Nadine's – he was wearing an acceptable suit. It made more sense to go with her now and wait at her apartment.

She lived close by, she'd been buying food locally. She had a pleasant apartment in a well-maintained building, the concierge was polite and wished her *bonsoir* with a smile. She left Roger in her sitting-room with a large glass of cool white wine and a fashion magazine, while she went to get ready.

He found a picture of her in the magazine, that was why she'd given it to him to look at – a photo of her in a glamorous off-the-shoulder dress by a moderately well-known name. Calf-length swirly skirt and long black gloves up her slender bare arms to her elbows.

Roger stared for a long time at the picture – Nadine's smooth bare shoulders and arms. And the long sleek black satin gloves. It was a well-taken photo, taken by someone of importance, such as the great Pierre-Raymond Becquet himself, perhaps. The flesh tones and texture were so expertly reproduced that Roger almost felt his hands stroke the real thing – Nadine's bare shoulders.

Desolated though he was by the events of the morning, he felt a certain familiar stirring down in his trousers. Especially at the idea of Nadine's hand, in a long black satin glove, sliding up and down his proud part, now swollen hard. His own reaction dismayed him – how could he even think of sexual pleasures when the woman he loved had deserted him?

He'd finished his glass of wine a long time ago. He looked at the little gold-and-blue Meissen porcelain clock on a cabinet – Nadine surely must be ready by now, she'd been gone for half an hour! At least that, he hadn't really noticed the time when he sat down.

Another ten minutes passed before he heard from her.

'Roger, do you have a cigarette?' she called, from somewhere in the apartment. He went searching for her.

'Nadine, where are you?'

'In here.'

The door was half-open so he went in and it was the bathroom. Nadine was standing naked by the bath, not even a towel round her, patting herself with a large white powder-puff. Under the arms, over her breasts. This was not Roger's first sight of her naked body, they'd been casual lovers in the past, although not for long. Even so, the vision of so perfect a body naked caused him to catch his breath.

Nadine had the classical model shape. Small round breasts set high, long narrow waist, delicately curved hips, slender thighs – if she had been as intelligent as she was beautiful she would have been the premier couturier model in all Paris.

Perhaps because they'd been lovers she was not embarrassed to be seen naked by him – not even the closely-clipped little tuft of blondish hair where her long graceful thighs met. She turned to look at herself in the mirror. Roger put his arms around her from behind and kissed the back of her neck.

She turned her head so he could kiss her cheek – wondering as he did if she wanted him to or if he wanted to. Her long blonde hair was shiny and smelled fragrantly of whatever she washed it with. In the mirror her face was pale without make-up. He moved his hands up her body to feel her perfect little breasts.

'I asked you for a cigarette, that's all,' she said huskily.

But the truth was, Roger told himself, she'd let him into the bathroom when she was naked – so she wanted him to make love to her. And, to be absolutely frank, he'd gone in after he saw she was naked, which could only mean that he wanted to make love to her. Even if he and she were both suffering the atrocious pain of love gone wrong.

He held her close to him, her back to his belly, his face in her sweet-smelling hair. There was face powder on his suit and he didn't care. She turned in his arms and pressed her mouth to his, her tongue slipped between his lips. And while he caressed her long bare back her hands were busy opening his trousers. In another moment her hand slid up and down his distended flesh.

She leaned back in his arms to stare into his eyes.

'I didn't want this to happen, Roger,' she said sadly, 'after all I've suffered, I can never trust a man again.'

'I make no promises, Nadine,' he said, 'but you know me for a true friend.'

'Are you?' she asked. 'Are you, Roger? Or are you the same as all the rest?'

In view of the undoubted fact that she was stroking his stiff male part, Roger thought it unnecessary to answer the question. An instant later they were in the bedroom, lying on the bed and locked in each other's arms, kissing and sighing. Roger's hands trembled as he stroked her body, she was warm to his touch from the bath, her flesh smooth and pliant.

She was waiting for him to roll her on her back and slide his belly on to hers. To relieve her sadness, of course. But in his mind there was an uncomfortable thought – what if Marie knew he was naked on a bed with another woman, stroking her between her thighs, fingering her chic little blondish tuft of curls?

Agreed, Marie had left him, and he was free to do what he wanted. But he'd begged her to stay and insisted he was in love with her. Now a beautiful blonde model was caressing his stiff length and his fingers were inside her slippery wet *joujou*. Marie would be rightfully scornful of his declaration of love if she could see what he was doing now to Nadine.

A man can't think about love all day long, he said to himself with a mental shrug. Nadine rolled on to her back without being prompted and opened her marvellous legs. Roger drew in a breath and slid on top of her – she sighed and put her arms around him as he pushed slowly in.

'Nadine,' he exclaimed, forgetting about Marie, 'oh Nadine!'

'*Ah cheri*,' she sighed, 'it is the best thing for us to do. I know you will be good for me, Roger.'

'Yes, yes, yes, Nadine,' he gasped, without the least idea of what she was talking about.

He had his hands on the neat little cheeks of her bottom and he was squeezing them happily. Her legs were around his waist, her ankles crossed and locked; with the strength of her thighs she pulled him deeper into her. She wasn't smiling, he saw, and that was unusual. In his limited experience of her he'd come to realize she had the habit of half-smiling when she had a man on her belly driving her to orgasm.

But he was too absorbed in his own sensations to be concerned about that. His breathing grew shorter, his thrusts were faster and shorter.

'Oh yes Roger,' Nadine panted, 'I needed so badly to feel you inside me!'

Roger thought it must be a dream. Only in a dream could a day start so badly and reverse itself to turn out so well. A dream, to lie on Nadine's beautiful belly and slide into her *joujou*, a fantastic dream from which one woke up with sticky pyjamas. But Nadine was real underneath him and this was truly happening. He was in her to the limit of his fifteen centimetres of hard flesh. He was sliding in and out of her and she was clinging to him with all the strength of her arms and legs.

'Faster, faster!' she cried. 'More, Roger!'

The moment arrived – Roger groaned as spasms of ecstasy shook him and he spurted into her hot belly. She shrieked and gripped him tighter, it went on and on in overwhelming sensations until he was at last drained of emotion and lay trembling on Nadine's exquisite body. Her legs released him, he raised himself on his elbows to kiss her – and was horrified to see the expression on her face. There had been no orgasm for her, no release, she was as nervous and unsatisfied as before they began – more so!

Fortunately Roger had encountered similar situations

with the occasional first-time client. Married ladies betraying husbands for the first time sometimes felt so guilty that their natural reactions were inhibited. It was necessary for him then to coax the reluctant orgasm.

He rolled off Nadine and lay beside her, very close, one hand caressing her pretty little breasts, the other hand between her thighs to caress her chic little *joujou*. She burst into tears.

'Why does everything go wrong for me?' she sobbed.

'With me it will go right, you may be assured of it,' he told her. 'Lie still and let me love you, Nadine, I am here for you, close your eyes and surrender yourself heart and soul.'

Five minutes and he'd restored her to an intensity of arousal that made her entire body shake and her heels drum on the bed. But there was no climactic release – she hung there in suspense and gasped and cried, unable to go forward or backward. Fingers were not achieving the desired result – but Roger was not ready yet to lie on her belly again.

She took matters into her own hands, so to speak; she jumped up and pushed him on to his back, she licked his hairy pompoms and tugged at his soft sticky shaft to make it stand up again. She licked his belly and sucked his nipples, she pulled so hard at his male part he was certain she'd stretch it another five or six centimetres. And perhaps ruin it so it never stood up again!

But he understood her anguish, this slim beautiful woman with the model face and figure, sought after by dress designers, and by wealthy men for other reasons. He was sad to see her in this condition, her face and eyes pink with tears of frustration and despair.

'I mean to have you, Roger!' she insisted fiercely.

She turned and flung herself face-down on him – her

93

head was between his thighs, her breasts were squashed on his belly. His beloved part was in her mouth, now she'd made it grow thick and long again. Her long slender thighs lay open, on either side of his head, her neatly-clipped blondish-haired *joujou* was a hand's breadth from his face.

Roger parted the long pink lips with busy fingers and raised his head to push his tongue into her moist depths, ignoring her little bud. To his relief she went into noisy orgasm instantly, shaking and screaming, her belly squirming on his chest.

'Yes yes,' she shrieked, *'je t'adore*, Roger, *je t'adore . . .'*

When her spasms seemed to slow down he decided not to let her stop yet. Not after all her effort to reach the racking ecstasy that had taken her. His tongue was in her *joujou*, licking fast over her wet bud. She shrieked, her perfect body convulsed, and she plunged back into orgasm. And again when she seemed to slow down, he flicked his tongue and kept her wailing and writhing – she was ten thousand kilometres up above the earth, floating on pink clouds!

But eventually she had to descend. She lay hot and trembling on him, her mouth released his throbbing stiffness. A minute or two more and he would have spurted in her mouth. As it was, her anxious sucking had made him desperate to do it in her. He slid out from under her slender limp body, the dew of perspiration everywhere on her, her belly, her delicious little breasts, her beautiful face. He turned her over and with his hands under her waist lifted her up on her hands and knees.

The writer Henri de Montherlant claimed beauty had nothing to do with desire – that ugliness was the most reliable stimulant. Roger had never found this so. He had no difficulty doing it to plain women clients, flabby breasts, big bellies, whatever. But he adored doing it to beautiful

women, their perfection of face and body inspired him to
new heights of passion.

Nadine was perfect in appearance. The small neat round
cheeks of her bottom, her delicate breasts hanging beneath
her – Roger was aroused to frenzy. He was on his knees
behind her, his long hard part pointing at her. He needed
her, he intended to become her lover for a long time, to
drive Marie Brantome right out of his head. Who better
to efface all memory of that ambiguous and emotionally-
withdrawn woman than beautiful, eager Nadine?

'Roger,' she gasped, her blonde head turned to stare
over her smooth and perfect shoulder at him, 'make me do
it again – you can, I know you can – you are the only one
who can!'

He put his arms around her, with his hands flat on her
belly. He held her tightly while he pushed into her, right in
till his belly was against the hot cheeks of her bottom and he
was fully sheathed.

'Ah, ah, ah,' Nadine sighed, 'that's so good! Give me all
of it, *cheri* – push right in hard. Ravage me!'

He slid in and out forcefully, his fingers were pressing
into the smooth flesh of her belly. She braced herself on stiff
arms and gave little squeals to the fast rhythm of his
thrusting. He couldn't see her face, but there was a hard
fixed smile on it – an unconscious grimace as she felt his
thickness sliding in her slippery depths.

She was going to experience a ravening orgasm very soon
now – she felt it coming closer and closer, her pretty mouth
was open to scream in delight.

Discovering

Madame Dubois lived across the Seine at Auteuil in an apartment off the Route de la Reine, by the Poets' Garden – an address of some consequence, Roger thought as he strolled along the street looking for the number. People of means lived in this district.

This was as it should be – ladies who made use of the special service offered by Madame Drouet were of means, it went without saying. Such particular services were expensive, partly because Madame was very selective about the young men she supplied to a restricted list of clients. They must be handsome and strenuous and intelligent, that was a minimum requirement. After that, it was essential they were discreet – which was another reason why Madame Drouet could ask for interestingly high prices.

Roger never troubled himself with questions about the motives of the women he was sent to call upon. Most were married, a few were widowed, some were divorced. Usually they were over forty, sometimes older. Their wish was to be entertained intimately by a good-looking young man and they could afford to pay. For Roger that was reason enough – he had no taste for philosophizing.

It was all very obvious to him, the married ones had husbands their own age, fat-bellied from good living and past it in bed. And with young girlfriends who endured them for their money. As for the others, divorced or widowed, they weren't able to find attractive young male friends. So the problem was solved in the time-honoured way – by a fee to Madame Drouet.

For Roger it was important to give value for money. Satisfied clients asked for him again. Some of them paid for his services twice a week, including the religious lady who liked to say her prayers naked. And as for Madame Dubois at Auteuil, he'd called on her before – five or six times at irregular intervals.

A straightforward roll on the bed, that was his assessment of Madame Dubois. Unimaginative, undemanding, that suited him well enough. Edmond Planchon had also called upon her – he and Roger checked with each other on clients as a way of avoiding awkward little surprises from strange women with strange ideas. Edmond had also visited the religious Madame Lenoir and helped her say her prayers.

But only once. After that Edmond refused to go. Madame Drouet spoke severely to him, cajoled him, threatened him, begged him. He refused. Roger laughed at him and had no objection to taking his place when she asked to be called on – he found her bedroom preferences amusing.

Edmond claimed he'd educated Madame Dubois in bed. Maybe, but the fact was that she'd asked for Roger this time. It must mean she preferred him to Edmond, or so he flattered himself. But it could mean she liked a change, no more than that.

He walked up the stairs – her apartment was one flight up and it was quicker to walk than wait for the lift. He rang the bell and waited, straightening his tie and smoothing a hand over his curly brown hair. The door opened, and although it was three in the afternoon, Madame Dubois was wearing a short white négligée embroidered with tiny blue flowers around the neck.

How different from the first time he had come here – it had been about three months ago. On that occasion she'd been demurely dressed in a black and white dress with buttons right up to the throat, as if to guard her body against male encroachment. Although she had paid a handsome fee to be called upon at home and subjected to bodily encroachment of an extremely intimate nature.

Naturally Roger played the little game the way she preferred. He charmed her out of her clothes by stages – she'd dived into bed when she was naked to hide herself, like a shy young virgin fingered between the thighs for the first time, although Madame Dubois would never see forty again and had two children – she told him that later, over a cup of coffee.

He had to dive under the sheets to get at her properly – even when he lay on top and rode her to orgasm she made certain they both remained decently covered. The second time too, not even a breast was bared above the sheets when Roger ravaged her again.

Since then her self-confidence had grown with each visit. She could now lie naked on top of the bed, legs open and nothing to conceal her. But this – to meet him at the door ready undressed for bedroom action – this was another great stride forward. And annoying though it was to give credit to Edmond, Roger knew it must be his attentions to Madame Dubois that were responsible.

She pulled him into the apartment and closed the door quickly to prevent any neighbour seeing her undressed in mid-afternoon. Roger noted the bright gleam in her eyes as he kissed the hand she held out to him. He gave her the five white carnations he'd brought for her and she set them down at once – there was to be no shilly-shallying today. She took his hand firmly and led him straight into the bedroom.

Only then did she seem to revert to her former ways. She turned her back to Roger while she took her white négligée off and she got into bed and drew the covers up to her shoulders. He smiled and chatted away to set her at ease. She smiled back nervously, or so it seemed to him – though he could think of no reason for her to be nervous.

After all, over the past few weeks he'd seen and fingered and kissed and stroked every naked centimetre of her body. What was there to be nervous about? Then she patted the bed to show him she wanted him to sit beside her.

His smile became broader when her hand was in his lap and her fingers were fumbling at his trouser zip – his first impression was the right one, she'd lost all her former housewife shyness. How could any woman be shy, when she had a man's fingers inside her, front and back – most of a breast in his mouth at the same time? It was ridiculous to imagine she could feel shy with him after all that.

While he was complimenting her on her elegant night-dress, she opened his trousers and tugged his shirt out of the way.

He was stiff, of course, she had his beloved part in her hand and was stroking it firmly. Edmond had worked wonders with her, that must be admitted – she'd hardly touched Roger anywhere below the waist before today. She'd held his part in her hand briefly – she'd looked at it sideways, so to speak. She liked it inside her, but she didn't want to play with it.

Now she was massaging it briskly. What had Edmond done to her to produce this dramatic change? Roger decided to find out. And while Madame Dubois lay there, propped on pillows with frilled edges, playing with his exposed length, she allowed the sheet to slide down until her bare shoulders were exposed. More than that, her breasts could be seen in her satin nightdress!

'It's warm today,' she said, 'don't you think so? Take your jacket off. And your tie – you'll be more comfortable.'

Roger eased himself out of his jacket and undid his tie – and all the while she held his strong part, her hand sliding gently up and down, making it leap and throb.

'Am I flushed?' she asked. 'It's so warm today, Roger.'

She seized his wrist and drew his hand into the bed and under her nightdress. She rubbed his palm over her hot belly.

'Ah yes,' he murmured as she pushed his hand down between her thighs, 'you are warm, Yvette.'

He used her name at the moment he clasped her plump *joujou* in the palm of his hand. These women he called on – in his mind he used their Christian names for the soft little openings between their thighs.

In the secret record book he kept for his own amusement, when he wrote *Visited Yvette* what he really meant was that he'd slid his beloved part into the brown-haired split between her legs – the *Yvette* he mentioned in writing was only the most vital part of the lady he went to see in Auteuil.

'What can I do to make you more comfortable?' he asked.

It was a question requiring no answer. Not in words at least. She raised her knees under the sheet and parted them – to allow him freer access. Between the legs she was moist and ready, but her hand on his stiff flesh was dry and hot. His expert fingers smoothed the thick curls between her thighs and parted the lips to find her wet little bud and caress it.

She became bold again at this delicate touch – she gasped and flung the bedclothes aside. Her nightdress was around her waist. She moved closer to where he sat on the side of the bed and to his astonishment, she planted a kiss on the pink-purple head of his sturdy length. Her hand pumped it non-stop, for her this was incredible. Whatever Edmond had done to her, he was worthy of the highest admiration!

If Edmond could perform these wonders of transformation, then so could Roger. He twisted sideways and in another instant had pushed his quivering shaft into Yvette's mouth. He was going to slide it into *little-Yvette-down-below* later. And make her very very happy.

She gurgled and a look of terror flashed over her face – only for a moment. Then she was using her tongue on him, as if she'd been doing it all her life – though Roger was certain it was the first time she'd ever had a mouthful of solid male flesh.

He slid the narrow straps of her nightdress off her shoulders to bare her breasts. Lying on her back, propped on pillows, her nightdress bunched around her waist, she was an average married woman of forty-odd, well-off, discontent. To Roger she represented a challenge, a point of professional pride. She had put herself in his hands, it was important to make sure she remembered this encounter for a long time.

And in the dark all cats are grey – after his fifteen centimetres slid into her the sensations would be the same as if he were on the belly of the prettiest young girl in Paris. Not the same as if he had it inside Marie Brantome – that was different because he was sure that he was in love with Marie.

But in the meantime the lapping of Yvette Dubois' tongue over the head of his pulsating shaft was very exciting and he wanted to proceed to the critical moments.

'Lie down, Yvette,' he said, pulling out of her mouth. He put his hands on her shoulders and pushed her down on her back. Her legs opened and she smiled up at him.

Three seconds and the rest of his clothes were off and thrown about the floor. His fifteen centimetres stuck out ferociously – and impressively. Yvette was reaching up towards him, hands ready to grip it and drag him down to her.

'Yes Roger,' she was saying, 'yes! Give it to me!'

He stared down at her, a smile on his face, and his throbbing length in his hand. Experience told him that she was very close to orgasm. It would be a matter of half a minute, no more, when he was inside her. It was astonishing, to think she had reached this intensity of arousal so fast – he'd hardly stroked her bud for more than a few seconds.

After her orgasm he'd give her a rest of twenty minutes – she would talk about her family. Then a second performance, slower, but equally satisfactory. He'd be out of the apartment, all his obligations met, inside the hour.

He got on the bed and lay on top of her. Her hands were there at once, down between her legs, guiding him into her. *Yes, Roger*, she said again, *Oh yes*! He slid into her with a strong push and swung forwards and backwards energetically, to meet her mood of urgency. She gave little moans of pleasure to feel the forceful drive into her slipperiness.

'You are strong inside me,' she gasped.

As Roger guessed, it didn't take long. She was overwhelmed by ecstasy – back arching and her belly bucking sharply up at him, her hot and clinging *joujou* sucking at his penetrating length. He gasped and spurted violently into her. Even after he had run his course and lay trembling on her, she still rammed her belly up at him.

Bravo Edmond, Roger was thinking, *I must ask you how you do it. How you transform an inhibited woman of forty into a ravening sex-machine. If I get the hang of it I can triple my income!*

While this interesting thought was passing through his mind – and Yvette was shaking underneath him in little after-throes of orgasmic pleasure, there took place the thing Roger had dreaded since entering this profession – he heard the bedroom door open behind him and a voice exclaim, *Well!*

He was off Yvette in a flash and round to face the intruder. It was a relief to him to see it was not Monsieur Dubois. Not a man at all – it was a woman. He heard Yvette chuckle beside him. Her hand slid under him from behind as he crouched on his hands and knees on the bed. She took hold of his wet and sticky part in a very proprietorial way.

'This is my friend Monique,' she said, 'she's been wanting to meet you ever since I told her about you, Roger.'

'Madame,' he said politely, though the position was absurd.

Monique was the same age as her friend Yvette – forty-something. She was thinner, she had smaller breasts and leaner thighs. All this was évident at a single glance because she was wearing her underwear and nothing else. Black bra and knickers. Stylish, of course, if unimaginative.

'I suppose Monique was watching us all the time,' said Roger. He was relaxed now he understood the newcomer was no threat.

'I said she could,' Yvette confirmed his guess. 'Like me, she has never seen a man and a woman making love. I couldn't say no to her – you don't mind, do you, Roger?'

It wasn't really a question, it was a statement. She had paid a fee for his services and he was at her disposal – entirely at her disposal – that was evidently how she saw it. Roger decided not to argue the point.

Monique smiled at him as she advanced to the bed and sat down on the edge of it. She took off her small black bra. Roger eyed her breasts closely, his interest more professional than it was personal, though like all men he'd never miss an opportunity to look at a pair of bare *nichons*.

He didn't touch them, though he knew she wanted him to. After all, the arrangement was for him to pleasure Madame Dubois, not her friend. But he smiled amiably at Monique to let her know he would be very happy to do whatever she wanted done to her – but on appropriate terms.

'Monique was in the kitchen when you arrived,' Yvette said to him, as if it were somehow important he should know. 'I left the bedroom door ajar so she could see us.'

'I took my clothes off in the kitchen and came to watch you,' Monique added helpfully. 'It was marvellous, beautiful, you and Yvette doing it with such enthusiasm.'

Roger made himself more comfortable with his back against the bedhead. Yvette closed her legs and sat beside him, the pillows at her back. Monique in her black knickers joined them, making a row of three, like sparrows sitting on a telephone line.

Roger was in the middle, the women sat close to him, each had an arm round his waist and a hand on the thigh nearest to her. Each had her face turned towards him with an expectant smile. He had no doubt at all what was expected, but an understanding had to be reached first. He put his palms flat on their bellies and massaged gently for a few seconds.

'I am greatly flattered,' he said, 'but I must confess that I am also slightly overwhelmed.'

He slid his hand down Yvette's belly, between her thighs, and clasped her warm wet *joujou*. He slid his other hand down inside Monique's knickers, to feel her at the same time.

The hand on his right thigh caressed upward – so did the hand on his left thigh. He looked down to see which would first grip his stiff-again part. Yvette let Monique have the honour – her thin fingers curled around his hardness and stroked it slowly, while Yvette cupped his hairy pompoms in her palm.

The three sat close together, knees well apart and hands down between thighs, playing with each other. The women were waiting for Roger to make the next move, he knew that.

'The agreement was for twice,' he said to Yvette, smiling his most charming smile to dispel any hint of commercialism, 'it is for you to decide who it shall be now.'

'Monique watched you making love to me,' she said, 'it's only fair for her to let me see you do it to her.'

Roger thought he understood now why Yvette had become aroused so rapidly before. It was because she knew Monique was watching at the door. She'd pulled his fifteen centimetres out and handled it to impress her friend. Then she'd let him slip it in her mouth to show Monique that she was clever enough to know of such things.

When she was on her back with her legs wide open, it made her reach orgasm almost at once, this knowledge that Monique was at the door, observing Roger on top of her, sliding in and out. No question in Roger's thought, there existed a lesbian attraction between Yvette and Monique. An unacknowledged attraction — that was clear, because otherwise they wouldn't need him there, they could have pleasured each other.

This analysis, right or wrong, brought him memories of Marie. Marie's liking was for women, he was sure of that. The image of her in his mind never varied — Marie lying on her back, naked, her thighs apart. Another woman crouching between them to probe her dark-haired *lapin* with her wet tongue. Marie's body shaking to tremors of ecstasy, sobbing and gasping in endless orgasm.

There was no time for such thoughts now, no point in regrets. Yvette helped him arrange a very willing Monique full-length on the bed. He was on his knees beside her and both his hands were inside her small black knickers. One hand under her to part the cheeks of her bottom and push a finger into her, the other hand down the front of her knickers, fingering her *lapin*, opening it and ravaging it to slippery wetness.

Monique's bottom was bouncing up off the bed, she was gasping and close to orgasm, astonished it could happen to her so fast. Roger deduced that it was the first time she'd been handled by an expert professional like himself. She had a lot to learn. And there was every chance she would become a regular client.

Her brown eyes bulged out unfocused as he drove her over the edge of sensation into ecstatic release. He heard Yvette beside him on the bed moaning under her breath — he glanced at her and saw she was staring wide-eyed at him, her mouth open, her hands on her own breasts, squeezing them hard.

Monique was still shuddering in after-tremors of ecstasy

when he dragged her round on the bed and made her lie with legs over the edge. She looked at him uncomprehending, but she let him do whatever it was he had in mind. Her bedtime experience had been on her back, but she knew there were other ways and was willing to have an expert demonstrate them.

Roger stood close to the bed and took her under the knees. He picked up her legs and rested them on his shoulders. And Yvette moved around the bed to seat herself alongside Monique – to get a clear view of the action. Roger leaned forward and guided his stiffened part into Monique's slippery opening, a long slow push took him in deep into her. He heard Yvette gasp to see what he was doing to her dear friend.

He rocked back and forth in a strong steady rhythm. *Masterful* was what he was aiming at – women expected that from an expert. Apart from pleasuring Monique, which was simplicity itself, his intention was to capture Yvette's imagination and make sure she asked for him on future occasions, not Edmond. This he was sure he could achieve by showing her what it was like to be attended to by him. She knew how it felt, of course, he'd done it to her enough times, now she was finding out how it looked.

On Yvette's face there was an expression of fascination – the look that said plainer than any words that her sexual fantasies were running wild. She was imagining herself in Monique's place on the bed – flat on her back with her legs hooked over Roger's shoulders, his shiny-wet part sliding in and out of her own wet split. Her hand was between her thighs, touching herself.

'Roger, you are beautiful,' Yvette moaned, 'I want you again, I want you!'

He gave her a grin and concentrated on Monique. Her

eyes were closed and her belly was bounding up to match his thrusts. She was very close to her moment, her mouth was open and she panted harshly. He leaned further forward, driving into her, her knees hooked over his shoulders, her heels drumming against his back.

He observed the moment when her orgasm began and responded to it with short fast jabs that sent his passion spurting into her heaving belly.

'Yes!' he heard Yvette gasping beside him, over the squeals of ecstasy from Monique beneath him.

Sitting on the bedside, Yvette's thighs were wide apart – she had three fingers deep in her *joujou*. When Roger was calm again he eased his slippery and dwindling part out of Monique and lay down beside her to rest for a little. She sat up with a look of content on her face and leaned over him with her breasts on his chest while she stroked his face and told him how marvellous he was.

Roger was pleased to hear her say that. Meanwhile Yvette had moved closer, her fingers trailed over his belly and slipped down between his thighs, she was reminding him he had a commitment to her. He laid a hand on her thigh to reassure her of his interest – she took his finger and made him feel how wet and ready she was.

But there were negotiations first. He reminded her delicately of that and Yvette said she understood perfectly – he need have no anxiety, all would be arranged with Madame Drouet, after the event.

He smiled at her encouragingly and reached up to twine a hand in her hair and pull her down to him. He kissed her with a very convincing sincerity and she stroked his chest. Then of her own accord she took up the same position, half-on and half-off, the bed, as he had pleasured Monique in. He slipped off the bed and stood between her parted knees, clasping his well-used part in his hand. It wasn't hard, not yet, it sagged half-stiff, trying to stand up straight and tall.

Yvette stared at it with a disappointed expression, her mouth turning down at the corners and her eyebrows drawn together. At this Monique grinned and jumped off the bed, breasts bobbing up and down – she stood behind Roger, her soft warm belly pressing against him and her chin on his shoulder.

She put her arms around his waist to hold his unready part in one hand and his pompoms in the other.

'We'll soon have it standing up hard,' she said, handling him briskly.

Roger leaned forward, his hands on Yvette's parted thighs. He looked at the long pink lips in her thatch of brown curls – and he knew it would require no great effort on his part to tip her over into orgasm once more. Which considering the circumstances was fortunate – he didn't want to exhaust himself.

'That's better,' Monique murmured in his ear.

She had him at his full fifteen centimetre length, she was pumping him busily. Yvette gazed up from the bed with glowing eyes.

'Ah yes!' she murmured, opening her legs wider to welcome it as Monique guided the swollen pink-purple head between her legs and pressed it against the soft lips.

Yvette's loins rose up to meet Roger's steady push and he was in a moment embedded in her hot belly. He bent forward with his hands on the bed, arms straight, only his belly resting on hers – her feet came up off the floor and her legs clamped round his waist. Monique's body was pressed against his back, her fingers were down where he was plunging into Yvette.

Her fingers were around the base of his stiff length,

feeling his rhythmic thrusting. She also had fingers inside Yvette, he felt their rub against him each time he slid in. The effect on Yvette of these combined efforts was dramatic – she screamed shrilly and her body heaved right up off the bed. She hung from Roger by the grip of her arms round his neck and her legs round his waist.

'Do it to her, do it to her,' Monique was panting in his ear, her belly ramming against his bottom and her fingertips rubbing at his embedded part.

Waves of wonderful sensation surged through him, so wonderful that however professional he thought himself he was overwhelmed almost as soon as Yvette – he cried out and spurted his passion into her swinging body.

Eventually he was finished and collapsed on top of her on the bed. The grip of her arms and legs did not slacken, even though she too had reached the conclusion of her ecstatic moments. Her sweat-slippery breasts and belly were close against him and her thighs held his waist – it was as if she wanted to be welded to him forever. He grinned secretly to think he had just given her the most powerful orgasm of her life. She'd never forget it.

It seemed that Monique too had undergone a release of tension of some sort; perhaps watching them and participating in their massive climax with her fingers had triggered off a mental – if not a physical – orgasm of emotion of her own. Whatever it was, she climbed on to the bed and lay with her head in the small of Roger's back. Her hand was between his thighs from the rear and she held his pompoms loosely.

It was fifteen or twenty minutes before they all came back to their proper senses. Yvette's tight grip was released, her arms and thighs fell away from him. He rolled off her and lay on the opposite side to Monique, both their heads pillowed on her soft belly. After another little while they were able to talk again. Both women informed Roger how marvellous he was – which he knew already. But it was always flattering to hear it.

So much for his plan to pleasure Yvette a couple of times and be out of the apartment inside an hour. He'd already been there longer than that, and he felt comfortably lazy and unwilling to move. He could lie with his head on her bare belly and doze off for a little rest after his recent exertions. But it was not to be so – Yvette insisted they took a shower. Monique was also in favour. He went along with the plan – they were paying the fee.

Fortunately it was a large shower-stall, certainly big enough for two, and with a squeeze for three. Roger leaned against the pink-tiled wall and enjoyed the feeling of warm water cascading down over his body. Yvette and Monique stood naked watching him and exchanging little remarks about his physique in voices that were too quiet for him to hear over the rush and hiss of water. Their interest was clearly directed at his cherished part, now dangling limply between his thighs though still of impressive proportions.

They got into the shower-stall with him, both of them, smiles on their faces. There was scented pink toilet-soap. They washed his body with it – four busy hands spreading thick white lather from his shoulders down to his knees. It was a game for them, a laughing and splashing game, their hands probing under his arms and between his thighs and between the cheeks of his bottom.

Roger understood that he was their toy, their big male doll – life-size and breathing, animated and responsive, warm flesh to be played with as they pleased. This was something neither had ever had before, he guessed, from the pleasure they were now taking.

He joined in their game, he laughed with them, he soaped four bare breasts and two patches of curls. Two bottoms to feel and stroke, two little knots between cheeks to press with a finger. They became sexually aroused, of course – although less than an hour had passed since the orgasm of a lifetime. Wet arms around Roger's neck, wet bellies pressed against him.

He backed them both against the tiles, side by side with feet well apart to open their thighs for him.

'*Roger cheri . . .*' they both murmured, trying to kiss his mouth, their noses together, their fingers groping for his limp part.

He was facing them, the hot water splashing down his back. He was so close to them his chest was against two pairs of breasts and each of his hips touched a soft wet belly. Two arms around his waist, pulling him closer, each trying to get him into her. But his pride was not ready for that, it dangled limply despite all their handling.

His right hand was between Yvette's thighs, his left hand was between Monique's. His fingertips played across curls flattened against warm flesh, then parted the lips of two *lapins*.

'*Roger cheri,*' Yvette murmured again when he found her secret bud. A moment later Monique sighed, '*Ah Roger!*' when he touched hers. His fingertips circled the buds slowly and deftly, making both ladies sigh again.

It was easy enough to satisfy them with his fingers, pressing both women back against the pink tiles, hearing their sighs and their little sobs as the touch of his fingers sent long tremors of delight through them. Their bodies shook against him, their hands gripped and fumbled. Which would reach her peak first, he asked himself, Monique or Yvette?

His guess was it would be Monique. Because Yvette had reached orgasm twice already and would take longer now than her friend, that was his reasoning. And like all reasoning about women, it was wrong. Yvette was the first to wail and shudder in ecstatic spasms.

She grabbed at his wrist and forced his fingers deeper inside herself – but before he could fully enjoy the sight and feel of her in orgasm, Monique arrived there too, her shrill cries rang round the shower-stall.

Was ever a man in so extraordinary a situation, Roger said to himself with a grin, two naked women impaled on his fingers and shrieking in orgasm!

When at last they were quiet again, they kissed his mouth and his chest, they sank to their knees to kiss his belly, hands on his thighs and between his thighs and between the cheeks of his bottom, as he'd done to them only moments ago. And by this time his cherished part was sticking out long and hard.

'Me first,' said Yvette, and she took it into her hot mouth.

Looking down at her, Roger noted no repetition of the look of apprehension when in the bedroom he'd pushed his hard part into her mouth. She was far beyond apprehension after what he'd made her experience since.

'Only a little while,' Monique said urgently, 'then my turn. I've never done it before, I want to know what he tastes like.'

Protesting

At the Agence Drouet the thin receptionist was talking into the telephone when Roger arrived. When she saw it was him she put a hand over the mouthpiece and smiled at him and asked him to sit down for a moment.

He took a chair and glanced round the office to make sure his photo was still on show. So was Edmond Planchon's, of course, a new one, slightly bigger than his own. He ought to do something about that, he decided. He'd get a new picture taken and have a bigger print made. Why should Edmond be more important?

There were glossy pictures of five or six other men he didn't know personally, the rest of Gilberte's stable. He gave them no more than a glance, none were as good-looking as he was – they were not serious competitors. To be perfectly candid, he didn't think Edmond was as handsome as he was, though he conceded that he had charm of a sort.

Almost as interesting as his own picture were the pictures of the dozens of beautiful young women the agency represented – as models, that is. Roger had never heard rumours to the contrary, and he'd never asked any questions about whether other services were contracted to middle-aged men. He didn't think so, men had no great problem in finding appropriate facilities.

The photo of Nadine Bernier had her in a slinky black evening frock – backless almost down to her elegant bottom, blonde hair arranged on top of her head and her long slender neck naked but for a diamond choker. Borrowed, if it was real.

She was marvellously attractive, Roger thought – until she began to talk. Then she became boring.

Ah, if only a chic little gag could be devised to prevent her talking! In black velvet perhaps, over her pretty mouth. To be worn all day, except when she ate – and all night, to make sure that only her legs were open. She would be the ideal girlfriend then, with a gag on, beautiful blonde Nadine.

But nothing in this world was ever perfect – Nadine had to be taken as she was. With all her irritating faults, she was well worth taking – he made up his mind to phone and arrange to meet her soon. Now that Marie was gone, he needed someone.

Celeste put the phone down and smiled at him again across the typewriter. She'd taken her spectacles off while he'd been busy with his thoughts about the photos on the walls. He smiled back at her and said she was looking very pretty – his words brought a faint pink acknowledgment to her cheeks.

'Madame Drouet is out,' she said, 'at the hairdresser. She'll be back quite soon now, if you don't mind waiting.'

'But of course I shall wait,' said Roger, getting up from his chair and drifting towards Celeste's desk.

He had no real interest in the receptionist, it was curiosity that urged him on. When one is an expert in the manipulation of women's bodies, he told himself, every woman becomes the object of continuing interest. It is necessary to understand, in order to form a professional opinion on how a particular female body must be handled to obtain the most satisfactory results.

Celeste was tall and thin – even when sitting down behind her desk she gave the impression of being tall. Perhaps because her arms were long and thin. And because she had a long face with a long nose and a long upper lip.

She was wearing a blouse like a shirt today, long-sleeved and close-fitting, buttoned down the front, open at the throat. Her neck was long and thin too, but she had a pretty face, now that her spectacles were off, long nose or not.

Roger perched on her desk – on her side of it – close to her. One cheek of his bottom on the edge, one foot on the floor, one foot swinging idly. His knees were well apart, his thighs open. He was making a demonstration of his masculinity by showing off the bulge in his trousers. Posing to impress her – to overwhelm her. Why else was he a model if he couldn't achieve that much?

Not that he went on many real modelling jobs these days – his career had taken another course after Madame Drouet discovered what his true talents were. But just occasionally he was still asked for to wear clothes rather than take them off.

Celeste crossed her arms over her narrow chest and stared up. Her breasts were small and hardly showed through her shirt, but she had a friendly expression on her face. Roger wanted to know about her breasts – how they appeared bare and how they felt to the fingers.

It was stupid to do anything that might annoy Madame Drouet – he told himself that while he slid off the desk and went behind Celeste's chair and stroked her hair lightly. And what could be more certain to enrage Madame than to find him playing with her receptionist? What he was contemplating was imbecilic, that he understood perfectly.

But it didn't stop him doing it. He stared down from over her head at the tiny mounds of her breasts under her striped shirt. He reached down over her narrow shoulders and felt them as best he could. He wanted to handle them bare, he wanted to know what it was like to have her warm flesh under his fingers.

'Madame Drouet will be back very soon now,' she said a little breathlessly when he started to unbutton her shirt.

'We shall hear her step on the stairs,' Roger assured her.

Her shirt was undone down to her waist. It took only a moment to unclip her tiny white bra and pull it up to her throat. Then his hands were on her bare breasts. The word promised too much – Celeste had two long pink buds set on swellings hardly perceptible to the naked eye. Nothing to hold or play with.

But she sighed in pleasure at his caress. Evidently her buds were sensitive to the touch and would react very satisfactorily to the flick of a warm wet tongue.

'Have you a boyfriend, Celeste?' Roger asked her.

'Yes and no,' she sighed. 'I do have someone but I'm not very serious about him.'

The invitation was very obvious. Roger stroked her and asked himself how far he wanted to go. Granted it was idiotic to risk annoying Gilberte Drouet – but on the other hand he was annoyed with her. The incident at Yvette's, when her friend Monique had appeared in the bedroom – it ought not to have happened.

He had coped, naturally, but that wasn't the point. There had been an agreement, so far as he was concerned – and that was to pleasure Yvette Dubois. Nothing was said by Madame Drouet about another woman at the same time –

evidently she hadn't known and that meant she had failed to look after his interests. Or so he believed. Therefore it would please him to annoy her.

He bent over to kiss Celeste's ear.

'Pull your skirt up,' he murmured.

'No, no – we can't do anything here,' she said hastily as she eased her skirt up to let him see her long thin thighs in nylon stockings. Roger wanted to run his hands up and down them.

'Higher,' he whispered.

'But no, this is impossible,' she sighed as she pulled up her skirt until he saw pale-skinned thighs above her stocking-tops.

'Ah yes, how charming,' he said, his fingertips moving slowly on the firm pink buds on her chest, 'I've been wanting to touch you like this every time I have been to your office – did you guess that?'

'Ah no!' she murmured, her face flushed pink. She pulled her skirt higher and he saw her knickers – creamy white and thin to almost transparency and stretched tight between her legs. There was a gap between her long thin thighs at the top. By putting a hand up her skirt he could touch her whether her legs were open or closed. To look at it another way, Celeste's legs were never closed.

At this pretty sight Roger suddenly knew how far he wanted to go with Celeste – to the ultimate. He would have those knickers off and her long thin thighs wide open – sit her on the edge of her desk and slide up into her . . .

She stood up quickly and stepped forward away from his hands, smoothing her skirt down, and hastily buttoned her shirt. Roger heard footsteps outside the office door, on the stairs, and knew it was Madame Drouet returning. He gave a sigh of exasperation; another ten minutes and he'd have had Celeste – and in some way that would have been getting his own back.

He was seated on one of the visitor's chairs, looking casual, when the door opened and Gilberte came in. To conceal the bulge in his trousers he had crossed his legs elegantly. All was well when he stood up to greet her and kiss her hand – nothing could be seen. Since taking up the profession of pleasuring women for a fee he'd changed the style of his underwear to something more likely to give middle-aged ladies a little thrill.

These days he wore a black silk posing-pouch for underwear, a tiny garment much like the *cache-sexe* worn by performers at the Casino de Paris or the Folies Bergère. The skimpy design showed off his strong thighs, all the way up to his hips – and it held his male pride in an upright position against his belly.

The silk clung closely to outline the shape and size of what he had to offer. And behind there was nothing except the thong, so his bottom was bare. They were not cheap to buy, these small items of underwear, but they caused interesting results. Madame Rocher, for example, the first time he took his trousers off in her bedroom, she fell to her knees and rained hot kisses on him through the thin silk.

She was fully dressed at the time, this Madame Rocher – Elise, her first name was. She asked him to take off his trousers and he'd guessed she liked to look at male parts and handle them to make them stand up. Pleasant enough – Roger liked being admired by women – but even he wasn't prepared for her wild enthusiasm. Her nails were digging into the cheeks of his bottom while she kissed him through the black silk – wet and hot kisses.

'*Zut alors*!' he gasped as her ardent kissing went on and on. After a while it intensified into licking through the thin silk and then into sucking – until his body jerked in sudden spasms and he was spurting into his flimsy underwear.

'*Bonjour Roger*,' said Gilberte Drouet, 'come into my office – there are matters to be discussed.'

Her visit to the hairdresser had evidently been a success. Her hair was a glossy chestnut, no more black with silver speckles. And it was in soft waves, parted on one side and arranged about her ears neatly. Roger thought it an improvement. He winked at Celeste secretly and followed Gilberte into her office.

She was wearing an expensive white jacket over a plain little black dress. She hung the jacket on a hanger and stood with her hands on her hips looking at Roger thoughtfully.

'About Madame Dubois,' she began, 'there was no suggestion of anything out of the ordinary when she phoned me to ask for you. I was surprised, to say the least of it, when she rang again to say she had included a friend in the session. I understand that you took it in your stride – she was so pleased she agreed to a very high fee.'

'So she should,' said Roger, 'but that's not the point. There ought not to be surprises – this time it was another woman, but next time it might be a client who wants to include her husband in the games. When I refuse and walk out she'll be on the phone to you to complain, isn't that so?'

'Never happened yet,' said Gilberte, raising her eyebrows. 'I suppose there's a first time for everything.'

'I want a plain understanding there will be no more surprises of any sort,' Roger insisted. 'You must make it clear when they phone that if they want me, I am there for one person only.'

'Well, well!' said Gilberte with a sly little smile. 'If you feel so strongly about it I will make a point of informing your clients of your stipulations. Was it exhausting, my poor Roger, two women in the bed? Madame Dubois didn't sound tired at all. She asked if you will go back there on Friday, to play with her and her friend Madame Santerre again.'

'What did you tell her?'

'That I must consult you first. I have promised to phone her, today or tomorrow. Well, Roger, what do you think? Shall I say yes to her? Or is it too much for you?'

'Friday,' said Roger, thinking about it, 'I don't know.'

'It is very simple,' said Gilbert, anxious to coax him into saying yes. 'Two ladies, two times each – but it is for you and only you to decide. I can always get one of the others to go.'

'Perhaps,' he said doubtfully. 'Have you got anyone else who can do it four times without a pause to draw breath? Then play with two women for another hour under the shower? After I got back to my apartment I slept for twelve hours non-stop and woke up starving hungry.'

'To tell the truth, I think you have lost weight from all the exertion,' Gilberte said with a chuckle. 'Stand up for a moment and let me check.'

He stood up, arms hanging at his sides, and she put her hands inside his jacket to stroke his chest and his sides, slowly and knowingly. She stroked his belly through his shirt and said she thought it was a little flatter than it had been. She bent down to run her hands up and down his thighs, outside and inside.

'You may have shed a kilo,' she said, straightening her back. Her hands moved round to his bottom, feeling the cheeks through his trousers – a long and thorough feel.

'You have a neat round bottom, Roger,' she said, 'it would be a calamity if it shrank or lost its shape. Do you like it to be stroked?'

She didn't bother herself to wait for a reply, she used both hands to unzip his trousers so she could rummage inside.

'I'm sure *this* hasn't lost any weight,' she announced boldly, her fingers inside his slinky black hold-all to stroke his hard and upright part, 'ah yes, it's as long and thick as I remember it from a day or two ago. The truth is that exercising it makes it stronger, don't you agree, Roger?'

She slipped his underwear down his thighs a little, to expose his interesting parts completely for her attention, stiff shaft and hairy pompoms.

'It's none the worse for wear, whatever use Madame Dubois and her friend made of it,' she said huskily, 'and to be frank with you, dear Roger, yours is the nicest and most thrilling of all the handsome young men on my books. But don't become conceited because of that – it's what you can do with it that counts.'

How it happened he didn't know, but she had him standing with his back to her desk – the very ordinary, brown, wooden office desk on which Gilberte had been pleasured more times than in bed. He guessed there was a psychological satisfaction for her in using the desk – it was involved with her determination to do well in business on her own. Compelling good-looking virile young men to do it to her on the desk was important as a measure of success.

But who cared about psychology at a time like this, when her hands were stroking him briskly up and down and his knees were beginning to shake. He gripped her waist and turned her around, so she was facing the desk and he was behind her.

'Bend forward,' he said, 'hands on the desk, Gilberte.'

'I see you are in a masterful mood today,' she said, her

tone mocking. 'You rebel against being a woman's plaything, do you? Very well, my dear Roger, I am your plaything this time.'

She placed her forearms flat on the desk and bent over, with her feet apart on the floor. Roger lifted her black dress up to her waist and pulled her knickers halfway down her thighs. She was wearing tangerine silk with black lace edging, for which he gave a sigh of pleasure.

She had described his bottom as round and neat – in return he could fairly describe hers as round and plump. Her cheeks were bouncy to his hands – he felt them and stroked them before he slipped his fingers between her thighs to stroke her *joujou*. The curls were the same rich chestnut as her head. He tried to recall if they had been black before, when her hair was black. Was it possible she'd had the curls between her legs dyed to match her hair?

'I am a man,' he announced, his fingers probing into her none too gently. 'I have had enough of being a plaything for middle-aged women. From now on I shall do what I please to them – they can complain all they want, it will make no difference to me.'

'Bravo!' Gilberte sighed, spreading her feet a little wider. 'Be a ram, *petit Roger*, be a stallion, rape and ravage and ruin every woman you go to – start with me!'

His fingers were inside her, he had her wide open and pushed his stiff flesh up into her without mercy. She gave a shriek of delight and her whole body shuddered to his urgent thrusting.

'You despise me, Gilberte,' he said forcefully, 'confess it – you despise me because I pleasure women for a living.'

'No, no,' she gasped, 'I like you very much, Roger, I admire you – your face and your body. And your remarkable abilities.'

'Lies,' he said, stabbing into her strongly, 'all those women who pay me to make love to them – they all despise me afterwards for taking money. And you despise me most of all, Gilberte.'

He was holding her shoulders and lying against her back while he slammed into her, his belly smacking against her bare bottom. It was of no consequence if she despised him, he told himself – at this moment he was a man asserting his natural rights over a woman, making her sigh and moan and thrill to his thrusting. He was not her plaything, he was her master.

'Roger, Roger,' she moaned, as if on cue, 'you are wonderful, the way you do this to me!'

He gripped her shoulders harder, his breath rasping, his legs trembling. Gilberte plunged into shuddering ecstasy, crying out shrilly as her bottom bucked back at him. He spurted his desire into her, determined to ravage her to a standstill this one time he was in control.

'Roger *cheri*,' she sighed in noisy pleasure, 'ah, but you are a marvel, my Roger! I want you for myself, I will not send you out to other women again. I want you here every day to do it to me on my desk – promise me you will!'

He said nothing, little tremors of ecstasy still shaking him. He didn't believe her, of course – Gilberte was not the sort of woman to put herself at emotional risk with a man, any man. Her chestnut-dyed *lapin* was talking, not her brain – her words came from between her legs, as it were, not her mouth.

On second thoughts, Roger decided it might be amusing to take her at face-value, to pretend to believe her, go along with her expressed wishes and see how she extricated herself from a rash statement.

'Gilberte *cherie*,' he murmured as he kissed her ear and

125

eased his wet and dwindling part out of her, 'it would make me happy, very happy indeed, to do it with you twice a day and never have to visit other women for a living. Morning and afternoon, yes? At eleven and again at three, would that be right for you? And if you wanted me in the evening as well, I'd come round to your apartment and have you naked on the bed.'

'But what a marvellous prospect,' she said thoughtfully while she pulled up her knickers and smoothed down her skirt. So much like Celeste making the same adjustments not twenty minutes ago that Roger almost laughed out loud.

Gilberte sat in her executive chair, Roger leaned on the edge of the desk, on the same side as her, his trousers unzipped but his black silk *cache-sexe* pulled up over his soft wet part.

'You can't really believe that women despise you, Roger,' she said, staring up curiously at his face. 'If only you could have heard Madame Dubois on the phone, she was raving about you. She could have been talking about a film-star or a footballer – the trumpets and drums were sounding in her voice.'

Roger shrugged.

'And what about Madame Lenoir,' Gilberte went on, 'she's even more of a fan than Madame Dubois! When she phones to arrange a visit by you she seems to be speaking of a saint. I think that I should inform her any halo you have is in your trousers – not around your head, *cheri*. But then I think it would be unkind to disillusion her. And Madame Lafoy, she's crazy about you. As is Madame Larose! They adore you, Roger, they are all besotted by you. It is absurd to believe they despise you.'

'All the same,' said Roger, and he shrugged again.

'To accuse me of despising you is incredible,' Gilberte said, eying him thoughtfully. 'I am a great admirer of yours, *cheri*.'

'But only one part of me,' he said, 'not me as a person – you needn't pretend, Gilberte, there is no need. Now we have agreed I am to be yours exclusively, I shall make very sure I give you every satisfaction.'

'Ah yes, that,' she said with a half-hearted smile – and then an idea occurred to her and her smile became broader. 'Roger, I think I understand the reason for your melancholy mood – you've fallen in love! Tell me truthfully, is it Nadine? I know that you've been with her. She's very pretty, what a pity that she's not intelligent too.'

Roger was horrified that Gilberte had guessed his secret. Did his shattered emotions and disappointment show in his face? It was absurd: he'd known Marie Brantome only a few days and made love to her twice – but apparently it had left marks on him for others to see.

'No,' he said in a tone as matter-of-fact as he could make it, 'I'm not in love with anyone, what a very strange idea! I like Nadine and she likes me. We are friends – sometimes we get into the same bed together, but that's all.'

Gilberte looked at him with her head on one side and a little half-smile on her face. Evidently she didn't believe a word of what he said.

'I'm pleased to hear that,' she said. 'Love is not a useful emotion in your profession, Roger, it gets in the way of proper performance with the ladies who admire you so ardently. And as for Nadine – play with her any time you wish. I don't believe a clever man could fall in love with her. Is she amusing in bed? Or does she lie on her back, silent, like a mannequin waiting for you to make use of her body?'

While she was speaking, Gilberte slid her hand into his open trousers to stroke his limp part through the thin black silk of his *cache-sexe*. Her fingers were agile and knowing, there was a slow stirring of his emotions that was pleasurable. But in view of the slighting way she spoke of Nadine, he was glad he hadn't mentioned Marie to her.

'Nadine in bed?' he said, determined not to let Gilberte get the better of him. 'She is like a leopard, savage and beautiful and dangerous. She fights and scratches and rolls over and over and bites at your throat with sharp little teeth. She screeches wildly when she arrives at her climax — a night with her is the most marvellous adventure possible.'

'Is that so?' said Gilberte mockingly, her fingernails sharp against the flesh of his lengthening part inside his underwear. 'She ravages you, does she, Roger, she makes you her prey? But we must be speaking of two different women, you and I. Or there is a twin sister, perhaps? The Nadine Bernier I know lies with her legs open and is pleased about it if a man sticks his thing into her — she has no talent for love.'

'You have been to bed with her, dear Gilberte?' Roger asked, his eyebrows rising in sarcasm.

'Of course not. Although I'm sure I could if I wanted to. She has so little personality of her own that she falls in with any suggestion. I understand her as well as I understand you — if I wanted her knickers off, I'd only have to tell her. Whether you like it or not, Roger, you and she are an open book to me.'

She was standing between his legs, pushing him back to sit on the desk fully, his knees well parted. Her hand was deep inside his little posing-pouch, massaging his upright part firmly.

'What nonsense!' he said shakily. 'You know nothing about me except I give satisfaction to women with money to pay for it.'

She released his stiff part for a moment while she pushed his jacket off his shoulders and down his arms.

'An open book,' she repeated with a smile. 'Let's read a page or two, shall we?'

To his surprise she pulled her little black dress up over her head and threw it on to the chair behind her. He was pleased to see her bra matched her knickers – tangerine edged with black lace. This he thought very chic and very provocative – even for a woman of her years.

She slipped the knickers down her meaty thighs and right off. All this undressing in the office, with Celeste just outside at her typewriter – Gilberte must regard the occasion as important in some way, Roger thought. But why? He reached down to stroke her plump bare belly, his finger strayed down into the chestnut curls between her thighs. With a murmur of pleasure she let him slide three fingers into her.

She was very warm and slippery from their first encounter. He tickled her secret bud for only two moments before she began to breathe loudly and jerk her body backwards and forwards. She was impaled on his fingers, and so hot and slippy inside that Roger thought she must be in the throes of orgasm already.

He dragged her nearer to him with fingers hooked deep inside her. She was unsteady on her feet – she really was in orgasm as he'd guessed. She put her hands on his shoulders to keep steady and not buckle at the knees.

'Lie down on your back,' she gasped.

She pushed him down flat and climbed on the desk to straddle him on her knees. *No, not like that*, he protested,

129

realizing too late she meant to use him as her plaything. But by then he was on his back and her weight was on his loins to hold him down.

She held his wrist and pulled his fingers out of her, smiling down at him. She gripped his stiff part between scarlet fingernails and held it at the proper angle while she parted her pink fleshy petals. *Yes Roger, like this*, she said, and she lowered herself on him slowly and forced him in deep.

She was a well-made, well-fleshed woman, this Gilberte, plump of belly and of thigh. She sat astride him and bounced strongly up and down.

'You refuse to be a plaything, Roger,' she said, smiling down at him, 'very well, I shall keep that in mind.'

She was quoting his very own words, laughing at his insolence in trying to oppose her. Her brief standing orgasm was over and she was ready for another.

'You must have confidence in me, Roger,' she went on, a little breathless now new spasms of pleasure were flicking through her belly, 'I understand you, I know what is best for you.'

'And is this best for me?' he sighed, feeling the sensations of delight surging through him. He couldn't help it – his hands were in her groin, his fingertips lay on the wet lips clinging to his hard shaft as they slid up and down its long length.

'But of course,' she sighed, 'this is the best thing for you, *mon petit Roger*, the best thing in the world...'

Her eyes were half-closed, she was panting, in a moment she would be shrieking in orgasm. Whether or not her actions were best for Roger it was clear the moment was very good for her. He reached up to pull her bra-straps off her shoulders and tip her breasts out of the cups. She was moving vigorously on him and her big soft pair flopped up and down in rhythm. The buds were red-brown against her pale skin.

She hardly knew what she was doing. She leaned forward with her hands flat on the desk on either side his head. Her breasts hung over his face. He seized one plump slack dangler in both hands and raised his head to suck the bud into his mouth.

I've won the bet, Edmond, he said to himself, *I've seen them.* And the thought made him smile so that her wet breast slid from his mouth. He stared down between their bodies to their groins, where his hard length was being plunged briskly in and out of her *joujou*. At this sight his hands clenched tight on the dangling breast he held.

Her assessment of him was right – he was forced to admit it. The woman he loved had left him. To be entirely honest, she had never really been with him, not as lovers understand it. It was a brief *affaire* of a hotel room and an hour on the divan in his apartment. And that was it. *Adieu Marie.*

As for beautiful blonde Nadine, she would drive a man insane if he ever stopped to listen to her chatter. Her pretty little mouth needed to be closed firmly on a stiff shaft. Which wasn't practical, day and night.

When you analyzed it, what was Roger Chavelle but a plaything for women who paid him? Gilberte was right. He stared into her face and saw her red-painted mouth drawn back in a fixed smile. He lifted his head from the desk to catch the tip of a dangling breast in his mouth again, and sighed to feel her slippery flesh gripping and milking him with ruthless skill.

'You like that, do you?' she gasped.

With hands that shook with passion she stuffed almost half of her left breast into his open mouth.

'Suck it, Roger!' she panted, bouncing up and down on him to a furious rhythm. A moment later she announced the onset of her orgasm with a wailing, cat-like shriek. Her soft *joujou* clung to him in a long sucking grip that pulled him deep into her belly, his body clenched like a fist and he spurted into her in spasms that racked him from head to foot.

When they were both calm again she lay forward on him, making him feel the weight of her solidly-fleshed body that pinned him to the desk. Her tongue was hot as she licked his mouth and grinned possessively down at him.

'Darling Roger,' she said, 'no wonder you are so sought after by the ladies who know you. You are superb, there's no question about it. So which day next week will you call on Madame Dubois and her friend Madame Santerre? I must phone her today.'

'I thought you wanted me as your own exclusively,' Roger said with a grin.

'You are in your prime, *cheri*,' said Gilberte. 'It would be a dreadful pity to monopolize you and restrict your career. Trust me – I am your friend and adviser.'

'Very well,' he agreed, knowing it was all settled in advance and there was no point in arguing with her, 'any day you like.'

'Good,' she said, and kissed his mouth, 'and before that I've arranged for you to call on Madame Rocher. She's absolutely mad about you, as you know – she offered to increase your fee to be certain she got you and not one of my others.'

On his way out, neat and debonair again, Roger smiled at tall, thin, bespectacled Celeste. She was standing at a filing cabinet with the top drawer open. He shrugged as he smiled – he had not the least doubt she knew what went on in Gilberte's office. She very probably had heard Gilberte's climactic squealing.

She was standing sideways to him, this Celeste, a hand inside the open cabinet drawer. How modest her chest was in profile, he considered, though he'd like to bare her doll-like breasts and tickle the buds again, when the chance arose. And lick them, to see just what it did to her – it would be interesting to see her long thin legs thrashing about in orgasm.

She didn't smile back at him, Celeste, she winked at him over her shoulder. *Any time you want*, she was silently telling him.

Retreating

On the phone Edmond Planchon said he didn't believe that Roger had won the bet. Gilberte had always evaded having her *nichons* bared, he insisted.

'For her it is psychological,' he told Roger, 'it would be an indication of weakness and subordination to let her danglers be handled by a man. Surely you must realize she uses her *lapin* as a weapon against you – she overcomes you.'

'Enough of the psychology,' said Roger, 'the simple truth you find difficult to accept is I've had them out and seen them and given them a thorough feel.'

'Fantasy, nothing more,' Edmond said firmly. 'If anyone could persuade her to get them out it would be me. She thinks well of me, she knows from personal experience how first-rate I am when it comes to push-and-pull. You haven't a chance.'

'Delude yourself as you wish,' Roger retorted, 'I've not only played with Gilberte's *nichons*, I've sucked them.'

'*Oh la la*,' said Edmond, his tone changing suddenly, 'this I want to hear about in detail. I'll concede the bet for the time being and buy you dinner on condition you tell me everything.'

'Agreed – and I shall make you turn bright green with envy.'

135

When it came to arranging which evening, there were problems. Edmond had professional engagements. Roger had a commitment for Madame Rochet. And an unspecified date for a visit Gilberte had talked him into with Madame Dubois and her friend.

In the end they agreed to leave their dinner together for a day or two. But Roger dreamed of Marie Brantome that night and woke up restless and discontented. He phoned Nadine – it was better to be miserable in company than on his own. Nadine said she had a busy day but nothing planned for the evening.

From her tone of voice Roger gathered she was pleased to hear from him – she was another who didn't want to stay alone in her apartment for an evening or go to the cinema on her own. He was surprised that so beautiful a woman encountered problems in her social life, but when he remembered how it had been with her in bed, what had happened and what had nearly not happened, it was perhaps understandable.

He suggested they might go to the little night-club they had been planning to go to the last time they'd met. Except they had never arrived there – he'd found Nadine naked in her bathroom and put his arms round her and that had been that.

This time he called for her at nine and politely declined her invitation into the apartment for a drink before they went out. He felt certain that if they sat down together for a drink, the furthest they would get that evening would be her bedroom. For the simplest of reasons: it was impossible to listen to her for more than a few minutes without sinking into a profound boredom – and the obvious way to stop that happening was to slip a hand up her skirt.

After which nature always took its course, so that in no

time at all beautiful blonde Nadine was naked on her back –
with her knees up. Roger had nothing against that, but he
knew it would take place anyway when they went back to
her apartment from the night-club. And he'd prefer to
enjoy a meal and a dance first.

Nadine looked perfectly stunning – she always did. Her
blonde hair was up on top of her head, braided through
with strings of stones which resembled diamonds but
weren't. She wore a short evening dress cut straight
across her breasts to reveal a most enticing valley between
them.

It was of silver lamé, the dress, it made blonde Nadine
look like an ice-queen from a Hans Christian Andersen
story. Remote, lovely, untouched, virginal. The stark
contrast between this appearance and how Roger remembered her in bed made him sigh; his precious part stiffened
and strained upwards in his trousers.

They'd played *soixante-neuf* on her bed, Nadine's blonde
head between his parted thighs and her breasts squashed on
his belly, his long thick part in her mouth and her slender
thighs open on either side of his head, her *joujou* two
centimetres from his face. His tongue had been in the long
pink lips and flicking over her bud, she had shaken and
screamed in noisy orgasm.

Now here she was in silver lamé, bare shoulders pale,
neck like a swan, looking as if she had never seen a man's
stiff thing in all her life and would be horrified and insulted
if she did. He smiled at the thought and touched his stiffness
through his dark trousers for a moment – this proud part
she'd had deep in her innocent-looking mouth.

And on that memorable occasion he'd refused to let her
escape in a short sharp climax. He'd licked her wet bud fast
and hard and made her shriek and convulse until she'd

collapsed on his belly and almost fainted. All of which he intended to do again to her when they arrived back at her apartment in the early morning.

'No one's taken me out dancing for over a week,' said Nadine. 'Dear Roger – I was so glad to hear your voice on the phone.'

It goes without saying that the food in the night-club wasn't very good but it was passable. The wine was acceptable; by the second bottle Roger's mood was cheerful. The three-man band for dancing was very good; saxophone, piano and drums. Nadine was a delight to dance with on the tiny floor; she danced expertly. She did everything with expert and polished ease, except fall in love, at which she was hopelessly bad.

But to dance with – what a joy! She didn't cling on tight as many women did, her hand was cool in Roger's hand, but her belly and her slender thighs brushed lightly against him to keep him in a state of permanent arousal. Her cheek lay lightly on his cheek, her perfume made him almost dizzy with delight. And best of all she kept her beautiful mouth shut while she danced.

In the dimness of the crowded dance-floor Roger's hand was on her sleek bottom – not clutching, not gripping, just fingertips straying almost imperceptibly over two perfect cheeks under the silver lamé, as proof to himself that in another hour he would undress her and roll her face-down on her own bed to kiss those smooth-skinned cheeks of her pretty *derrière*.

'Ah Roger,' she murmured into his ear, 'I melt when you touch me – my legs start to feel shaky.'

Roger was enjoying himself, but as thinkers have pointed out down the ages to anyone with time to listen to them, there is a certain maliciousness that keeps interfering in human destiny. A design-fault in the fabric of the cosmos causes all that can go wrong to go wrong – and at the least convenient time.

At about midnight Roger suddenly noticed that Marie Brantome was sitting on the other side of the dance-floor in a party of four. How long she'd been there he had no idea, or if she'd spotted him – the night-club was very dimly lit. Night-clubs are always dimly lit – so male customers can slide a hand unnoticed up the skirts of their female companions.

Which was precisely what Roger was doing at the moment he saw Marie across the room. His hand was up Nadine's silver lamé skirt and he was stroking the smooth inside of her thigh. In a little while he'd feel a few centimetres higher – to where her slender thighs met – and touch her neatly-clipped patch of soft blonde curls. Play with her while they drank another glass of wine and dance with her again. And when the third bottle was empty, take her home and undress her.

Seeing Marie drove all that out of his mind instantly. He sat open-mouthed, his hand motionless under Nadine's skirt, staring across the room, between the dancers, catching glimpses, saying to himself, *Yes it is her*, and then, *No it's not her*.

But it was Marie, and she looked delicious enough to make his heart ache. She wore a shiny black dress, sleeveless and nearly backless. Her dark hair was glossy even in the dark – cut short in a mannish style and parted neatly on the right, as ever. She presented a mixture of masculine and feminine traits that Roger found enchanting. He wanted to rush across the room to drag her out of the club into a taxi.

It would be impossible to wait as long as it took the taxi to reach the Place Denfert and into his apartment. Before the taxi moved away from the kerb he'd have her dress up to her hips and her knickers down and sit her across his lap – his hands on her pretty breasts, his stiff part up inside her. The driver could complain all he liked, a few francs would shut him up.

The other woman at Marie's table must be her lover – and very striking she was too. Ten years older than Marie, and almost as blonde as Nadine, with a fine big pair of breasts in the white lace top of her dress. She wore a four-row pearl choker, the real thing, very probably, not an Oriental imitation. She was holding Marie's hand and talking to her intimately, their heads close together.

The two men at the table were nobody, both about forty, well-dressed, smooth-faced, with money to spend. Roger ignored them completely – they had no part in his thinking about Marie, only the blonde woman, murmuring to her and smiling.

'Shall we dance again?' Nadine asked, smiling at the feel of his fingers high on her thigh, under her dress, almost into her knickers.

'Not just now,' he said, obsessed by his thoughts.

He had a face now for the figure that haunted his fantasy – a face for the woman in his dreams who leaned naked over Marie to kiss her breasts. A 35-year-old blonde with a big pair of her own. This was Marie's lesbian lover – this was the woman she'd gone back to after his embraces.

She was attractive, this big blonde woman. Roger could easily imagine her in his own bed with him, naked on her back with her legs spread. His hands squeezing her soft round breasts and his belly flat on hers. But a malign fate had reversed these roles. She lay under no man, this woman, she took Roger's place in the affections of beautiful Marie. And between her legs, her blonde head down between Marie's thighs, her skilled tongue in Marie's dark-haired *lapin* to send tremors of ecstasy through her.

In another ten minutes Marie got up and went out of the club. The blonde and the two men stayed where they were at the table. Roger murmured his excuses to Nadine and got up. It was obvious where Marie had gone. A discreet door in the entrance lobby led to a small cramped room where the usual hag in an apron guarded two cubicles, a saucer at her elbow for the tips she expected.

One cubicle door stood open, the other was closing. Roger had a bank-note ready in his hand, he winked at the hag as he threw it into her saucer and pushed his way into the cubicle a moment before the door was bolted. Marie glared at him, astonished and nervous – it is not customary for beautiful young women to find themselves accosted in toilet cubicles, even by men they know.

The space was tiny – they were standing so close that Marie's breasts touched his chest, and he could see down the front of her shiny black dress that she wore no bra that evening. Seen close – not just across a smoky, crowded night-club – Marie was so very beautiful that Roger felt he might almost burst into tears.

Her skin was clear and pale, her eyebrows thin and black, her lips full and dark red. He put his hands on her narrow hips and bent his head a little to kiss her mouth.

'Get out of here,' she said angrily, turning her head to stop him kissing her. 'What do you think you're doing?'

'In two words,' said Roger, 'I'm dying. Does that answer your question? I cannot live without you, Marie, I want you back.'

'This is ridiculous,' she said.

Indeed, the situation was totally absurd, this declaration

Marie-Claire Villefranche

of love in a cramped night-club toilet. But love does not concern itself with absurdity and Roger was beyond rational thinking on the subject of Marie Brantome.

'I notice that you're dying in the company of a fancy blonde. She will comfort your final moments, I suppose,' Marie said, in a tone that boded no good for Roger.

'She is a colleague, another model,' he said, trying to sound convincing. 'We have the same agent. And you, Marie, I see that you are here with your lover.'

'My lover?' she said, shaking her dark head, 'I am here with my husband and two friends. I have no lover. Not since you.'

'Ha!' Roger exclaimed, not believing a word of it. 'You deny the blonde woman at your table is your lover – am I supposed to accept your word for that?'

'Believe what you like,' she said, 'let me go, Roger.'

'I want to know her name,' he insisted, 'tell me.'

'Her name is Michele Legarnier and her husband is there with us – the man wearing glasses.'

Roger's hands were gliding over her hips and round her bottom and down the outsides of her thighs. In another moment his hand would be up her dress.

'No, don't do that,' she said firmly, 'there is something you don't know.'

'I may not know but I can guess,' he said sadly. 'Do you want to break my heart again by making me live your love-making with her in my imagination? What I invent by myself is bad enough – the reality of what she does to you will destroy me.'

'You must be mad,' she said.

Roger took her by the shoulders and shook her.

'No lies,' he said indignantly, 'I refuse to be made an idiot of. Tell me the truth now – how long have you been lovers?'

'Keep your voice down!' Marie exclaimed, with a nervous look at the bolted door. 'You don't know who may be listening.'

'I am a desperate man,' he warned her, 'you can't hope I'm in a mood to be discreet or reasonable. I love you to distraction, Marie, I want you to come back to me.'

'Impossible,' she said. 'We were lovers for a week but now it is finished. Get that into your head.'

Roger thought he heard an underlying plaintiveness in the way she spoke that was at odds with her ostensible meaning. He shook her again, but more gently this time.

'But you love me too,' he announced, 'I'm certain of it.'

'All this talk of how you love me and do I love you – it adds up to nothing, a mouthful of words,' she said. 'There are other considerations, but you are too self-centred to see that.'

'You are in love with this Michele – is that it?' he asked.

'What a fool you are!' she said bitterly.

Without bothering to answer he reached down between her knees and put his hand up her dress. She caught his wrist and stopped him as his fingers reached the smooth, bare flesh above the tops of her stockings.

'No, Roger, not this time. I told you there is something you don't know about – stand away and you shall see what I meant.'

He thought it was a trick to escape him. He took a step back, a very small step as there wasn't room for a full one, and kept his back to the door to trap her. She lifted her dress with one hand, up to her hip, and with the other she pulled down the top of her shiny little black knickers.

Roger sighed. She'd been wearing black satin knickers

the day he first met her, in the Avenue de l'Opera. This he'd found out when he had taken her to the little hotel near the Gare St Lazare to undress her and play with her for an hour. But these she had on tonight were even smaller, hardly more than a triangle of satin front and rear.

She held one side down and he saw something was different now – there on the smooth flesh of her belly, near her tuft of dark curls, almost in her groin: a red and blue mark. It was small, two centimetres in diameter, or thereabouts, and round. True, the lighting in the toilet was better than in the club but not good enough for Roger to make out what this curious mark was.

He squatted down on his haunches for a close look. Marie held her knickers down and her dress up for his inspection. It was a tattoo, he was astounded to observe – placed as near her *joujou* as it could be without infringing on the long thin pink lips.

Roger leaned forward a little, his hands holding the backs of Marie's thighs, and pressed a heart-felt kiss to her belly. And then he realized what the design was and swayed back and gasped – it was a monogram, a device of two interlocking initials: an M and an M.

'Finally the truth is out,' he said, standing up again, 'two letter Ms entwined – Marie and Michele. One done in red and one in blue. A sign of true love, presumably an identical tattoo is to be seen on Madame Legarnier's belly?'

'Just for one moment stop feeling sorry for yourself and hear what I want to tell you,' Marie exclaimed, sounding impatient. 'Neither M stands for Marie or for Michele – we have never been lovers. This mark was put on me because of you, Roger – you are to blame for this atrocity.'

'Me? What do you mean?'

'It's a long story,' she said with a shrug, 'and one that is

144

very familiar. My husband suspected I was meeting someone, and he was right: it was you. He had this mark of
ownership put on me. Need I explain to you why he chose
to have his monogram put on that particular spot?'

'What is his name?' Roger demanded, not knowing if he
should believe this bizarre tale or not.

'His name is Martin.'

'Martin and Marie, two initials enlaced,' Roger said
dismally, 'not Michele and Marie. Or so you tell me.'

'Again you're wrong,' she said, 'the other M is for
Messager. His name is Martin Messager – he has set his
brand on me to let me know who I belong to.'

'Then your surname is Messager, not Brantome?' Roger
said, a frown wrinkling his forehead. 'That explains a lot.'

He meant it explained why he hadn't been able to trace
her in the Paris telephone directory. No point in explaining.

'This man is a monster,' he declared. *If what you say is
true* were the words he didn't speak. 'Why do you stay with
him?'

'All part of the same long story,' she said, as she pulled up
her tiny knickers and smoothed down her short black dress.

'Do you have any real feeling for me,' he asked, 'a trace
of affection? Perhaps even a hint of love? You can be as
truthful as you like.'

'If I do, what of it?'

'Your body is not your own – you said that to me once
and now I understand what it meant. Let me help you
escape – you cannot wish to be someone's chattel. Meet me
tomorrow and tell me this long story of yours and we will
decide what can be done.'

'There is nothing to be done,' she said.

'We all have a choice, Marie.'

'Tomorrow – I will come to your apartment.'

'Come early,' he said quickly, 'about eleven.'

'The morning's not possible. Nor the afternoon. But Martin is going out about seven and I'll come then.'

'I'll be there and waiting,' Roger said fervently.

He kissed her forehead and slipped out of the toilet. The hag in the apron gave him a fearful leer and muttered, *Vive le sport, Monsieur*! but he didn't give her any more money.

His mind was full of hope and doubt; he couldn't stay another minute in the club only a few metres from Marie and her husband – or her blonde lesbian lover. He didn't know what he believed now he'd seen the little monogram tattoo. For what reason would any sensible man want his beautiful wife to cut her hair like a man and dress in masculine suits in the daytime?

If he was that way inclined he'd surely not have a wife to be jealous of but a young boyfriend. However Marie explained it to him, Roger couldn't entirely liberate himself from those first conclusions of his about her – that she loved women rather than men. Or as much as. He'd seen how she and blonde Michele talked so very intimately at the table with their heads close together and how Michele held Marie's hand.

He emptied his glass, then refilled it by emptying the bottle, finished that and asked Nadine if she was ready to go. She said yes, though if the truth were told she would have liked another dance first. As they got up and left, Roger made a huge effort not to stare at the table where Marie was sitting with the others.

In the taxi taking them to Nadine's apartment he was confused and uncertain. His arm was about Nadine's waist, of course, but he was asking himself what he really wanted to do. *I am in love with Marie*, he said to himself. *Tonight she let me kiss her belly and tomorrow she's coming to my*

*apartment and I shall make love to her for hours. Do I want
to be with Nadine tonight? I don't love her, that's certain – I
don't like her all that much.*

But while he was debating what to do, Nadine laid her
hand on his knee and turned her face to him to kiss him.
The soft scent of her perfume and the soft touch of her lips
enraptured Roger. He felt her long-fingered hand glide up
his thigh and rest over the bulge in his trousers. He was stiff
in a moment and had no more questions about which bed to
sleep in that night.

When they reached Nadine's apartment she asked him to
wait in the sitting-room for a moment – she would call him
into the bedroom when she was ready. Roger sat in an
armchair with a glass of cognac and his complicated
musings. Even though he'd seen the woman he was madly
in love with and she'd promised to be at his apartment
tomorrow, his thoughts were not happy.

It was all too absurd – how could anybody take seriously
this story of an angry husband branding an erring wife with
his name as a sign of ownership? To receive the tattoo,
Marie had to be willing. She had to co-operate, it wasn't a
question of holding her down on a table while the expert
with a needle put the mark on her – especially not in so
intimate a place.

All this *blague* about initials – it must be an invention! To
have a husband named Martin and a girlfriend named
Michele, and to be named Marie yourself – ridiculous! All it
needed was for Michele's husband to be named Maurice –
that would give four Ms in a row.

Roger was sure his first deduction was correct – the
monogram of two intertwined Ms stood for Marie and
Michele. He suspected they'd gone to a tattoo parlour
together to prove how much they adored each other.

They'd lain side by side with their knickers off, holding hands, probably, while the mark of undying love was inked into the soft flesh close to their bared *lapins*.

As for the tale of the husband, Roger conceded that there was a Monsieur Messager, a well-off man, who played a role of some importance in Marie's life. He paid the bills and he had her in bed when he had a mind to. He understood her love lay elsewhere and with another woman, it was of no great significance to him. Marie lives in a *ménage a trois* Roger concluded.

The most usual version was a man with a wife and a mistress – in this instance it was a woman who had a husband and a lesbian lover the man knew of. How could there ever be room in Marie's affections for a male lover in addition? Tomorrow evening when she came to Roger's apartment she'd explain this to him and say *adieu* for the second time.

Before he could devise more gloomy complications for his tale of woe and heartbreak, Nadine called from the bedroom that she was ready. He drained his glass and got up, not in the best of moods to accommodate her.

She had undressed and was lying on top of the bed in a haze of perfume and a wispy and practically transparent silk mousseline nightdress. Its low neckline was ruffled and almost exposed her breasts – she was posing for effect on one elbow, head back and lips slightly parted.

Roger shed his clothes in seconds – he was very good at that. He lay beside Nadine and kissed her hand, murmuring the correct compliments for an occasion of this type. She was not as stupid as many believed her, she guessed all was not as perfect as she wished. Perhaps there was no gleam in Roger's eyes, perhaps the softness of his male part warned her.

'You are sad,' she said. 'Tell me why.'

Roger shrugged as he tried to devise an answer that would not be too hurtful. The simple truth was that he was sad because he was in bed with a beautiful woman but she wasn't Marie.

'I have no coherent reason,' he said, 'it is only a mood that takes us all at times if we consider the impossibilities of our lives and expectations.'

It didn't seem to mean much, even to Roger as he said it, but Nadine took it seriously.

'Yes, it is true,' she said, 'we think we have found love and then it is gone. Our hearts are broken, we weep and suffer. But we never lose our belief in the possibility of love, that would be to lose interest in life itself.'

'What do you regret most?' he asked, to turn the questioning away from himself.

'I have nothing to regret,' she said, 'only that nothing ever lasts. Everything fades out after a week. And you, Roger, what do you regret?'

She held his dangler in the palm of her hand while they were exchanging these meaningless comments. Roger thought she was too boring to retain the interest of the men who took her to bed – she thought he had excess of charm and insincerity. Both were right, of course, and both were wrong.

One thing Nadine was entirely right about was his reaction to her hand stroking his male part. He could be as sad as he liked for all she cared – she was determined to have him. Rejection by any more men would be too painfully destructive to even think about. She played with his soft length and watched it growing long and thick in her hand.

'Am I the most beautiful woman you've ever made love

149

to?' she asked, needing a boost to her self-esteem after his slow start.

He leaned over her and delicately kissed the pink buds of her breasts showing through her wispy nightdress.

'Yes!' he said. 'Ten times yes, Nadine!'

'Do you know,' she sighed as his kisses continued through the thin silk, 'when you were here the last time I began to believe there's a possibility you and I could be the right partners for each other. Have you ever thought of me in that way, Roger?'

While he was wondering what he could say to that she released his hard length and lifted her flimsy nightdress over her head. He stared in rapture at her perfect breasts, the elegant curve of her hips, at her long smooth thighs.

And that neatly-clipped little patch of blondish curls where her thighs met – she was perfection itself for making love to. To live with, that was a very different pair of shirt-cuffs. He had to say something – she was waiting for an answer.

'*Moi*?' he said, putting surprise into his voice. 'How could an ordinary sort of person like me aspire to the most beautiful woman in all Paris?'

So that she couldn't expect him to say anything else he threw himself down flat and pressed his lips to her pretty *joujou*.

'But Roger...' she began, but the tip of his tongue slid into her and touched her secret bud. The conversation faded out fast in the glow of thrilling sensation.

He'd always known the best way to shut her up – he parted the long pink lips of her *joujou* with his fingers and held her wide open while he flicked his tongue over her little bud. Last time he'd been in bed with her she'd had difficulty in reaching orgasm, and he wanted no misery or remorse from her tonight – he had enough miseries of his own since the bizarre events in the night-club.

His wet tongue worked deftly – this was something he knew how to do very well, he had sent many a bored wife into frantically squealing orgasm this way. He wanted to finish Nadine as easily as possible and satisfy himself and go to sleep with no chatter about the absurdities of life and love. He knew all about that.

It didn't take long before Nadine was shaking and moaning and squirming about on her back.

'Oh yes, yes,' she sighed, '*je t'adore*, Roger, *je t'adore ...*'

And in less than a minute her beautiful body went into spasms of ecstasy, her legs were up in the air kicking out wildly. She had both her hands on the back of Roger's head to push his face into her open wetness. *Yes*, he said in his head, *yes, Nadine, shriek your pleasure at the top of your voice – let me hear it*.

When her legs fell back on the bed and she stopped shrieking, he knelt up to take her slim ankles in his hands and force them wide apart. He wiggled himself close to her on his knees, until his stiff and twitching length was looming boldly over her soft belly. He slipped his hands up her legs, from her ankles to her splayed thighs, he hooked two fingers between the long wet pink lips and flipped them so widely open that her bud, swollen and moist, was fully exposed.

'Not so soon,' she gasped, 'I can't!'

'You can,' he said, 'I shall make you.'

And he was on top of her in a flash, guiding himself into her with eager fingers.

'Oh,' she squealed as he slid all the way into her and put his belly flat on hers, 'no, Roger, I can't so soon.'

But she lay still and let him thrust away, a pleasant in-and-out motion he could keep going for a long time if he wanted to. Nadine's head had rolled to the side, presenting him with an ear and a cheek. Her eyes were closed, her arms lay loosely down by her sides. Now and then a tremor ran through her belly under him.

She was so still that in the middle of it all, Roger recalled that Gilberte Drouet had asked if Nadine lay silent on her back while he did it to her – like a dress-shop mannequin. Ah – only Gilberte hadn't seen how Nadine spread herself over him to play at *soixante-neuf*!

Whether Nadine was ready or not, her feet came up off the bed suddenly and her legs closed over his back like a trap. She was moving underneath him, matching him thrust for thrust – pushing her hot loins up at him with nervous little movements.

'Yes, Roger,' she gasped, 'you know how to make me do it!'

He went into overdrive, plunging in and out, her legs clamped tight about his waist, holding him with his belly tight to hers and her breasts squashed under his chest. He stared down at her beautiful face on the pillow, wondering what went on inside her head. Her dark blue eyes were set in a stare of amazement.

Roger got there first – he wailed as he spurted his desire up into her. But he wasn't ahead by much – three seconds later she gripped him so hard with her arms and legs that the breath was almost squeezed out of him. Intense and thrilling sensation had him helpless, an automaton that jerked and spurted and panted.

There was a little smile on Nadine's face as she became calm again – a smile of ecstasy transformed into satisfaction. '*Je t'adore,*' she whispered to him, '*Je t'adore, Roger.*'

'*Cherie*,' he murmured back.

At that moment he really did like Nadine more than he thought possible. Then a curious and disturbing question came into his head, why had Marie been wearing those tiny black satin knickers she'd showed him in the night-club toilet? Not proper knickers at all – they were hardly more than a *cache-sexe* for the stage.

In the times when he'd been with her before, she'd never worn underwear like that. Small, yes, provocative, yes. But never as small and blatantly sexy as tonight's tiny satin triangle. Why, Roger asked himself – who was she wearing them for?

They were an open invitation, designed to leave her belly and the cheeks of her bottom bare. They didn't conceal, they showed off her pretty *joujou* – that was their express purpose. Someone was going to take them off tonight, by now they were off, most certainly – someone had taken them down and stroked her *lapin*.

But who? Her so-called husband? But surely not, women didn't put on knickers like that for husbands, not in Roger's opinion. Though it must be said that his experience of married women was restricted to the well-off discontented ones who paid him a fee to pleasure them.

If not Messager the husband, was it blonde Michele Legarnier who had the advantage of taking off Marie's absurd little black satin *cache-sexe*? Or if, as Marie claimed, they were not lovers at all, she and the blonde woman, then who?

Who Roger moaned, *who*? In his distress he spoke aloud.

'Who what, *cheri*?' Nadine asked, her arms around his neck.

Wavering

Madame Choisy had a little surprise for Roger when he called on her by appointment at eleven in the morning. It wasn't that she led him straight into the bedroom without a word beyond *bonjour*. He expected that; this wasn't the first time he'd visited her fine large apartment just off the Boulevard St-Germain.

Nor was it a surprise when she put her hands on his shoulders and pressed her mouth to his in a fierce kiss. She was a woman of hot passions, this Elise Choisy, he knew that. She had a lot of money and lived apart from her husband. Perhaps these passions of hers had become too much for him to manage comfortably after they both reached the age of forty.

She had taken to Roger the first time he was scheduled for an afternoon visit to her. On that comical occasion there had been five minutes' chat before she invited him into her bedroom – her self-restraint was very limited in the presence of a young man. In the bedroom that first time she'd given an artificial little laugh and asked him to take his trousers off.

Naturally, his assumption had been that she wanted to see what she was getting for her fee – he'd unbuckled his belt and dropped his trousers. What had happened then struck Roger as very comical. This elegant lady of mature years had stood transfixed and stared round-eyed at the little black satin posing-pouch which contained his most precious parts.

After an incoherent murmur or two she'd dropped to her knees on the bedroom floor – without consideration for her *haute-couture* skirt or stockings. She'd sunk pink-painted fingernails into the cheeks of his bare bottom while she'd showered wet and hot kisses on him through the black satin. And very soon her ardent kisses had become a continuous licking through the fragile material.

The licking had eventually turned into sucking – a vacuum-cleaner strength sucking that had drawn his hard and bucking part right into her mouth and his satin pouch with it – and then his body had shaken in uncontrollable spasms and he'd spurted. Her nails had dug into his bottom harder yet and her sucking became frantic.

It was some time before she'd let go of him – he'd started to go limp by then. She'd sunk back on her heels with a long sigh and stared at the soaked silk of his little black pouch.

'*Formidable*,' she'd said in a murmur like a cat purring after a saucer of cream.

On subsequent visits to her apartment Roger found she handled him just as wildly. He thought it amusing that she found her chief pleasure in doing things to him rather than the other way about – but he'd been in this select profession for two years now and so he'd come across more variations on the belly-to-belly theme than he'd ever expected.

Always with the least likely women, the unconventional games. Well-to-do women, elegant, well-educated, married to important men, mothers of teenage children. The more conventional on the outside, the more unlikely the little games they wanted to play in the bedroom. He never troubled himself to ask why, he simply shrugged and went along with what they enjoyed.

So when Elise dragged him into her bedroom this afternoon and dragged his clothes off his body, he grinned. She had him naked in seconds, his clothes were strewn about the floor and she had her hand down the front of his black satin triangle to get hold of his prize part. It was still dangling, all this had happened so fast it hadn't begun to stand upright.

'I have a little present for you,' she said, her smile bright and her eyes gleaming, 'don't let yourself go stiff yet.'

She pulled open a drawer in the bedside cabinet and there was her surprise. She'd bought him a fancy *cache-sexe* to wear. More for her pleasure than his, naturally, but it was her privilege. It was very small, so small he wondered if he could get into it – and if he tried to cram his belongings in, would anything be really covered or contained?

The fancy little pouch Elise held out for his examination was made of white silk, the most expensive type. And words had been embroidered in purple on the front of it. *Mon petit Roger, je te baise, je t'adore.*

'What a charming gesture,' he said.

She was down on her knees to strip off his black silk *cache-sexe* and slide the new white one up his legs and into position. Her long fingers flitting in his groin were making him go hard – she was laughing while she crammed his upright flesh into the tiny pouch. When she sank back on her heels to inspect her work he stared down and grinned – she'd made him so big and hard the little pouch was strained impossibly tight.

'Fantastic!' said Elise, hands on her hips. 'I've never seen so impressive a bulge, Roger.'

157

She was fully dressed – she was wearing a white blouse tucked down into a dark blue skirt. She wore a thick necklace of polished white coral and a flat, gold wedding ring. And she sat there on the floor and stared in silence as if entranced by Roger's bulge.

She sighed and ran her fingertips very gently over his smooth flat belly. She didn't touch his bulge, not for an instant. She ran her fingertips down his thighs. It didn't need the touch of her fingertips or her lips through the silk of the little pouch to convince Roger – he knew perfectly well she was devouring it with her eyes.

At their first meeting she'd ravaged him with her mouth – and he'd made up his mind she was a predator, a sort of sadist, one who battened on young men and sucked them till she drained them dry, for her sexual pleasure and her spiritual nourishment. But at later meetings he wasn't so sure.

She was fascinated by the stiff male part – as the embroidery admitted, she adored it. And more than that, she worshipped it. It was her habit of getting down on her knees when his part was exposed that made him question his own first assumption. To get down on one's knees indicates submission, that was Roger's view. So was she a willing victim, perhaps, anxious to undergo sexual aggression?

If she was at heart a predator surely she'd have made him lie on his back so she could sit over him or lie on him – to assert her superiority. She'd have made him a victim beneath her while she sucked out his virility and spat it on his belly. One woman he'd visited by arrangement had done exactly that to him. Only later did he learn she had recently been divorced – and that in circumstances of considerable acrimony.

But Elise displayed no open aggression, on the contrary, she wanted to abase herself before a stiff male part – more or less any young man would do as the provider of the upright object of her fascination. Roger guessed there must have been many before him, though none as good-looking or as expert as he was.

It went without saying that he himself was most par- ticularly agreeable to Elise Choisy. She liked the look of his naked body and the touch of his flesh. She liked his manners and his never-failing readiness to oblige her in her whims and desires. And she was enraptured by his strong part standing stiff and bold.

It was bold indeed at its full magnificent stretch – fifteen centimetres in length and twelve centimetres around. To be more precise, fifteen and a bit. Fifteen and two millimetres at the least, perhaps even three millimetres. It was impossible to be exact when one tried to measure because it bounded and throbbed excitedly when handled.

Elise sighed to observe Roger's muscular thighs move a little further apart to give her a better view of the pompoms filling the lower part of his pouch. She gave a tiny sob, her trembling hand slid slowly up the flesh of his bare thigh. He was certain she wanted to be a victim, a sex-sacrifice. He also knew how to fulfil her desire.

'Confess it now, Elise,' he said in a commanding tone, 'never in your life have you seen anything as beautiful or exciting as my body. You've been to the Louvre often enough to stare at the naked marble statues of gods. Broad chests and flat bellies for you to admire. And especially the danglers between their legs.'

'Oh yes,' she murmured, her eyes glowing.

'But when you see me naked,' Roger continued, 'you understand they are nothing, those stone statues. Look at

159

me, Elise, look close – I am warm strong flesh you want to reach out and touch. Perhaps I shall let you. But first I want you to read aloud the words embroidered in front of you.'

'*Mon petit Roger, je te baise, je t'adore*,' she read from his silk underwear, her voice husky with emotion.

'But are these words sincere?' he asked with just a touch of disdain. 'Tell me truthfully what is in your mind, Elise, while you are staring with those huge eyes at me.'

'I hardly know what I think,' she stammered. 'I have no words to describe my feelings, Roger.'

'But you have already said that you adore me.'

'Oh, yes, yes,' she whispered, mesmerized by the bulge inside his white silk *cache-sexe*, 'that's true, I swear it.'

'Prove it,' he said.

She loved the way Roger was playing with her – and she adored him for understanding her enough to devise the game. She swayed forward on her knees and pressed her lips against his bare thigh.

'A proper start,' said Roger. 'Higher now.'

As if in a dream, she slid her mouth upwards a little to kiss his thigh nearer his straining silk pouch. Her breath was warm on his skin, she was sighing rather than breathing.

'Higher,' said Roger.

She gasped and kissed inside his thigh, so far up her flushed cheek was pressing against his bulging *cache-sexe*.

'Tell me you adore me, Elise,' he said, his hand stroking the top of her head. Her hair was soft to the touch, a middle-brown colour, thick and wavy.

'I adore you, Roger,' she murmured, and her hot tongue licked lightly over the silk covering his upright part.

'Kiss me higher,' said Roger again, parting his thighs wider.

Her lips had reached the object of her worship. Her mouth was pressed over the hard fleshy shaft under the silk.

This was how it always was when he called on Elise Choisy. He was contracted to perform twice for her, in any way she wished. Inevitably she wanted it in her mouth the first time, she on her knees in submission. Without words she was conveying he was the dominant one, the superior being – she was his sex-slave, there to pleasure him.

It was all make-believe, of course; he knew it, she knew it – but it was what she wanted and so it was what she got. Perhaps her missing husband had never understood her.

'Ah!' Roger sighed as he felt her drag his little pouch down his thighs to bare his rearing pride.

She held the shaft firmly between red-nailed fingers and slid her hand up and down – the unhooded purple head was deep inside her mouth and her tongue was hotly at work. Roger couldn't see her face, his guess was that her eyes were closed in rapture at what she was doing to him.

Today she didn't sink her nails into his bottom, she held his hairy pompoms in her other hand and rolled them about while she was busy with her tongue. It didn't take long – Roger gasped in sudden spasm and his body jerked as he spurted into her sucking and eager mouth.

When she was ready she released him and stared up at his face with gleaming brown eyes. Roger smiled to see the white trickle down her chin and she smiled back at him, a look of fulfilment on her face.

'Would you like to move in and live with me?' she asked him, 'we could do this every day. I'd buy very smart clothes for you – you like to dress well. And money when you wanted it.'

The invitation was one Roger had received often from women in the after-throes of pleasure. He assumed that Elise had reached orgasm while she was licking him – it was impossible for him to tell whether she had or not. But judging by her invitation, she had done so.

And naturally she wanted more. And more. Which she could have if she was willing to pay the fee. As for moving in with her – he hadn't the least intention of living with any woman, rich or very rich. Except one. Marie Brantome. But the prospect of that was very remote.

Marie had promised to come to his apartment that evening. She would keep her promise, he honestly believed that. He would see her and hold her in his arms and kiss her – how marvellous that would be! But he had no great hopes of the outcome. Not after the tangled story of the husband and the tattoo on her belly.

An M and an M entwined, a blue and a red on her smooth flesh. Her own initial and the blonde woman's initial. It must be – he was sure Marie hadn't been truthful at their bizarre encounter in the night-club toilet. In fact, desperately as he loved her, he didn't believe she'd told him the truth about anything – not from the moment they met in the Printemps department store.

He lay naked on Elise's bed and watched her undress. Off with the white silk blouse and then her white bra – her breasts were slack without the bra, but still worth a feel. She took off her dark blue skirt to reveal white knickers matching the bra, with an edge of pink lace. She kept her knickers on but took off her stockings.

She lay on the bed beside him, facing him and very close. She had her stylish knickers on and her thick white coral necklace, her hand was gliding up and down, to coax him to full stiffness again.

'Now I shall have the truth from you, Roger,' she told him in a voice trembling with delicate emotion. 'Will you come here to live with me? Will you be my lover every day?'

'Am I your lover?' he asked, smiling gently. He knew he was no such thing. Exactly what he was could be argued and debated; her living plaything perhaps, her scapegoat for the whole race of men on whom to inflict all the sexual indignities she chose. Or was he her masculine god with a long hard item to be touched and kissed in reverence?

He managed to shrug slightly at his own question, even though he was lying on his side propped on an elbow while Elise amused herself with him. What did it matter what he was to her, god or doll? Enough amateur psychologizing, he said, it is impossible to understand women's thoughts or motives.

He ran his fingertips lightly over her elegant knickers – not to arouse her or himself, but to check the quality. Superb, of course, Elise could afford the best.

'Answer me, Roger,' she said dreamily as her fingers pumped up and down, 'give me a real answer, not another question.'

She was always sun-tanned, an expensive golden shade, and not only her face. Now she was undressed all her body was tanned to the same attractive tint – breasts, belly and thighs. All over, there were no white patches on her body. In winter she followed the sun to the Middle East and in summer she stayed on the Côte d'Azur. In between she had herself tanned artificially. Naked.

From her knickers Roger's idle fingers strayed to her slender thigh, a gesture that meant nothing much – but he

163

wasn't really able to stop himself touching her body. Her closeness and the clasp of her hand had made him excited again, and he wanted the feel of smooth female flesh under his fingers.

Elise took little notice of his hand on her thigh, very close to the strip of thin silk that concealed her *lapin*, she was too involved in the pleasure she got from stroking his stiff part.

'You still haven't given me an answer,' she said, her fingers sliding briskly. 'Do you want to come here and live with me?'

'You would tire of me in a week,' he said, his palm flat upon her thigh and stroking expertly to divert her attention.

'Never! We'd make love in the morning and in the evening and I know you would be happy with me.'

Her long red-nailed fingers stroked him very lovingly while she watched his expression, her mouth open and the pink tip of her tongue showing. That tongue had done devastating things to his swollen part when she was kneeling in front of him. Perhaps she meant to do the same now they were on the bed together, and was showing him in advance her intention.

But he didn't think so. When he had been with her before, she had made him spurt once into her mouth and once into her *joujou* – she evidently thought it best to receive him and pleasure him in both openings. If one were unnecessarily realistic about the matter, to pleasure herself by taking him into both openings.

'You suit me very well,' she murmured, 'tell me you adore me, Roger.'

'I adore you to distraction, Elise – you know that,' he said, feeling his male pride buck furiously in her hand.

'Ah yes,' she said, giving it a fond squeeze. Her

tantalizing fingers released it as she told him she wanted him to take her knickers off. Roger's hands were trembling as he slid them down her legs and bared her brown-haired *joujou*. She lay on her back with her knees up and apart.

'Come to me, Roger,' she said, 'let me see how you adore me.'

He kissed the thin pink lips between her thighs and rolled on to her belly. But before he could slide into her, she took hold of his jerking length.

'On your elbows,' she ordered, and he took his weight on his forearms and his knees.

His belly was over hers – his fingers felt for her *joujou*, to part the lips for his penetration of her. Her hand was there first – she opened herself for him. He slid forward to press the head of his stiff part between those long, thin lips – he was shaking with excitement, hardly more than a heartbeat or two away from the sexual crisis.

But Elise's other hand held his throbbing length tight – so it was not possible to slide in. She kissed his face, little pecking kisses like a bird, almost mocking his eagerness, while her fingers were sliding up and down his shaking part. He knew what she was doing, it was not the first time she had done this to him.

She was deploying her power over the hard male part – perhaps the naked display of power was to impress him, but he suspected it was to persuade herself she wasn't a sexual victim – even if that's what she really desired to be. Or had he got it totally wrong? His thoughts were whirling like a carousel, he was in a delirium of sensation.

'Elise!' he gasped, 'Elise . . . !'

From his shuddering she knew he was *in extremis*. She steered his bounding part between the moist lips between her legs. Even in these moments she kept a firm hold of him as she let him slide into her slowly, centimetre by centimetre.

It was too much – his desire spurted frantically while he was sliding into her. Her eyes were staring into his, her mouth was open in a grin. It was all over for Roger before he was fully inside her. Her grin became wider, her belly shook and her own orgasm arrived.

'*Cheri, cheri!*' she was moaning, her arms about him to clasp him tightly to her jerking body.

Roger lay still, letting her enjoy her moment to the full. At the final instant of his slide into her, he had lost touch with the actuality of his surroundings – he'd forgotten whose thighs he was between. The hot belly under him had become Marie's, the soft wet *joujou* into which he was spurting his desire was hers.

It seemed so real and vivid that it astonished him now, as he lay on Elise's hot belly in the sticky aftermath of ecstasy. My mind played a trick, he concluded, and he took comfort from the pleasing idea that he was so wildly in love with Marie that he couldn't help but think of her in moments of furious emotion – such as when he was in the throes of pleasuring another woman.

The alternative was far too absurd to even think about – that he was losing his wits. That there was a little spider spinning a web on his ceiling, as the saying went. And he could prove it conclusively – this evening when he lay between Marie's parted legs he wouldn't suddenly imagine he was doing it to Elise. Not for one instant. He would be utterly certain whose belly he was lying on and whose *joujou* he was spurting in. There could be no better proof of his clear-mindedness than that. Could there?

He was right about that, of course. When Marie arrived at his tiny apartment, just as she'd promised, he had her

clothes off in the first minute and a half and she was on her
back upon his divan while he kissed and kissed and kissed
her naked body from her eyebrows to her painted toenails.

Not for even half a second did he think she was Elise
Choisy, or any other of the many women he was paid to
pleasure. She was Marie Brantome – tall, slender, beautiful
Marie, with glossy hair so dark brown it was indistinguish-
able from black. Short like a man's hair and parted on the
right. Long-bodied Marie with the perfect round breasts –
long-thighed and satin-skinned woman he dreamed about
at nights.

Ambiguous Marie, who claimed she had a husband and
denied she had a woman as a lover, although Roger was
sure it was the blonde woman Marie made love to and the
so-called husband was merely a bill-payer who slept alone
in a separate room. Or to get nearer to Roger's miserably
complicated state of mind, he was sure for some of the time
that he was right about her. But then for some of the time
he believed what Marie told him.

What did he believe now, when she lay on his divan,
naked and beautiful, open to his kisses and caresses? And
returning them – her fingertips trailed down his bare chest,
her mouth pressed against his in long, hot kisses. He was
confused, this Roger, he didn't know if he believed her or
not.

He'd stripped her naked except for her wristwatch – and
that he left on her arm as a piquant reminder of the first
time they'd made love, in the little hotel near the St Lazare
station. Its thin gold case, its mottled snakeskin strap –
what a wealth of memories that expensive little item on her
wrist held for him.

He rolled the wet tip of his tongue over the pink buds of
her breasts and heard her little gasp of pleasure. His hand

stroked up the inside of her bare thigh – he was persuading himself all was the same, that nothing had changed, that Marie would be his just as she'd been that first time he'd mounted her on the hotel bed and she'd lain with her arms stretched out sideways, looking as if she'd been crucified.

Something had changed, he couldn't pretend any longer when he trailed his mouth down her soft belly. There on the smoothness, on the satin skin, very close to her tuft of dark curls, almost in her groin. The tiny red and blue tattoo. A monogram of M and M twining. He licked it with the tip of his tongue for a moment and then drew back.

'So Monsieur Messager is responsible for having this barbaric mark placed on your beautiful body?' he asked – his tone light but doubtful.

It was the story Marie had told him in the night-club toilet. But he couldn't entirely give up his own theory, which was that one M stood for Marie and the other for Michele. Blonde Madame Legarnier; he'd seen her murmuring into Marie's ear and holding her hand.

'No, Roger, it is you who are responsible,' Marie answered as she ran her fingers through his hair, 'if we had never met, you and I, there would have been nothing to make Martin jealous and angry. He suspected there was another man – that I'd been with someone else. He had his initials tattooed on me as a warning.'

'A warning that you belong to him and worse may follow if you forget that and meet me again?'

Roger wanted very much to kiss the little red and blue tattoo on her belly – but he didn't. It would have been to acknowledge another man's ownership rights. That was impossible.

'Perhaps it is intended as a warning to me,' said Marie, with a shrug of her bare shoulders, 'but it may be a warning

to you, have you considered that? So be warned, Roger –
my husband has a devious mind, nothing he does can be
taken at face value.'

'Does he know who I am?' Roger exclaimed.

'He doesn't know anything for certain but he suspects I
had a lover. Every time I went out and came back, no
matter what time of the day, he made me strip naked so he
could examine my body, head to foot. Every centimetre,
every millimetre.'

'But this is insane!' Roger said, amazed by what he
heard.

'Whatever proof he was looking for, he never found it.
There was nothing to find. But it didn't end his suspicions.
Which is why he dragged me to a sordid den in a
backstreet, where a bald man with a heavy moustache
used needles to put this monogram on me. I was branded
like an animal.'

'But this is incredible, hideous, brutal beyond imagining.
We are not living in Bulgaria in the Middle Ages – this
husband of yours compelled you to undress in front of a low
type while he stuck a needle into you?'

'He told me to take off my skirt and knickers, and lie on
the man's table. I closed my eyes to shut out the horror but I
could feel the man's stubby fingers touching between my
legs. And I knew he was leering down at my naked body.'

'*Bon Dieu!* Your husband watched this?'

'He sat on a rickety chair – and he pulled it up close to the
table to oversee the tattooing. He enjoyed it, watching how
his initials were put on me. And the other, the tattooist, I
opened my eyes for an instant when the pain of the needle
was too much to bear – but before I could complain I saw a
long bulge in his trousers and I knew he wanted to fling
himself on top of me and rape me to death on his table.'

It was too much for Roger to bear – with a moan of despair he dropped his head between her open legs and slid his tongue into her dark-haired *joujou*.

'He was going to put the tattoo higher, near my belly-button, this backstreet skin-artist,' she said, her voice trembling as thrilling sensations flicked through her from Roger's caress of her secret bud, 'but Martin ordered him to put it as near as possible to my curls.'

'Ah,' Roger murmured indistinctly, his tongue inside her.

'Martin did this out of cruelty and spite,' Marie moaned, 'he is a sadist – he wanted to see me writhe in agony as the needle pierced this sensitive part of my body.'

Roger moaned as he flicked his tongue over her bud – he would have given anything himself to see her on the tattooist's table with her legs apart. And his own fingers stroking the long pink lips between, while the bald man with the moustache drew in her satin-skinned groin his own initial – an R close to her *joujou*.

She had already been hot and moist when he slipped his tongue into her. Now she was wetter. Her sharp fingernails clawed down his bare back.

'I denied Martin the satisfaction he wanted of hearing me cry out in agony, but my face was wet with tears when the tattooist finished. His fingers had been inside me, feeling and probing – it seemed like hours. It was almost as bad as if he'd raped me. When he stood back from the table the bulge in his trousers was monstrous.'

Roger moaned quietly into her *joujou* to hear this.

'Martin stood up and bent over me to inspect the work. He was grinning; he liked what he saw – the way he had ruined my body. He paid the tattoo-man and sent him out of the room. Before I could get up and put my underwear on he jumped on me, he pinned me to the table with his weight. He forced me – I was screaming in fear and pain but that only seemed to urge him on. It was a nightmare.'

'Ah yes, yes,' Roger gasped, turning around quick as a cat to fling himself flat on Marie's soft belly.

His mind was ablaze – it seemed everyone had the woman he was madly in love with, except himself. It was more than unjust, it was grotesque. Her beautiful *joujou* had been fingered and felt by a greasy tattooist with a moustache. Her beautiful body had been ravaged by her so-called husband – a madman who sat by and watched her being fingered by a stranger. It was too much!

Her legs were wide apart. In an instant Roger's stiff length was inside her – he went in to the hilt with a single push. Her arms were around him and clasping him to her as he stabbed hard and fast, desperate to do it.

His mind was full of the image she had conjured up, the dirty tattoo den where she lay on a table, naked from the waist down. A sweating bald man bent over her and fingered her *joujou* with one hand while he traced a monogram on her skin with his needle loaded with coloured ink.

'Yes, Roger, hard and fast,' she moaned, 'wipe out the past.'

Ah, if only that were possible. He shut her mouth with a kiss, her tongue pushed into his mouth and fluttered wildly. This was going to be very fast, it was almost happening now. Deep in his belly he felt the stir of a huge brutal climax hurtling at him.

Marie felt it coming too – she was jerking underneath him and moaning, pushing herself at him in urgent little spasms. Roger gasped at the first ecstatic throb in his belly and he pulled out of her at once. She shrieked as he rubbed the unhooded head of his shaft on the smooth soft skin of her belly.

An instant later he spurted on to her little monogram – again and again and again – as if he was trying to wash it off. Erase it from her flesh and from her mind. She understood what he was doing with the fast sliding and spurting of his stiff length on her belly – she shrieked to feel the warm flood on her skin.

Substituting

An evening was finally arranged for dinner at Edmond Planchon's expense to celebrate Roger winning the bet concerning Gilberte. They had agreed in advance it would be at the Brasserie Lipp on the Boulevard St-Germain – they both lived very strenuous lives as stars of the Agence Drouet stable and in consequence they always preferred solid food of the type to be found at Lipp.

As ever, the place was full to bursting. They had to wait for half an hour to get a table – no phone reservations were taken at Lipp's. While they were waiting they found a table outside on the pavement where they could order a drink and talk.

Over a glass of *pastis* Edmond demanded to be told the epic of getting Gilberte's *nichons* out for a look and a feel – he still claimed not to believe Roger had succeeded where he had failed.

'You have too good an opinion of yourself,' Roger retorted at once, 'everyone agrees I'm better looking than you – apart from being better at it than you.'

'And hens have teeth,' said Edmond, 'you'll have to do better than that, *mon brave*.'

'It happened,' Roger insisted, 'I flipped them out of her bra and – *hopla!* – there they were, two long *nichons* swinging about over my nose.'

173

'You must have been down on your knees – she makes you grovel to her, does she? I've often wondered about you, Roger.'

'I wasn't down on my knees, I was flat on my back on her desk at the time. I swear that desk has seen more action than a bed in a brothel. Gilberte was at her usual trick of straddling me – a position you've found yourself in plenty of times.'

'Hah!' Edmond exclaimed with fine contempt. 'She gets on top of you, does she?'

'And you,' Roger retorted, 'you've never had her on her back, so don't try to pretend. As a matter of fact I'd just given her a stand-up, bent double over the desk – and that's something you can't do because you're not tall enough to get it in her.'

'What nonsense,' Edmond said, 'I've done it standing to that woman more times than you've had hot dinners. But go on, I want to know how you persuaded her to get them out.'

'I softened her up by first having her standing,' Roger said, knowing it annoyed Edmond to talk about doing in that position. 'I held her by the shoulders and rammed into her until she told me I was wonderful and started moaning.'

'Don't believe a word of it,' Edmond said, teeth clenched.

'When we got our breath back she asked me if I'd mind getting on the desk to let her have her usual.'

'Now that's an outright lie,' said Edmond smartly, 'Gilberte never *asks* anyone. She does what she wants, whether you mind or not. She pushed you down flat on your back, that's the truth of it, isn't it?'

Roger shrugged and grinned and emptied his glass. He waved at the waiter to bring two more *pastis*.

'Anyway,' Roger went on, 'so there we were, me on my back and dear Gilberte squatting over the top of me sliding up and down. I forgot to tell you – she took her dress off with her knickers and all she had on was her bra and her stockings.'

'This is a fairy-tale,' Edmond interrupted, 'she doesn't take her clothes off in the office, only her knickers. And sometimes not even those – I've known her to pull them down to her knees, when she's pressed for time, and expect you to manage.'

'Evidently you are under-privileged,' Roger said with a broad grin. 'She doesn't take them off for you. I can understand why. You haven't made as big an impression as you believe.'

Edmond said a rude word. 'Go on with your fairy-tale,' he said, 'I've heard nothing so far to justify paying for dinner. We'll share the bill.'

'No, you're paying – I won that bet fair and square. There we were on the desk with Gilberte rattling away with her eyes shut and I reached up and slipped her bra-straps off her shoulders. Her *nichons* fell out of the cups – a long soft pair flopping up and down over my face. I grabbed one in both hands and stuffed the end into my mouth.'

'*Bon Dieu* – is this true?' Edmond demanded breathlessly.

'I give you my solemn word.'

'Gilberte Drouet let you do that?'

'She was panting and moaning and begging me to suck it while she bounced up and down on me like a yo-yo. She shrieked like a cat on a roof-top at midnight when I gave her the works. I was certain skinny Celeste outside could hear her squawking.'

'I shall never recover from what you've told me,'

Edmond said slowly, 'this shows everything in a new light. From now on I'll treat Madame Drouet very differently. She won't have it all her own way quite so easily.'

'*L'audace, et encore de l'audace*,' Roger quoted to him with a smile intended to encourage Edmond in his dream of independence and masterful approach. 'Skinny Celeste in the outer office,' Roger followed a train of thought of his own, 'have you ever considered having a belly to belly with her? Not in the office – her place or yours.'

'She's got no *nichons*,' Edmond was dismissive, 'and bony hips – it would be like doing it to a boy. And that doesn't tempt me in the least. Don't tell me you've had a go!'

'No, I was only speculating – just imagine her long thin legs wrapped tight round your waist, it might be interesting.'

But Edmond was hardly listening. His interest was in Gilberte and not her receptionist – he refused to be diverted.

'So Gilberte really went for it when you sucked her *nichons*,' he said, half question, half statement, 'she wanted you to keep on doing it to her?'

'My dear friend, she liked it so much that she stuffed half a big *nichon* into my mouth so far she nearly choked me to death! What a comical way to die, flat on your back with your trousers round your ankles and two kilos of female flesh in your mouth.'

'Formidable!' Edmond said.

His tone made Roger realize that Edmond was more than usually interested in Gilberte. It seemed strange he should have tender emotions about the woman who made regular sexual use of him, as she did of every young man who had dealings with Agence Drouet.

What made it even more amusing was Edmond's habitual cynicism in all matters to do with women and sexual games. After all, he was a professional, like Roger, and knew more about such things than most men would find it comfortable to know. But attraction between men and women does not depend on beauty or esteem – all the world knows that.

They were still talking about Gilberte and her *nichons* when a table became vacant in the restaurant. And though Edmond seemed greatly struck by the tale of how Roger handled them to win the bet, he was still in two minds about paying up.

'We'll have the *plat du jour*,' he said, not troubling to look at the menu.

'I've never heard such meanness!' said Roger. 'You can have the *plat du jour* if you wish as you're paying, but I'm going to order something very expensive. And a couple of bottles of good wine to go with it. You owe it to me.'

Edmond conceded the point and decided to make the best of the situation – he too ordered a substantial meal. Harmony reigned, conversation was suspended while they ate. Eventually they were considering which cheese to finish the meal with and were ready to talk to each other again.

Not without misgivings, Roger mentioned a certain tattoo that had appeared in circumstances not properly explained – a tattoo of two intertwined initials on the body of a beautiful woman.

Edmond raised his eyebrows and looked interested.

'This woman – is she a regular client?' Edmond asked.

'No, not a client, a dear friend.'

'If she agreed to let you put your initials on her then she's devoted to you. Where is this tattoo – on her shoulder? On her thigh? Or perhaps on her backside?'

'Close to her *lapin*,' said Roger.

'Well! In that case she is madly in love with you – there is no other possible explanation. Do you love her?'

Roger explained in some embarrassment that the initials were not his but the husband's. Or so she said. He told Edmond most of the story, leaving out names and places.

Edmond's eyebrows rose higher and higher as he listened.

'You've made the entire thing up,' he said when Roger had finished his story of his unsatisfactory love-affair.

'I wish I had,' Roger said gloomily, 'as things stand I don't know what to believe.'

'Let us consider this sorry tale of yours,' Edmond said. 'You are in love with a mysterious woman married to a man who became suspicious and carried her off to a tattooist.'

'Yes.'

'Then this furiously jealous husband makes his wife lie half-naked on a table and watches the tattooist feel her while he is etching his monogram on her belly near her *lapin*. Have I got it right so far?'

Roger nodded disconsolately and Edmond burst out laughing.

'Forgive me,' he said, 'but I've never heard so extraordinary a tale. But you, my friend, you are being naïve to believe this woman – she is leading you by the nose, or some more sensitive part of your body. No woman would allow herself to be abused in so blatant a manner unless she enjoyed it – and to enjoy it she must be in love with her husband.'

'The man is a sadist,' Roger objected, 'he did it from spite, to make her suffer mentally as much as physically.'

He had said nothing to Edmond about what took place after the tattooing was completed – when according to

178

Marie the tattooist was sent out of the room and her husband jumped on top of her.

'Sadist!' Edmond scoffed. 'What does that mean? Women enjoy a little sadism in sex, you understand that. This business with the tattoo – if it ever took place – was a game between him and her, nothing more.'

'Of course it took place – I've seen the tattoo.'

Not only seen it, he'd tried to erase it from Marie's body in a very special way that achieved nothing beyond pleasure. Of that episode he said nothing to Edmond, in case he laughed.

'You've seen a monogram tattoo, that I don't dispute. But you have only the woman's word for the circumstances of its etching on her belly. With women truth and fiction are the same – it is the driving force of their passion, the confusion of unreal and real, everyone knows that.'

'If she is so in love with her husband, why does she visit my apartment and let me make love to her? Explain that to me.'

'Easily,' said Edmond with a superior smile. 'She lies on her back for you to make her husband jealous. Then she is sure that he adores her.'

'Perhaps,' said Roger, by no means convinced, 'there could be another explanation.'

He described Marie, her short hair parted on the side and her beautifully tailored suits. He admitted that when he first saw her, one afternoon on the Avenue de l'Opera, the thought in his mind was that this superbly sexy woman had no interest in men, only in other women.

That impression had been so strong that he'd imagined her naked on her back, with her legs apart, and another naked woman lying between them, her body shaking as the other woman's tongue slid over her secret little bud.

'Aha,' said Edmond, 'that puts a different complexion on it. But besides your poetical impressions, which are moon-dust, has there been anything to seriously suggest that your *femme fatale* prefers the touch of a woman's hand between her legs?'

Roger told him about the accidental meeting, and the blonde woman he had seen holding Marie's hand.

Edmond shrugged. 'Holding hands doesn't mean much,' he said, 'if the hand were up your little friend's skirt that would be more convincing. Is she young or old, pretty or plain, this rival of yours?'

'About thirty-five and attractive.' Roger tried to be objective. 'Chic and elegant – and she had a pearl choker, real pearls, three or four rows. A fine big pair of *nichons* – the type that cause you to go stiff on sight.'

'Have you asked your girlfriend about this other woman?'

'Of course I have. She denies there is anything between them. But I can't get it out of my head that the initial could easily stand for the blonde woman's first name. What is one to make of that?'

'What were the circumstances of this hand-holding? On a café terrace, in a shop, in a cinema – fill in some detail for me.'

Roger explained it was in a night-club where by chance he had taken Nadine Bernier. The two women had been accompanied by men who might or might not be their husbands.

'A night-club!' Edmond exclaimed. 'That suggests more than a casual acquaintance between them, holding hands there.'

'You think so?'

'The night-club atmosphere is not that of a church,' Edmond said with great authority. 'It is no secret what goes on in the dark corners of night-clubs. People do intimate things to each other under the tablecloth. Middle-aged men have no hesitation about groping about in young women's underwear.'

'This is true,' Roger agreed.

'Take you, for example,' Edmond went on, 'just where was your hand when you saw your mystery girlfriend sitting with a blonde who has big *nichons*?'

'That has nothing to do with it,' Roger insisted, 'but if you must know, my hand was up Nadine's skirt at the time – but only in a casual sort of way. It had no particular significance.'

'But of course not,' Edmond grinned, 'stroking Nadine's *lapin* is neither here nor there, it's much the same as holding hands, it doesn't imply that you're going to jump on top of her later. Hypocrite – I've heard you've been seen out with Nadine lately. I was interested in her myself once, but not for long.'

'She mentioned someone who had ill-treated her and abused her emotions,' Roger countered, 'I didn't guess it was you – what a dirty beast you are to exploit her body and ravage her soul!'

'All in a day's work,' Edmond grinned and shrugged, 'but tell me, how does getting astride Nadine fit in with this new love of yours, Roger? I find that a little difficult to follow.'

'Ah, there you come to the heart of it. Nadine wants me – she makes herself very agreeable to me and almost drags me into her bed. What a delight that is after the women we call on, you and I, in our everyday business, what a joy it is to make love with someone as lithe and beautiful as Nadine!'

'She is neurotic,' Edmond pointed out.

'Not when she's on her back. But in truth I don't really want Nadine. The woman I do want, I can't have, or so it seems. She turns up at intervals, when it suits her, and bewilders me with bizarre excuses about a jealous husband. And secretly I believe she is in love with another woman.'

'Yet she lets you take her knickers down?'

'One time she came to my apartment she left her knickers with me – a fragile little garment of orchid-pink silk.'

Edmond was shaking his head and grinning in wonder.

'Your little friend sounds fascinating – but she is certainly deceiving you, one way or the other. What will you do?'

'Then you have no advice to offer me?'

'Oh yes, from my unsurpassed experience of women in all their moods I can offer you very sound advice. Which is this: go with your instincts. It will not change the outcome but it will give you a more enjoyable time while it lasts.'

The cheese was finished, an excellent Roquefort, and they sat drinking a final glass of wine. Edmond glanced at his watch, it was gold and Swiss and very expensive and evidently a gift from an outstandingly satisfied client.

'I have a booking at midnight,' he said in explanation of his otherwise discourteous act.

'At midnight?' Roger grinned, not quite believing him.

'One has one's admirers,' Edmond said, 'my position demands a certain *noblesse oblige*.'

It was Roger's turn to say a rude word.

'Naturally it is tedious to be asked to make a call so late,' said Edmond with a slight shrug, 'but what is one to do – there is a certain lady who loves to believe that she is seduced and exploited by an unknown lover in the night.

By good fortune she is rich enough to pay extra for late visits.'

'Who is this mad woman who has you at midnight,' Roger asked, 'and how do you go about seducing her? Does she play at being a young virgin?'

'Her fantasy is more complicated than that,' Edmond explained with one eyebrow raised. 'I arrive punctually at twelve and the door is left unlocked for me. The apartment is in darkness, for Madame has gone to bed and is fast asleep. I know my way to her bedroom – there is one bedside lamp on, but shaded and very dim – and by its glow I stand by the bed and strip myself naked.'

'Is she really asleep?' Roger enquired.

'Of course not, but she gives the appearance of it. She is on her back, eyes closed and breathing regularly – but I know that she is watching me from under her eyelids as I undress, looking at my body, gloating to herself to see how masculine I am.'

'You flatter yourself, dear friend. I've been told by someone with inside information that you only have ten centimetres to offer.'

'That's a lie!' Edmond said furiously. 'Who told you that?'

Roger shrugged airily and begged Edmond to continue with the tale of his midnight encounters. Edmond scowled and said he was certain it was that bitch Nadine telling lies about him. But he went on with his curious story.

'I turn back the bedclothes with care – so as not to disturb her pretended sleep. I lie beside her, moving slowly. She wears very short silk nighties, little-girl style, arms and shoulders bare, hem not even halfway down her thighs. To be precise, the hem is arranged so that it only just covers her *lapin*, her legs are completely bare.'

'Is her body attractive? Is she plump or thin, dark-haired or blonde?' Roger asked, visualizing the scene in his mind and intrigued by the strangeness of it.

'I've never seen her in the light and I've never even spoken to her in the dark,' was Edmond's astounding reply. 'Before the first meeting everything was arranged between her and Gilberte. I was told in detail what was required – I carry out my orders to the letter.'

'But this is bizarre!'

'What of it? It makes Madame happy, she pays the double fee, that makes me happy. What would you do?'

'You're right,' said Roger, 'who are we to despise the dreams of others – especially those who seek our assistance to realize their dreams. What happens next?'

'I take her nightdress carefully by the hem and lift it over her breasts. I touch them, I sigh in rapture to feel the weight and softness of them – she adores hearing sighs of rapture over her body. I glide my palm over the curve of her belly – but so lightly as not to wake a sleeping woman. If she were sleeping.'

'Even in the dark you can tell if she's plump or thin,' Roger objected, 'and if she's dark or blonde.'

'She is in every way average,' Edmond told him, 'neither thin nor plump, average. And in the dim lighting her hair is average brown, not fair and not dark. Does that make you happier?'

'How old is she?' Roger persisted.

'Between thirty and fifty, as far as I can make out. The average.'

'But from what you tell me, her desires are not average, are they?' said Roger. 'In effect, they sound very uncommon to me. How often do you make these midnight calls?'

'Once a week, regularly. I understand from Gilberte that

when I take my month's vacation at St Tropez later this summer it is you who will substitute for me. So listen and learn.'

'I'm breathless in anticipation! You'd got as far as lifting her nightie and feeling her *nichons*. What next?'

'I stroke her belly gently down to the curls below. She sighs in her sleep and slides down a little more comfortably with her legs lolling apart. And still she maintains every impression of sleeping calmly. I lay my cheek on the broadness of her belly, I lick slowly from her button down to where the curls begin.'

'How long is this taking?' Roger was genuinely interested.

'From the moment I lie on the bed with her until the moment I touch her *lapin* – fifteen minutes at least. I finger the fleshy lips and for her benefit I murmur little idiocies such as, *Ah it is so sexy I cannot control myself, I am going to ravage it – I hope she won't wake up in time to stop me, this pretty lady!*'

'I've got the hang of it,' Roger assured him, 'I'm sure I can do it better than you, when you're away by the seaside.'

'Never!' Edmond declared firmly. 'After you've botched it up once Madame will be praying for my early return. But to resume, by now she is wet and ready, but it is necessary to keep up the pretence of sleep by licking your middle finger and pressing it gently into her. As soon as her bud is touched the tempo of her breathing quickens and her body twitches – as I play with her I can see her belly jerking in quick little spasms.'

'I wonder what is going on inside her head while all this is being done to her body?' Roger murmured. Edmond ignored him.

'I slide myself on top of her,' he said, 'taking my weight

on my arms – and I push very slowly into her. Once in, all that is needed is an easy little movement of three or four centimetres, no heavy pounding. This little movement is enough – she becomes very hot and slippery.'

'Does she ever wake up?'

'She seems to sleep on,' said Edmond, 'right up to the moment her orgasm overtakes her – only then do her eyes blink open for an instant or two. They are round with surprise to find a naked man lying on her belly and a length of hard flesh up her – four or five ecstatic tremors shake her from head to foot and that's it. Even in this orgasm she is silent and quiescent.'

'What do you know of her?' Roger asked, playing the scene in his vivid imagination. 'Is she married or is she divorced, this woman of the sleeping thrill? There must surely have been some interesting experience in the past that set her on this course. Perhaps as a young girl there was a man who crept secretly into her bed at night and first taught her the pleasure of love. She may be trying to recapture that experience.'

'How do I know?' said Edmond indifferently. 'As I said – I've never spoken to her. She is a mystery to me, as your girlfriend is a mystery to you. But what she wants me to do to her, that's no mystery – I do it and she is pleased. *Et voila tout!*'

'Just the once and then she really does go to sleep?' Roger asked. 'You get dressed and sneak out, yes?'

'Your choice of words is insulting – I have never sneaked out of a bedroom in my life. But to answer your question, imbecilic though it is, Madame requires the standard twice for her money. You're right to think she really falls asleep after her orgasm, I pull the bedclothes over us both and doze off with her.'

'That's interesting,' Roger commented, 'I've never heard of a client who let one of us stay in her apartment while she slept. It's not being raped that they're afraid of, so they must think we'd steal their jewels.'

Edmond explained how the sleeping encounter always continued, according to plan. Sometime during the night he was woken up by a hand caressing him to stiffness – though no hand was touching him when he awoke. Madame's back was towards him and she seemed fast asleep. But her nightie was well up her back and her plump bottom was bare.

'See!' said Roger. 'She has a plump bottom – you said before that you've never seen her in the light and have no idea at all of what she looks like.'

'What are you, an examining magistrate?' Edmond demanded. 'I know her bottom is plump because I've felt it often enough. And in the dark I press my length against it, in a warm deep crease between soft cheeks.'

Roger listened intently while his friend told him how long he lay close to Madame X's back, knowing she was becoming aroused. He waited until she sighed and turned over as a sleeper would – a complete turn that left her facing him and close – and in the process her leg lay over his thigh.

Because her short silk nightie was up above her waist, almost at her breasts, the head of his aroused and very stiff part was touching her bare belly. And hardly moving his hips he was able to rub it gently against her warm flesh. For a long time.

'You are slower this second time?' Roger asked, his eyebrows arching upwards in amusement.

Edmond surprised him by saying his instructions from Gilberte before each midnight visit to Madame X were to make it last – a whole hour if possible. That was all very well and good, but he was not a sex machine, he complained, he was a man of flesh and passions – strong passions!

After ten or twelve minutes his hot nature took charge and he was pushing lower down – at the lips of her *joujou*, in fact. And soon he was inside. Not deep, just a few centimetres. There was no stir or reaction from Madame when her flesh was penetrated – her breathing remained regular and she appeared to sleep on.

Yet Edmond could feel the little spasms that were starting to shake her. He would clench his teeth hard and force himself to lie motionless – the tiny nervous quaking of her body was enough to bring them both to the point of sexual climax if it was allowed to continue.

Another ten minutes of this – two people joined by the least possible insertion of hard flesh into wet flesh. By then Edmond was almost out of his mind with raging desire. Two long thrusts and he would spurt into her but his instructions were clear and so he tightened his muscles and lay still as a marble statue on a monument.

Then would come a gasp so stifled that it was practically inaudible – she would shudder and her orgasm sweep right through her. Edmond would be instantly released by the sudden wet grip of her *joujou* and spurt furiously into her.

'Extraordinary!' said Roger. 'I suppose when she wakes up in the morning all alone she persuades herself it was a dream?'

'I imagine so,' Edmond agreed. 'This is the way she distances herself from the reality of what men and women do to each other in bed. She goes to bed alone and she wakes up the next morning alone – and what takes place in between has no reality. It is a strange quirk of hers. I hope she never thinks of talking to a psychiatrist. That could ruin a profitable relationship.'

About eleven-thirty Roger and Edmond took leave of each other outside the brasserie. They shook hands on the pavement. Edmond was going to find a taxi to take him to his midnight tryst with Sleeping Beauty; Roger had decided on an encounter of his own – with Nadine Bernier. Her apartment was not far, close enough to walk, it was a dry mild night. He strolled along the Boulevard St-Germain, smiling and politely declining the occasional tarts who pressed forward to offer their services.

He tapped lightly at Nadine's door. There was a long wait and no response – could she be out with someone? he asked himself. The thought was displeasing, now he'd made a special effort to call. He knocked again, louder this time – she could be asleep, although it wasn't midnight yet. At last he heard steps inside, then the door opened slowly.

She'd been in bed asleep and he'd woken her. She'd dragged on a pale-blue negligée over her nightdress and held it closed at her waist with both arms. Her long blonde hair was tied at the back in a ribbon and hung to her shoulders. She stared at Roger uncertainly, her beautiful face shiny with a beauty preparation she'd applied before going to bed.

'What do you want, Roger?' she said.

'To see you, Nadine. It has been days since we met and talked to each other.'

'Are you drunk?' she asked. 'Goodnight Roger – ring me after midday tomorrow.'

'I'm not very drunk,' he said with a smile and a light shrug, 'you could at least give me a glass of cognac to keep me going. It's a long ride on the Metro from here to the Place Denfert.'

'You can come in for a minute,' she said, not very

189

enthusiastically, 'but you can't stay. I'm on an early photo-shoot in the morning and I have to be up at five and out of here before six.'

She stood aside to let him in. And closing the door behind him she realized what she'd done.

'What am I saying?' she exclaimed. 'You won't go when you've had a glass of cognac – I must be an idiot to believe that!'

'You're the most beautiful woman I know,' Roger told her.

The total lack of relevance and logic didn't trouble her. She stared at him with big, dark blue eyes – he grinned and pressed her back to the wall with his belly on hers. She let go of her negligée and put her hands on his shoulders, expecting a kiss.

He didn't disappoint her – but while he was kissing her mouth he reached down to get his hand under her nightdress and feel up between her legs. He clasped her warm blondish *lapin* in the palm of his hand.

'No, Roger,' she said, 'I have to get up in a few hours to go to work.'

'I adore you,' he said, his middle finger caressing her.

'And I thought we were friends,' she said, 'is this an act of friendship, to wake me in the middle of the night just for that when tomorrow would do as well?'

'True friendship is as spontaneous as love,' he assured her.

He picked her up and carried her into her own bedroom. He was convinced that women surrender to the man who carries them, and indeed one client he visited had gone into light orgasm in his arms when her feet left the carpet. She was an extreme case, no doubt, but the principle was the same.

He kissed her eyes as he placed her on her bed and sat beside her – her eyes stayed closed as he opened her negligée like two big, pale-blue wings and pulled her thin nightdress up over her perfect breasts. But her thighs moved apart for his fingers.

'Nadine – has it ever been done to you in your sleep?'

'In dreams?' she murmured. 'Many times.'

'No, I mean has a man ever got on top while you were sleeping and done it to you in reality.'

'Of course not, it's impossible. I'd wake up straight away if you tried that. What are you talking about, Roger?'

There was something wrong with his theory. He'd swept Nadine off her feet and carried her to the bedroom and was kissing her elegant breasts – but she didn't seem to be very interested in making love.

'*Je t'adore*, Nadine,' he said hopefully.

'I adore you Roger but I want to go back to sleep,' she said, her eyes closed. 'Do it if you must and let me sleep.'

'What,' he said, 'you believe I am an insensitive lout who'd jump on you and thump away for my amusement, without regard for your feelings? Am I an animal, a brute?'

'You are a wonderful caring person,' she said, with a sigh of exasperation, 'now please stop arguing and get on with it so I can get some sleep before the alarm clock goes off at five.'

'You have shamed me, Nadine,' he said, 'I shall never be able to look you in the face again.'

She said nothing, she spread her legs wide. Roger was sitting on the side of the bed still fully dressed. He flung his jacket off and loosened his tie – he ripped his trousers wide open and pulled his shirt up to his chest.

'Nadine, you are the most beautiful woman I know,' he murmured quickly as he laid his bare belly on hers.

Indifferent to him she might be but he pushed into her easily enough. His hands slid under her to grip the taut cheeks of her bottom, she breathed out deeply and spread her legs wider.

They wouldn't be around his waist tonight, those long slender legs of hers, holding him to her tightly. Her belly wouldn't be jerking up at him to meet his thrusts. He wasn't going to hear her sobs of ecstasy this time.

What of it? he said to himself as he slid in and out of her passive body. When she talks it is a disaster but when she lies on her back she is perfect. To do it to Nadine asleep would be the ideal, but she said herself that is not possible.

She lay limp and still under him, only his own thrusts making her limbs jerk a little – it wasn't difficult to believe he was mounted on the strange woman Edmond Planchon named his Sleeping Princess. That thought was as electrifying as it was perverse – it would be fascinating to deputize for Edmond when he went on holiday, and service the mystery woman as she lay in mock sleep with her nightdress up round her neck.

And it was easy to persuade himself that Nadine was also fast asleep underneath him – short rapid jabs took him to his critical moment and he spurted into her unresponsive belly. The gasps he heard were his own, she was silent and still while he finished and his spasms slowed and stopped.

He lay quietly on her soft body and listened to the rhythm of her breathing. He slid a hand between his chest and her perfect breasts and felt the rhythm of her heartbeat – she was asleep.

'I adore you,' he murmured, 'and when Edmond said tonight you are neurotic, I defended you by saying you're not neurotic when you're on your back. I think now that I was wrong.'

But Nadine didn't hear a word he said. And in a little while Roger slid off her body and managed to get his shoes off before he fell asleep with his head between her splayed thighs.

Conspiring

This time when Roger went to Madame Dubois' apartment in Auteuil it had been arranged in advance that her friend Madame Santerre would be there as well. He had agreed with Gilberte Drouet that he would oblige both ladies, but the fee was necessarily high.

Yvette Dubois had evidently given some advance thought to the visit. She opened the door to him wearing a short kimono in red silk with embroidered chrysanthemums in gold. She offered Roger both cheeks to be kissed and took the flowers he'd brought her. There being two ladies, his present was ten small pink roses.

The friend, Monique Santerre, was in the sitting-room, on the long sofa. All she had on was her stylish underwear – black bra and knickers. Against her pale skin this stark black caused her to look thinner than she was. The impression was of lean thighs and a narrow belly.

Roger kissed the hand she extended to him and stared with his well-practised look of admiration at her small breasts in their black silk half-cups – this was to make her feel desirable. She at once turned her face up towards him be kissed on the mouth – he did so, meaning it to be brief, but she flung her arm around his neck and held him while she kissed him long and hard.

By then Yvette Dubois had put the roses into water and

thrown off her kimono to reveal herself also in her underwear, a black bra and knickers almost identical to Monique's. To Roger this seemed a lack of imagination – why did so many women think that only black was *chic*? For himself he preferred vivid colours.

Yvette's underwear was a size or so larger than her friend's – her breasts were fuller and her hips broader. But the women were a pair – a matched pair; elegant, pampered. Roger sat beside Monique and looked at Yvette for a lead. Something was going on in her mind he could only guess at – it was sensible to wait for a cue from her.

'No little surprises this time, Roger,' she said with an easy smile, 'perhaps it was naughty of me to invite Monique secretly when you were here before – but it all turned out for the best. And she and I are such good friends that we like to take our enjoyment together, when we can.'

He thought he knew what she wanted – but thinking and knowing are far apart. It would be imbecilic to make a mistake, besides being unprofessional. His opinion was that Yvette was attracted sexually to her friend Monique, but was timid about approaching her in case she was rebuffed.

They were married women, both of them, and he was fairly sure neither had any experience of lesbian love-affairs – otherwise, why would they need him? Yvette wanted him there as an excuse, a reason for being naked with Monique, to get her accustomed to the idea of shared sexual activity. If they shared Roger, then it wasn't an impossible step to share sexual pleasure without his participation.

Yvette gave him a little glass of cognac and sat on his

other side and smiled graciously. She seemed in no hurry today to get him into the bedroom, she began a conversation in which Monique also took part, a conversation about nothing much, as if it was an ordinary social visit between friends.

It was noticeable that Yvette looked at Monique more than she looked at Roger while they sat talking on the sofa. At her lean thighs and at her little breasts inside the black cups. It only went to reinforce Roger's views – what Yvette really wanted was to flip Monique's *nichons* out of their half-cups and kiss them.

If she had her way, this Yvette, she'd be down on the carpet on her knees to drag Monique's *chic* black knickers down to her ankles and stroke her *joujou*. Perhaps she dreamed at night that she was playing with her dear friend.

'Are you in good form today, Roger?' Yvette asked.

She didn't expect an answer and she certainly didn't wait for one. She reached into his lap and unzipped his trousers. He was already stiff and ready – sitting between two perfectly groomed and expensively perfumed women in their silk underwear had done that for him.

'Ah yes, I see you are,' she said.

She pulled out his fifteen centimetres of hard flesh.

'Look at that, Monique – have you ever seen a better one?'

She was handling him to impress her friend. To arouse her and sweep away any reservations. She held the head of his straining part between her thumb and forefinger.

'Men are by nature so uncomplicated it is very easy to make them reach a climax,' she told Monique, her fingers flicking up and down, 'two minutes of this is all it needs to satisfy them.'

197

Roger let himself lie back easily against the sofa and spread his legs – it was very clear to him he was not required in this conversation, he was only the living object Yvette was using to indoctrinate Monique. Now he had heard the opening statement he could predict how Yvette was going to prove the superiority of female sexuality.

She would point out that women's orgasms were deeper and more forceful, that they had more emotional meaning than men's fast little spurtings, that men were done for after twice or three times but women could do it again and again. And so on, and so on – he'd heard all this many times before.

He rested a hand on a bare thigh on each side of him, a plump and rounded thigh to his left, that was Yvette – a long slender thigh to his right, that was Monique. They both had smooth, soft flesh, they were warm and comforting under his palms.

'But it swells up so big when you hold it,' Monique murmured, staring fascinated at his rearing part in Yvette's fingers. 'It looks very strong and determined!'

'The bigger the better,' Yvette said, 'but however big it may grow, it can be contained by even a small woman. I love to feel a big solid one inside me, all the way in, stretching me open.'

'Me too,' Monique agreed.

It was a source of wonder to Roger how very far Yvette Dubois had come in the few months that he'd known her. The first time he'd visited her apartment she was wearing a dress buttoned right up to the throat, he remembered it clearly. And when he got her clothes off she dived into bed and hid herself like a shy young girl. Now she was giving her friend Monique sex lessons!

'Ah, see it jump in your hand,' Monique said softly, 'you're right about it only taking two minutes – though I've never done that to a man, not all the way, I mean.'

'No?' Yvette said, a one-sided smile on her face. 'Would you like to take over and finish him off?'

Roger was always amenable to women's whims but he didn't want to be exploited – he decided it was time to take an active part in this three-handed game. There were strong cross-currents of emotion that fascinated him. He slid his palms gently along the two dissimilar thighs they lay on, over smooth warm flesh until he clasped two *lapins* through fine black silk.

'Dear ladies,' he said, 'a far more comfortable place for our exciting little games would be Yvette's bedroom.'

He slipped a hand into Yvette's knickers. They were small and it was easy to feel down her warm belly. She opened her legs as if by reflex action when his fingers touched her *lapin*. She let him stroke it for a while, but as soon as he tried to press his finger in between the lips, she grasped his wrist.

'Not so fast, Roger,' she said.

'He's right,' Monique said, 'let's lie on the bed, Yvette.'

Roger smiled affectionately at both of them and gave them an amiable squeeze between the legs. Yvette abandoned what she was doing, but with reluctance, and got up with them. Roger put his arms round their waists and as they moved into the bedroom gave Yvette a secret wink to let her know he understood her desires. And would help her achieve them.

All three stripped naked and lay on the bed, Roger was in the middle, of course. The women lay on their backs, legs apart, he was on his knees, stroking a warm soft *joujou* with each hand. A series of small sighs indicated he was on the right track – and he spoke to Monique while he pressed two fingers into her.

'When Yvette was playing with me you told us you'd never done it to a man all the way,' he began. 'Have you ever done it to a woman, Monique?'

His fingertips were gliding over her wet little bud, her legs were trembling – but she blushed at his question.

'Of course not!' she said, 'Never, never, never! I think I'd die if another woman touched me between the legs.'

'But when I feel your *joujou* you love it,' he said, 'and when I put a finger inside you to tickle your little bud you get wet and slippery in no time. And if I were to put my tongue in you, it would make you have a lovely long noisy orgasm.'

'But that's different,' Monique exclaimed, staring up at him.

There was a broad smile on Yvette's face as she realized what Roger was trying to achieve. To make sure she remained happy he flicked a fingertip over her secret bud and heard her gasp.

'Fingers are fingers,' he said with a smile and a shrug, 'and a tongue is a tongue. If you closed your eyes you couldn't tell who was feeling you, me or Yvette.'

'Of course I'd know,' she said, 'what an absurd idea!'

'Perhaps,' he said with an easy shrug, 'and even if you could, it doesn't affect what I said – I see no reason why two women who like each other shouldn't pleasure each other in bed.'

He was saying it for Yvette's benefit, of course. And because he was curious to find out if Monique could be persuaded to let her friend make love to her. And because it would be amusing to watch them playing together.

Against that, suppose they did it to each other and concluded that they preferred it like that, he would lose both of them as clients. Gilberte Drouet would be furious about it.

To tell the truth, he could think of reasons why women should not play with each other, good friends or not. But only because of Marie Brantome and her blonde friend.

He put his hands between two smooth pairs of thighs, one lean pair, one plump pair, both pairs spread to allow his fingertips to tickle two patches of curls, a dark brown patch and a mouse-brown patch. He stroked two sets of soft lips, little to choose between them, he opened both *joujous* and saw one bud was bigger than the other. Not by much, but Monique had the advantage.

'You're wrong, Roger,' Monique said, 'I'd know.'

He wondered what she meant, then he realized she was thinking about what he'd said about fingers and tongues.

'Your fingers are touching me now,' she went on, 'and even if my eyes were closed I'd know it was a man touching me. There is a difference between the natural and the unnatural.'

Yvette and Roger glanced at each other and grinned.

'A little test,' he said, 'we'll blindfold you and see if you can tell whether it's me touching you or Yvette – agreed?'

'That's a good idea,' Yvette joined in, 'as you're so certain you can tell the difference – prove it, *cherie*!'

She fetched an expensive silk scarf from a drawer and wrapped it around Monique's head twice and tied it at the back. She and Roger arranged Monique on the bed between them, legs well open.

'Can you see anything through the blindfold?' Yvette asked.

Monique said she couldn't. Roger checked to be sure and

asked her to put her hands under her head. He nodded at Yvette across the long naked body between them, she put her hand down between Monique's thighs and stroked the lips of her *joujou*.

'This is how it feels when I caress you, Monique,' he said, a grin on his face, 'you must remember it exactly so you can tell the difference when Yvette touches you.'

'I shall know instantly,' Monique sighed, her legs trembling, 'and much as I like you, Yvette *cherie*, dear friends as we are, it could never be exciting to be touched by another woman.'

'We shall see,' Yvette murmured, her fingers caressing inside Monique's slippery wet *joujou*. She winked at Roger and she said she thought it was time she took over, to see if Monique could tell the difference.

'Not yet,' Roger grinned, 'a little longer to be certain that she knows the touch of my fingers.'

But by then Monique was too far gone in her ascent to ecstasy to know who was touching her, or to care. With Yvette's fingers teasing her bud, her hips jerked up off the bed and she wailed, a long moaning sound of climactic pleasure.

'*Ah mon Dieu*,' Yvette gasped, staring wide-eyed at her friend in her ecstatic throes, 'ah, Roger – help me!'

He too was almost wild with excitement at observing how she'd played with blindfolded Monique. His stiff fifteen centimetres stood throbbing upright, he reached out for Yvette and scrambled over the naked woman between them to get at her.

And she too flung herself down flat on her back with her legs wide apart. In an instant his belly was on hers, he was pushing into her wet and open *joujou*. He could feel her body squirming under him as he moved in long steady thrusts to bring her to her peak. *Ah ah ah* she was moaning, *ah Roger, I know you understand . . .*

She was right – he understood what she really wanted. To have her friend Monique kneel between her legs and use her tongue to bring on her orgasm. And do it the same way to Monique. She had become enormously aroused while she was taking secret advantage of Monique – but Monique wasn't ready yet, more seduction would be required before she accepted the sexual role Yvette intended for her. This was clear to Roger while he sprawled on Yvette's hot belly and slid in and out strongly.

Yvette's hands were on his shoulders, gripping him tight – he felt another pair of hands on his bottom as it rode up and down. He glanced over his shoulder and saw Monique sitting beside him with a curious smile on her narrow face. She'd pulled the silk scarf down, not bothering with the knot, it hung loosely around her neck.

She ran her hands over his body, stroking his sides and back. She stroked his bottom, she pinched it and slapped it, she slid a finger down the crease. She felt down between his open thighs to touch his hairy pompoms as they bounced to his movements.

'Yes, Roger,' she said softly, 'do it to her good and hard!'

Yvette reached her climax and writhed on the bed, moaning and sighing. Roger thrust short and hard five or six more times and spurted ecstatically into her shuddering belly.

When he and she were calm again he rolled off and sat up with his back to the polished wooden headboard. Yvette stayed as she was on her back, a contented smile on her face. Monique crawled up the bed and sat with her head on Roger's shoulder and a hand between his legs, holding his limp and sticky length.

'It's me next,' she said seriously, 'but not yet – I want you to rest and get your strength back, Roger, so that you can make me shriek and thrash about like Yvette did.'

'With pleasure,' he said – and all the charm in the world was in his voice, 'I shall drive you insane with ecstasy.'

'You almost did that before,' she said, 'with your fingers, I mean. It was you all the time, wasn't it? You were joking when you said you were going to let Yvette take over. I'd have known at once.'

'Are you sure about that?' he asked gently.

From where he sat, the smile on Yvette's face was upside-down as she listened to the conversation between him and Monique. He was scoring points with Yvette, no question about that, but how would Monique react when she learned the truth. Or a version of the truth – perhaps that would be more acceptable.

'I'm absolutely certain,' Monique said, but her tone was very doubtful now in the light of his questioning.

'You are certain that Yvette never touched you?' he asked.

'Tell me the truth – did she?' Monique blurted out, her face turning pink with embarrassment at the implication.

'The truth,' said Roger, 'but what use is that to anyone? We intelligent people live only for our passions and our pleasures – we leave matters of truth to philosophers and policemen.'

'I must know!' said Monique, her face scarlet. 'Yvette, tell me – did you touch me when I was blindfolded?'

Yvette was enjoying the game.

'Did I touch you, *cherie*? You ask me that now – but you were so very certain you knew the difference between a man's fingers between your legs and a woman's fingers.'

'But I want to know!'

'And so you shall,' Roger assured her, 'but first, a question or two – did you at any time while you were being caressed feel a change of emphasis in the pleasure? As if one set of fingers gave way to another set of fingers?'

'No,' Monique admitted, 'if there was a change at some point, if you let Yvette take over, then it was done so skilfully that it wasn't possible to say where you stopped and she started. If she did. Did you, Yvette – did you stroke me?'

'That's for you to decide, *cherie*,' Yvette said with a smile, 'you are the expert.'

'Roger – tell me if she did!'

'I shall tell you everything,' he said, his hand down between her thighs to soothe her. She was leaning against the headboard with her knees up. He pressed his middle finger into her *joujou* and touched her slippy bud very lightly.

'Before all is revealed,' he said airily, 'there is a second question you must answer. When you lay blindfolded on your back with your legs apart, did you truly enjoy the experience?'

'I suppose so,' she conceded, 'but that's not the point.'

'Perhaps not – but to Yvette and me it looked as if you had a marvellous time. You arched your back up off the bed and moaned and sobbed – it was very impressive.'

'Which of you did it to me, you or Yvette?' she demanded.

'We both did,' said Roger, distorting the truth expertly, 'we changed over five or six times while we were playing with you – and you never knew. Sometimes my fingers were in you, sometimes Yvette's. And the pleasure you felt was the same.'

'That's impossible,' Monique said, 'it couldn't be! Yvette – is that what happened?'

'Exactly as Roger said,' Yvette lied boldly, a sideways smile on her face.

'In the final moments,' Monique said, 'when it all happened – whose fingers were doing it to me then, yours or his?'

Roger answered the question, not sure if Yvette could without upsetting her friend.

'Both of us,' he said pleasantly, 'there were fingers rubbing you at the great moment, one was mine and one Yvette's. Pressed close together and touching the exact spot. Now you know.'

'My god – I'd never have believed it!' Monique said faintly.

The feel of his fingers inside her had already aroused her to the point of action. She had been holding his limp and dangling part throughout their curious conversation – it was standing up again, long and thick in her hand, jerking a little against her palm. Her hand beat up and down firmly.

'You cheated me,' she said, 'but now I'm going to have what I came here for.'

She pulled him away from the headboard and down on his back – he had to grin when she threw her long slender leg over him and sat astride his belly. His hard-upright part was held firmly in her clasped hand while she massaged it up and down fiercely.

'I won't let you cheat me this time,' she said, 'I'm going to have you, Roger.'

He wondered if she'd ever done it this way before and thought it unlikely. But she seemed to understand what to do. She rose up to position his straining part between her thighs, then sank down slowly – he felt her warm slippery flesh swallow him. She lowered herself all the way, till his entire fifteen centimetres had gone into her belly.

'Now you can pay me back for cheating me,' she said, starting to ride him.

'Well done!' Yvette encouraged her from where she lay beside them on her side. 'Make him pay his debts, *cherie*!'

Monique's rhythm was fast and twitchy, as if she was nervous of the initiative she was taking. Roger was convinced now she'd never done it like this before – she must have seen pictures in books, the *Sixteen Positions*, or some such tourist nonsense. He put his hands on her thighs and stroked up to her stretched and penetrated *joujou*.

It was too much to expect that Yvette would rest content with watching her dear friend pleasuring herself sexually with a man – not now that she'd pleasured Monique herself, although it had been by stealth. Roger grinned again to see Yvette mount behind Monique and squat across his outstretched thighs.

Yvette's arms were around Monique to hold her close while she squeezed her full breasts and belly against her long bare back. Her hands were kneading Monique's little breasts like dough.

'What are you doing?' Monique screamed.

'We'll share him,' Yvette gasped, 'we'll have him together.'

Her hands slid down Monique's lean belly and were between her splayed thighs, a fingertip stroked the long wet lips parted by the penetration of Roger's thick shaft.

'He's had both of us, now we'll have him,' Yvette panted, her face red and her eyes bulging. Roger stared up in huge arousal, wishing he had two shafts, so that he could pleasure both women at the same time.

'No!' Monique squealed, but Yvette held her about the

waist and slid her up and down Roger's hard length, bounced her on it in a jolting rhythm.

This vigorous handling plunged Monique into orgasm very fast, to a fierce shuddering and wailing. The urgent contractions of her clasping *joujou* pushed Roger over the brink of sensuality – he spurted into her in sensational spasms.

'Yes, Monique, *cherie*!' Yvette was moaning. She alone of the trio was not thrashing about in orgasm – a mild flicker of pity stirred Roger, but he was too involved in his own ecstasy to do anything to relieve her solitary anguish.

Monique sagged forward on Roger, momentarily exhausted by the ferocity of the orgasm she had experienced. She lay weakly upon him, her *nichons* flattened on his chest, her knees bent double underneath her, her bottom in the air.

Roger was content to let her lie, it was pleasing and somehow comforting to feel the weight of her hot body resting on him. A living blanket, so to speak. He felt himself go soft and small, and slip out of her wet, warm flesh. Then her body jerked on him and she murmured *not again, not yet...*

He peered over her shoulder and saw that Yvette was crouching behind her. The expression on her face was of eagerness, almost of desperation, her fingers were busy at Monique's very wet and exposed *lapin*.

'I can't – I can't,' Monique gurgled, her body trembling upon Roger. Yvette said nothing to that – she went on doing what she was doing to Monique, her expression more and more intent, till Roger feared she was becoming demented.

Monique groaned and shook in orgasmic convulsions, her bottom jerked up against Yvette's busily interfering fingers. *Yes, yes, Yvette*, she sobbed, in place of the *no I can't* of a minute ago.

Roger lay underneath her twitching body wondering what Yvette would do now. He was finding this unusual encounter interesting – and exciting. If Yvette would be patient for a few minutes he was certain he'd be able to pleasure her.

Yvette couldn't wait. She seized Monique's limp left hand and pressed it between her open thighs with both her own hands. *Ah ah ah*, she was moaning, holding Monique's fingers to her bud and rubbing herself rapidly against them.

It didn't take long – Yvette jerked in intense spasms and she screamed as if being murdered. Roger took it to signify she had reached total satisfaction. For the time being.

The three of them lay for a time resting. Monique was in the middle, which to Roger suggested Yvette intended to do far more to her when they recovered. He couldn't tell whether Monique's attitude to being touched by another woman had been modified by what had been done to her so far – time would tell.

The two women were whispering to each other, which gave him to think Yvette might perhaps be winning her campaign. He found it an amusing speculation – and he closed his eyes for a short and refreshing semi-doze before it became necessary to complete his contract by offering his services to both women again.

When he opened his eyes he saw Yvette half-lying over Monique to kiss her on the mouth, with a leg between Monique's legs. He moved cautiously, not to disturb them in their devotions, as he turned on his side and raised himself on an elbow to watch what would develop. He noted with interest that Monique didn't pull away, after a pause she opened her mouth to let Yvette's tongue slide between her lips.

I think I may have lost not just one client but two, he said to himself in great amusement, *but what of that, there are plenty more where these came from – Gilberte has a great talent to find women who need a handsome young man to pleasure them.*

Watching his charming companions was making his precious part stir into renewed life – he clasped it fondly in his hand while he heard Yvette telling Monique she adored her. Monique looked troubled for a moment, but when Yvette kissed her breasts their dark red buds were prominent and firm.

What followed was far beyond his expectations. Yvette pressed Monique down on her back with her legs apart and lay in between them, her fingers playing over Monique's belly and the patch of brown curls. She kissed inside Monique's thighs and licked them until Monique was writhing in delicious sensation.

Well, now she knows if there is any discernible difference at all between a man's touch and a woman's touch, Roger thought as he saw Monique's eyes close and her hands clench. *She said that she could tell – now she knows for certain*. She was gasping and her belly arched upwards in an urgent plea for more.

Yvette laughed as she pushed her friend's thighs wider apart. She put her face between them and used her tongue. Monique was squealing now – a shrill continuous noise that Roger found both curious and amusing. Personally he preferred women who sang out loud and clear in sexual arousal.

It was obvious to him that Yvette was making the most of

this fortunate chance to have her dear friend. She kissed and licked her *joujou*, stopped and let her cool down, resumed and took her another two or three steps up the mountain of pleasure. For one with no previous experience of playing with other women she had great finesse and dexterity.

Roger asked himself if he was wrong about Yvette. Perhaps she had been with other women before, though his instincts told him otherwise. He reached the conclusion she had learned her tender skills fingering her own *joujou* in private.

She played with herself at night in bed, no doubt, lying flat on her back with her nightdress up round her waist, legs apart and her hand down between her thighs. Or perhaps on the sofa in her sitting-room, in the afternoon. Knees apart, her hand under her dress and inside her knickers. A wetted fingertip pressing between the lips of her *joujou*, a slow and gentle stroking till she gasped and shivered in fast little spasms.

True or false, it was irrelevant now she was using her tongue on Monique's exposed and pink little bud. Making her shiver and gasp. And however long Yvette tried to spin it out, the moment had to come when human endurance could stand no more pleasure. The thrilling moment arrived when Monique's loins bucked up off the bed in orgasm and her back arched like a bow. She shrieked in her ecstasy and enchanted Roger by it. But finally her cries diminished, her convulsive jerking faded to a trembling of legs and belly.

'Yvette, what have you done to me?' she sighed, her face red. 'I've never been touched by another woman before.'

'And I've never done that to another woman,' Yvette murmured, so confirming Roger's assessment of her. If she was telling the truth – how could anyone ever be sure about a woman in bed?

Monique was wrung out, emotionally as well as physically. She put an arm over her eyes and lay limp and trembling. Not bad at all, Roger thought with a secret grin – four orgasms in half an hour, for a woman who's never been past twice before until now. She has personal proof of what Yvette was telling her about how women can go on doing it for hours.

Meanwhile Yvette saw that there was nothing to be gained from Monique until she had rested. She couldn't wait that long – she reached out over Monique's bare body and took hold of his stiff shaft. It twitched in her hand – he was aroused from seeing her pleasure Monique. She chuckled a little nervously while she was sliding her fingers up and down it.

'Monique must rest,' she said, 'but you never tire, Roger, do you? You know much more about love-making than I do. You were very interested in what I did to Monique. I was too excited to know what I was doing – do you think it might be the end of the friendship between her and me?'

It wasn't a real question, Roger knew, she was only making an excuse for herself. She had revealed her true feelings in front of him, the strength of her desire for Monique, and didn't know how a male witness would take it.

'At first she was troubled by the strangeness of it,' he told Yvette, 'but then she adored it – she had her legs so far apart I was afraid she would split up the middle. When she has rested a little I'm certain she will do the same to you.'

Yvette laughed and spread herself on her back on the bed, her legs well apart. Roger gave her an encouraging smile and sat up. He got off the bed and walked round the foot and climbed back on beside her – all this not to wake Monique by scrambling over her! He stroked the brunette *joujou* she was offering him, his fingers explored the prominence of the fleshy mound between her plump thighs.

'You like to look between women's legs,' she said, 'I've seen you do this before. You were staring at Monique in the same way – what are you looking for, Roger; the perfect *joujou*?'

'But they are all perfect,' he assured her, while his fingers opened her impossibly wide.

'Some more than others,' she sighed. 'In my view the good God was exceptionally kind to men when He designed this part of the female body.'

And she spread her legs wider, to be sure he was in no doubt of the enormous favour a woman bestowed upon a man when she let him enter her. Roger knelt between her thighs, with his upright part in his hand.

'Superb,' he said, grinning as he probed her wetness with the fingers of his other hand. 'Enchanting!' Then his belly was on hers and he was sliding up inside her.

'Hard and fast, Roger,' she panted, 'I'm dying for it!'

With short fast strokes he rammed her till she was jerking so strongly he had to cling to her shoulders not to be dismounted. The psychological effect of her powerful reaction sent waves of sensation surging through Roger – he adored it when women moved and sobbed underneath him, it was very flattering to his pride. And brief as the time was since he had penetrated her, he felt his crisis arriving.

'So soon, so soon!' he gasped as his sticky passion spurted into her quaking belly.

Yvette cried out when she felt his surge inside her, her body jerked in ecstatic spasms. The orgasm was fierce and short. Her arms were tight around his neck holding his cheek down on hers, her hot breath panted into his ear. He thrust a few more times, just to make her twitch, and waited for her to calm down.

'Now you've had both of us,' he said lightly, 'Monique and me – which of us do you prefer?'

'I don't understand my own feelings,' she said, sounding very content with the situation, whether it puzzled her or not, 'you made me do it so easily and it was marvellous. When Monique lay with her legs open and let me kiss her, that was marvellous too – why should I choose between you?'

'No need to,' he said cheerfully, 'you are a fortunate woman, you can have either of us whenever you please. Or both of us if you choose.'

He slid off her and stretched out beside her – now she was in the middle. He saw Monique stir a little. Her eyes were closed, but she had moved her arm away from her face. She turned on her side and lay so close her little breasts touched Yvette's arm.

'Don't misunderstand me, Roger,' Yvette said discreetly, 'you mustn't think I'm a lesbian. I adore the feel of you inside me, your long thick *thing* sliding up and down. I am normal in every way. Monique is a friend.'

'Of course she is,' Roger agreed with a smile.

Excusing

Roger had promised to phone Gilberte at the Agence Drouet after his visit to Yvette Dubois and her friend Monique. Gilberte was interested to know how he had handled the situation, whether he would go there again if Madame Dubois asked for him – she had a sharp nose for business, Gilberte, especially when there was an opportunity to increase future fees.

But Roger didn't bother himself to phone the next day. He was not sure what to tell Gilberte. He'd stayed longer than he needed to because he wanted to see the outcome of the *affaire* between the two women. And yes, they pleasured each other spiritedly, after they'd rested a while.

That seemed to dispose of a need for his presence in future – but before he departed Monique Santerre insisted she wanted him there the next time she came to Yvette's. Yvette agreed – which left him thinking that neither of them were confident, as yet, of their bedroom relationship and wanted him there as the catalyst to bring about an explosive reaction between them.

When he phoned Gilberte two days later, Celeste told him that Madame Drouet was out all day. While he was chatting to Celeste he thought he detected a note of sadness in her voice and asked if anything was wrong.

'Nothing,' she said. 'My boyfriend promised to take me to see the new Jean Gabin movie tonight, but now he's dodged out of it to go somewhere with his friends.'

'The boyfriend you told me you were not very serious about?'

'Just as well,' she said, 'because he's not serious about me, that's clear enough.'

'Come with me to see the movie,' Roger offered.

He felt sorry for Celeste, he wasn't sure why. He felt sorry for himself and knew exactly why. Over a week had gone by since Marie had come to his apartment and told him the incredible tale of her tattoo. When she left she refused to make any promise about seeing him again – or even phoning him.

He didn't want to spend the evening with Nadine. She was more neurotic than ever about how she was treated by men – they were only interested in her body, she said, they wanted one thing, then they were gone. Roger shared the view himself, so he knew what she was talking about, although it was impossible to explain to her why her men friends moved on so quickly.

What a pity, he thought, because Nadine is a stunner and it's an erotic dream come true when you get her in bed. Then an hour later when it's over you realize how boring she can be when she starts talking again. The best thing for her would be to find a rich boyfriend who is stone-deaf. Failing that, a foreigner who speaks no French.

So it was to be an evening with Celeste, the thin receptionist, and an opportunity to continue the exploration of her tiny breasts and lean thighs begun in Gilberte's outer office.

'Do you really mean that?' she breathed down the telephone.

'Certainly. Where do you live – you know where I am from your Agency records. Are you anywhere close?'

She told him she lived in Clichy. To Roger that was a suburb as unknown as Madagascar or Timbuktu – it was just a name on a map of the Metro.

'Meet halfway,' he suggested. 'Do you know the Opera Imperial in the Boulevard des Italiens? They show all the new movies.'

She was waiting for him on the pavement outside the cinema at seven thirty. It was a warm summer evening, she looked as attractive as she ever would, in a loose coffee-brown blouse and a grey skirt, her long brunette hair tied back in a pony-tail. She gave Roger an eager stare through her big round spectacles – he kissed her cheek and wondered if he was being sensible. Encouraging her in this way might make her too eager, this Celeste.

She proved him right as soon as the lights went out. Her head was on his shoulder and she held his hand hotly. He put his arm round her narrow waist. She responded with a hand on his thigh. Mentally he shrugged and thought, *Why not?* and he cupped a tiny breast in his hand as she stroked the bulge between his legs.

That day at the Agence he'd felt her breasts, standing behind her typist's chair and reaching down over her narrow shoulders. He'd unbuttoned the shirt she wore that day and unclipped her bra to put his hands on her bare breasts – but Celeste had only two big pink buds set high on her chest, no fleshy delights to play with or squeeze.

That was why she was wearing a loose blouse this evening – to disguise her thin figure. But Roger's fingertips found her buds through her thin blouse. She had a soft and fragile garment of some sort under the blouse, though it didn't feel

217

like a bra. A slip, he assumed as she sighed in pleasure at his touch.

The movie was a typical Jean Gabin gangster story. Roger kept half an eye on the screen; his interest lay elsewhere – between Celeste's legs now she'd aroused him by caressing the length in his trousers. That day in the office he'd persuaded her to pull her skirt up to show him her long thin thighs – and he had seen they didn't press together at the top, as most women's did.

She had a charming gap between her thighs, Celeste, room for a hand when her legs were together – in fact, her legs never were closed and never could be completely closed, however she tried. The thought excited Roger – he settled her comfortably against him with an arm around her and put his hand up her skirt.

Oh la la! he exclaimed softly when his fingers told him that she was not wearing knickers.

In the dark her face turned towards him – she had a broad grin and he saw the glint of her big spectacles. His fingertips slid over smooth flesh and soft curls and warm lips – she had spread her legs wide on the seat.

'Is this how you usually go to the cinema?' he whispered.

'Do you approve?' she murmured.

'I find it charming,' he said.

He assumed that her missing boyfriend had first persuaded her to go to the movies with him like this, to make it easy for him to play with her in the dark. A man who knew what he wanted and made sure he got it. What else had Celeste learned at the hands of this enterprising friend?

That question was answered when she flipped his trousers open and slipped her hand inside. Needless to say he'd been as stiff as a broomstick since the moment she first put her hand on his thigh. She felt his upstanding fifteen

centimetres casually, fingers seeking an opening in the thin
silk of his posing-pouch, to get to his bare, hard flesh.

While she explored his underwear thoroughly Roger
pressed his middle finger into her and found she was moist
already. By then her hand had moved to the top of his little
silk pouch and down inside – she clasped his bounding part
full-handed and firmly.

'Ah, a little *cache-sexe* for underwear,' she said, 'you are
a real performer, *cheri*, an artiste – I guessed that much.'

Her fingertips were gliding lightly over the unhooded
head of his throbbing shaft.

'Be careful, *cherie*,' he sighed as he stroked her secret
bud, wet and slippy to his touch. The evening was turning
out better than he'd expected – only five minutes into the
movie and they had achieved this exciting state of intimacy.

'When I get you home,' he told her, 'I shall strip you
naked, Celeste. I shall do things to you – marvellous things
that you have never imagined.'

*And that your missing boyfriend has never imagined
either*, he added to himself.

'What will you do to me?' she sighed. 'Ah no, don't tell
me – let me guess...'

From this moment, as if they'd agreed silently about it,
they handled each other with great delicacy. Their objective was to excite and to thrill but no more; to go to the edge
and totter above the precipice of climax – but not to push
each other over it into release.

Time passed, minutes of sensation that seemed to stretch
into hours, the two of them lost in their silent pleasure. The
movie was about three-quarters over and they had both lost
touch with it long ago – Celeste sighed and implored Roger
to take her out of the cinema.

To his apartment, to a dark corner, to a hotel, anywhere

that he liked, she couldn't wait another second. And indeed, between her lean spread thighs Celeste was very wet and hot – Roger had two fingers between the lips of her *joujou*, hardly touching her bud now. He was keeping her at the point of detonation just by having his fingers inside her.

He pulled her hand out of his trousers, zipped up and led her out of the dark cinema, up between the rows, out into the foyer. The sudden light almost dazzled them – they clung together as they went out into the street. It was a good place for a taxi, there was no question of going by Metro when they were both hot for each other. Arm-in-arm they almost ran to the cab rank near the corner.

From the Boulevard des Italiens to Roger's apartment near the Place Denfert-Rochereau is a journey of some distance – and by taxi very expensive. Right down the Avenue de l'Opera to the Louvre and across the Seine, evening traffic all the way, along the entire length of the Boulevard Raspail. A long ride, it was unrealistic to expect sexually-aroused Celeste to be still.

True to form, the taxi was hardly moving before her hand slid between his thighs and cupped his bulge. For a moment Roger was worried that she meant to unzip him – not a good option while a driver was sitting in front of them, and it was not a large car. But she compromised by sliding her hand into his trouser-pocket – not an easy manoeuvre if a man is sitting, but she managed to do it.

Her fingers plucked and worried at his stiff part through the pocket-lining and the silk of his little posing-pouch. Her palm was hot and he gasped at the touch. And then it was her turn to gasp when his hand was under her skirt and moving slowly upwards between her thighs – until his fingers were pressing inside her wet little *joujou*.

This is absurd, he said to himself, surprised by his own

actions; I am a professional, an expert in love-making, highly paid by women to give them pleasure. And yet I am playing with this girl in the back of a taxi as if I were a boy with my hand up a skirt for the first time!

And what makes it even less comprehensible is that she is not even attractive. I could have been with Nadine this evening and chose not to be. At this very moment I could be feeling beautiful Nadine's *lapin*, that perfect little *joujou* that pouts and opens delicately for me to slide my shaft in.

Instead of that I'm playing with Gilberte's thin receptionist in a taxi. A girl with big spectacles and a flat chest. And I'm taking her home with me for the night. It will be like lying on a billiard table – I think I must be going out of my mind.

The truth was, he admitted to himself, he'd not been behaving at all normally or intelligently since that day he fell in love with Marie Brantome. Or whatever her real name was. She was to blame and he hated her – even though he was in love with her.

As pleasant as it was to play with Celeste in the taxi, and to let her stroke him, Roger took care not to let their little game go too far. He had his professional standards, there were to be no sudden shuddering accidents in the dark. Celeste would reach her climax of passion when he wanted her to and not until then. It was something he wanted to observe, long thin Celeste in the throes of ecstasy. So he wasn't going to let it happen to her until he had her in his apartment. Sprawled on her back, on his divan. Naked. Legs wide open. Then he'd make her and watch.

He heard her fast intake of breath – five more seconds and it would be too late! At once the gentle motion of his fingers in her slippery little *joujou* stopped. She moaned and put her free hand up to his face to stroke his lips. She kissed him with her mouth open on his, her wet tongue vibrating between his lips.

Celeste was so formidably aroused that her body was shivering against him – her hand in his trousers was plucking at his hard length as if to force him to resume his caress between her legs and take her all the way. But Roger was not to be persuaded. He refused to let her reach that urgent orgasm for which her whole body was screeching.

A few more touches of his fingers between her thin thighs and the crisis would be precipitated – her tongue flickered against his tongue in mute and desperate appeal. And through the lining of his trouser-pocket he felt her finger-nails digging furiously into his stiff flesh. The cruel pleasure almost did for him, he reached down and grabbed her wrist to make her stop it.

'Not yet!' he gasped into her ear. 'Just a few more minutes, we're almost there!'

'I think I'm there already,' she sighed, her thighs trembling against his unmoving hand.

'Not yet, *cherie*, I won't let you,' he said firmly. There's the corner – once we're inside that building there are no rules at all, absolutely none. You can scream and writhe and kick all night long. And I shall do the same, you may rely on it.'

'You'll do things to me that I've never imagined before,' she said in a hot whisper, 'you promised!'

The taxi swerved across the Place Denfert-Rochereau, ignoring other traffic, and braked hard by the kerb outside the building Roger had designated. Celeste behaved well enough while he paid the fare, but when she was inside the apartment building and on the stairs, that was another matter.

It was not late, not yet ten o'clock, and there might well be other tenants and visitors about, coming or going – but Celeste didn't care. They reached the second landing, their arms around each other's waists. She was clinging to Roger very tightly. She pushed him against the wall and pressed herself close, her hand busy with his zip.

'Here?' he said. 'But we're almost there.'

'I told you,' she gasped, 'I'm there already!'

Roger was amused, he leaned back against the wall, his hands on her thin shoulders while she wrenched his trousers wide open and his posing-pouch down. Her painted nails sank like claws in the stiff flesh of his upstanding part – that made him gasp and flinch, then her clenched hand was sliding up and down.

'You've got me in such a state, Roger,' she moaned, 'I want it now, now – do you hear me?'

Her free hand hoisted her skirt to her waist to bare herself. She steered him roughly into her *joujou*, he grinned and pushed. Celeste pushed harder and longer – she was so wet and open that he slipped all the way into her. Instantly she was thumping her lean belly at him.

'I can't believe I'm doing this,' she gasped, 'somebody might come up the stairs and see us!'

'Ah yes,' Roger murmured, bracing himself against the wall as she rammed away – the situation was absurd and entertaining, he thought. He wondered if Celeste was always this desperate.

He stared curiously into her face. Her eyes stared wide open behind her round spectacles, her bright-painted lips were drawn back over regular white teeth – it was an expression of intense emotion. He recognized that Celeste had left this world and was soaring high in a pink whirlwind of sexual frenzy.

From which there was only one way back to reality. She had to undergo the destructive thunderstorm of orgasm.

His hands gripped the cheeks of her bare bottom, so small and taut that it needed an effort to sink his fingertips into their leanness. There was nothing to be done, nothing he could assist her with – she was like a sex-machine fitted over his shaft and sliding furiously up and down it until she got what she wanted.

It didn't take long – she pressed herself tighter against him to stay upright on shaking legs, her fingers hooked in his belt for a grip – then an ecstatic wail announced the arrival of her crisis. Roger stood firm while her pleasure ran its course, not letting himself be carried over the edge by her enthusiasm into a quick thrill. She was sobbing and shaking, slamming her belly against his in her urgent orgasm.

When she calmed down her legs were so weak under her that he picked her up bodily, his hard fifteen centimetres sliding wetly out of her. She was tall, as tall as him, but her thinness made her light and easy to carry up the remaining flights of stairs. She lay limp in his arms, breathing as heavily as if she'd just run a marathon.

Ah no, that was only a 250-metre sprint, Roger said to himself with a mental grin. *There are surprises to come, Celeste. In an hour or two from now you will be completely screamed out and all you will desire will be to turn over and go to sleep – that I promise you.*

Inside his tiny apartment he kicked the door shut behind him. He carried Celeste to the divan which was also his bed at night and laid her on it. She grinned up at him. He sat beside her on the edge and looked at her with raised eyebrows.

'Well?' he asked humorously.

'That was ridiculous,' she said, 'but it was something that I never imagined doing, so you kept your promise, I suppose.'

She took off her big round spectacles and handed them to him. Roger put them in a safe place on the floor under the divan. He knew it was as overt an invitation as if she'd taken off a pair of knickers, if she'd been wearing any. Her gesture was charged with a bizarre eroticism.

He nodded and grinned and opened her coffee-brown blouse. She was wearing a close-fitting black lace basque, the pale tint of her flesh gleaming through. He pulled the ribbon straps off her narrow shoulders and a moment later he was licking the long red buds that were all she had by way of breasts.

'Oh Roger!' she said and started to wriggle as he sucked the bud nearest to him. After a minute or two he transferred to the other one and drew it as deep into his mouth as he could, while the tip of his tongue flipped over it.

'Oh Roger,' she sighed again, 'oh *cheri*!'

His hand was up her skirt and between her thin thighs – which lay open for him. His fingers probed her and parted the lips of her *joujou* – she was very warm and slippery inside. He stood up to shed his clothes, and sat down naked beside her. From between his thighs jutted his fifteen centimetres of hard flesh.

Celeste rolled over on her side to take it into her mouth and suck so furiously that Roger's determination to control her was almost undermined. After being ravaged by her on the landing he was so aroused that it would take very little to make him spurt into her mouth.

It would have been so delicious to let her continue, and she was demonstrating a most flattering enthusiasm for

225

what she was doing to him. But Roger put his hands on her thin shoulders and pushed her gently away. She rolled onto her back, smiling up at him. Her pale eyes were unfocused without her spectacles – she looked younger than she was and vulnerable.

'Not so fast, *cherie*,' he said, 'I mean to keep you here with me all night.'

She sighed and smiled blindly at him.

He undid the waistband of her skirt and slid it over her hips and down her long lean thighs. The black basque reached to just below her belly-button, from there on down she was naked to her stocking-tops. A patch of wispy curls, a light ash-brown shade, split by long thin lips, slightly parted – he drew a fingertip down the split and into her groin.

'Do impossible things to me, Roger,' she murmured, eyes half-open but unseeing, 'you said you would.'

He pressed two fingers into her slippery-wet *joujou*, to touch her secret bud lightly and make her squirm in delight and gasp. The black lace basque had an expensive look about it; that sort of underwear came from boutiques in the rue Cambon – there were never any prices shown in their windows – if you had to ask the price you couldn't afford it.

He didn't think for an instant Gilberte Drouet paid her staff enough to go shopping in places like that.

'It's very elegant, your basque,' he remarked, observing with particular interest her facial expression as his clever fingers sent thrills of delicious sensation through her body.

But she wasn't going to discuss underwear at that moment.

'I want you to take it off,' she sighed, 'make me naked!'

It was the work of a second, to slip the little lace garment under her back and over her flat chest and up over the head

226

and off altogether. She lay on her back, legs slightly apart, hands by her sides, a vague smile on her face. Seen completely naked, Celeste was exquisitely thin. There was hardly any flesh on her bones – Roger ran his hands over her jutting hips and along her thin thighs and wondered if he'd ever seen so slender a woman.

She began to breathe hard when he held her ankles and pushed her feet right up to her lean bottom, forcing her knees outward and opening her thighs wide. She exhaled in a long sigh when he put his bare belly on hers and let her feel his weight upon her thin body.

'How well can you see without your glasses, Celeste?'

'Hardly at all,' she sighed, 'your face is just a blur.'

One long push took him deep into her, fifteen centimetres of stiff flesh penetrating her narrow belly.

'But I see you perfectly,' he told her, starting his slow strokes, 'when you reach your climax I shall study your face, Celeste – in the critical moments I shall see how ecstasy is expressed on your face.'

'Ah no!'

'I shall observe if your eyes are wide or shut, and if your mouth hangs open. I shall see everything and remember, so that when we meet in the office I'll know how your face looks at the first moment of orgasm.'

'Ah no no, that's unfair,' she sighed, her thin loins jerking up at him to receive his thrusts, 'I won't know how you look!'

Roger had said the right thing to capture her imagination and drive her wild with desire. She gasped and writhed beneath him, her flat belly bucked fiercely upwards to drive him in deeper. And then it happened to her – she was squealing and tossing her head from side to side.

Roger raised himself on his elbows to stare down at her

227

face. Her mouth gaped open and her eyes were starting from her head. The look on her face was of happy bewilderment – she loved what she was feeling, the surging of indescribable sensation through her, impossible though it was to make sense of it. Roger almost laughed at her expression.

'The face of Celeste in ecstasy,' he said out loud – or tried to say. But the contractions of her thin belly were so powerful on his throbbing shaft – squeezing and pulling like a soft hand playing with him – that he gushed his passion into her in short hard strokes. She screamed as her back arched up off the bed in frantic spasms.

'*Je t'adore* Roger,' she squealed, '*je t'adore!*'

Roger was flattered to see how long it took after that before she was calm again. When she was breathing normally and able to speak rationally he fetched a bottle of cognac from the kitchen and poured them a little glass each. Celeste turned herself on the divan and propped her back against the wall while they were drinking and talking.

'So now you know how I look when I reach a climax,' she said, staring at him short-sightedly, 'were you impressed?'

'The moment was charming,' he told her. 'So much so that in a little while I shall observe your face again.'

'Is it part of your job?' she asked, sounding interested. 'I mean, do you observe the faces of all the women you take to bed to make sure they're really enjoying it and will want you again when they phone to make an appointment?'

Roger looked at her thoughtfully. He'd never believed she was the receptionist for Gilberte Drouet without suspecting another type of posing was managed from there besides fashion.

'No,' he said, giving her his most charming smile, 'it is not to do with my profession – I hardly ever recall their faces. It is only when I am with someone special that I want to see their expression of pleasure – it makes me feel that I have been able to delight them.'

'You surely delighted me,' Celeste said, 'and you can delight me again whenever you want. Do you observe Madame Drouet's face when you do it to her in the office?'

'No,' Roger said, more or less truthfully, and he smiled.

'I suppose you couldn't,' Celeste said, 'none of you, because her favourite position is bending forward over her desk.'

'How do you know that?'

'I used to look through the keyhole when good-looking models like you came to see her. Nowadays I don't bother – it's always the same, whether it's you or Edmond Planchon, Henri Dublanc or Pierre Poitier or any of the others.'

'Ah, we do not impress you,' said Roger. His hand lay lightly on her lean thigh.

'Remember that day when you'd been doing your duty and Madame Drouet went to the washroom and left you alone in her office,' Celeste asked.

Roger shrugged. One day with Gilberte was much like another.

'Yes you do,' Celeste insisted, 'you'd been at it a long time with her and I thought a cup of strong coffee might perk you up so in I marched with the tray.'

Roger chuckled. He remembered now.

'You were sitting in Madame's swivel chair,' Celeste went on, 'with your knees apart and your trousers undone, everything was dangling out. When you saw me you went into a panic and ran the chair forward till your body was against the desk – you didn't want me to see your trinket.'

'Trinket!' he exclaimed, 'I'd remind you, Mademoiselle, that I have more than fifteen centimetres of good solid flesh to offer.'

'Not that day, you didn't,' she grinned at him. 'From where I was standing it seemed to be about the size of my little finger – and I remind you, Monsieur, that I had my glasses on that day and could see perfectly.'

'Appearances can be deceptive,' he told her as he stroked his limp part to make it grow to more impressive dimensions. 'Since we arrived here you've had it in you twice – once on the stairs and once on this divan. You know from personal experience that it is a great deal longer and thicker than your little finger.'

'I never doubted it,' she said, 'I'd seen you sliding it into Madame Drouet plenty of times before that day. In fact that was the first time I'd seen it when it wasn't stiff.'

'And at present,' he said. 'But only briefly.'

'It was a comical afternoon, that's why I thought of it,' she said, grinning as she watched him handling his limpness. 'First you tried to hide your little treasure from me. As if I'd never seen it before. Then an hour after you left in came your friend Edmond Planchon. Madame was pleased to see him, even though you did your duty by her. And that time I did look through the keyhole – Madame had never had two of you on the same day before.'

'Really?' Roger sighed. 'She had Edmond after me? But it is incredible, what goes on in your office, *cherie*. Tell me more – tell me everything.'

He turned and half-sat, half-lay against her, as she sat with her back against the wall. His wet tongue licked delicately at the long pink buds on her flat chest.

'I can't believe I'm telling you all the office secrets,' she whispered, but before she thought better of it his fingers were between her legs. Her feet moved apart on the divan, he clasped her *lapin* in his hand and squeezed it pleasantly.

'Well, two days ago Madame went out to dinner with him,' she confided, 'and I've never known her to go out with a model, not while I've worked there.'

Dinner with Edmond Planchon, Roger thought, half-stupefied so that his tongue was motionless on Celeste's prominent buds. *What's he up to? It's since he lost the bet about her nichons. He wants to have them out and handle them to prove he's as good as me. But taking her to dinner isn't necessary – there's more to it than that. I must drag it out of Celeste even if it means making love to her all night non-stop!*

Celeste was most certainly not going to have any objection to that – his tongue on her chest and his fingers between her legs were making her sigh and shake. He pulled the divan cover from underneath her – there was a small dark wet patch in the middle – and dropped it on the floor. He put his arms about Celeste to pull her down away from the wall and on her back. He rolled on top of her, belly on belly.

He reached under her thin thighs with both hands and pulled her legs up till her bent knees touched her flat belly. She was wider open than ever she could have imagined. Her short-sighted eyes peered up as he positioned himself to plunge into her warm wetness. She began to whimper, her belly strained up at him.

'No, wait!' she gasped, and she crossed her shins to stop him getting into her.

She twisted from beneath him and was up on her knees, pushing him onto his back – she straddled him with her long thin thighs impossibly splayed across his hips.

'You watched my face,' she gasped, 'I want to see yours.'

She opened herself deftly with two fingers and held his stiff shaft between finger and thumb, to guide it up between the long, wet lips between her thighs. She was breathing raggedly as she sank down on him to impale herself. Roger held her by her bony hips to steady her. She rode him fast, her face split in a grin of concentration.

'You saw me,' she gasped, 'now I'm going to watch you.'

Roger didn't think so – from where she sat above him his face must be only a blur to her. But Celeste was ready for that, she lay forward on him, her chest on his and her face just a hand's-breadth above his. While she slid forcefully along his embedded length she gripped his head in her hands so he couldn't turn it.

'Now I've got you!' she panted. 'You can't look away now. I shall see the look in your eyes – then we'll be quits!'

In the event, he saw her expression first. What she was doing to him aroused her so fast that in a very short time she gave a long wail and her eyes rolled upwards – her thin body went into sharp spasms of ecstasy that milked Roger of his surging desire in quick little spurts.

Poor Celeste, she missed it, was the thought that slipped into his mind when he was rational again.

He found it amusing – but when he opened his eyes Celeste was staring down at his face, and she was the one who was grinning.

'You nearly cheated me again,' she said, and her fingers were tracing the shape of his mouth, 'you made me do it first so I'd miss your big moment – but I forced myself to concentrate and I came back in time to catch the tail-end. I'll never forget the stunned look on your face.'

Roger laughed and took her slender arms to roll her off him. She lay at his side in the crook of his arm, pressing her belly to his hip. Her skin was damp with perspiration, he felt it on his side and where her arm lay across his chest. He put a hand down and touched her flat wet belly.

Before they fell asleep he did it to her once more – slow and gentle this time. She gasped out it was impossible, she'd never done it so often, she couldn't ... her little protests continued almost to the moment when her back arched off the divan and she sobbed in ecstasy. She went to sleep holding his small wet limp part in her hand – she didn't stir when he pulled the bed-sheet up over them both.

He woke up in the morning light, to find himself lying on his back. His cherished part was standing stiff and bold. Celeste's head was on his thigh. She was staring at a distance of only a few centimetres at the hard length she was stroking.

'What are you doing, *cherie*?' he asked lazily – not a useful question, it was perfectly obvious what she was doing.

'I've only your word for the size of it,' she said, 'you took my spectacles away and hid them somewhere before you undressed, so I haven't seen what you've got, Roger. You could be lying to me about fifteen centimetres – how do I know?'

'From that close, you must realize I was telling the truth,' he told her, somewhat surprised at how aroused he was already.

She had thrown the bed-sheet aside, they were naked together. Her thumb and forefinger closed around his bulging shaft and he sucked in his breath as she began a firm manipulation. He moved his legs further apart to let her hold his pompoms in her other hand.

'I shall be late for work,' she remarked, 'there's no time to go home and change. I'll have to take the Metro from

233

here. Even if I left now I'd be late. Madame Drouet will not be pleased to see me arrive after her. Shall I go now, Roger?'

'Not yet,' he sighed, 'another few minutes won't matter.'

Her hand closed about the full length of his upstanding part, the up-and-down motion sent delicious sensations flicking along it and through his belly.

'Suppose Madame wants to know why I'm late,' she said, 'shall I make an excuse or shall I tell her the truth?'

'Tell her the truth. Tell her you were in bed with me – tell her I wouldn't let you go before I made love to you.'

'But that wouldn't be the truth, would it?' Celeste said.

Her clenched hand pumped up and down busily and the effect on Roger was dramatic – she had been doing it to him for some time before he awoke. She could tell by the way his shaft strained up towards his chin that he was almost at the critical moment.

'What do you mean, Celeste?' he gasped. 'In a moment I shall push you on your back and roll on top of you.'

'You won't,' she said calmly, and without missing a beat she sprawled alongside him, her face over his. Roger moaned to feel the muscles of his belly clench in ecstasy and an instant later he spurted his sticky desire up onto his chest.

Celeste was grinning down at him, her eyes very close to his, watching his expression.

'Got you,' she said happily. 'I only caught the tail-end last night – now I've seen the lot. I'll be thinking all day how you look at the interesting moment, Roger.'

And that was when the phone rang. Roger hardly had his breath back yet or was thinking properly. All down his chest and belly was spattered the result of Celeste's activity. The phone stood near enough for him to reach out an arm and pick it up. Celeste was grinning as she used a corner of the bed-sheet to wipe him.

'It's me,' said a distant voice in the receiver he pressed to his ear.

She didn't have to identify herself – it was Marie Brantome's voice.

'Yes,' he said – he could hardly believe she was calling him.

'That little hotel by the Gare St-Lazare you took me to,' she said, 'I shall be waiting for you in the same room at midday.'

Without another word she rang off. Roger dropped the phone on the divan beside him and lay bemused while Celeste gently dried his wilting part with the sheet. Marie wanted to see him. Today – the woman he was in love with wanted to see him!

'If Madame Drouet asks me why I'm half an hour late,' Celeste said cheerfully, 'I shall tell her I've been handling something she thought belongs to her – and if she asks what that might be I shall say it's something supposed to be fifteen centimetres long.'

Deceiving

The man behind the reception desk of the small hotel gave Roger a knowing wink as he accepted the banknote skilfully slipped to him. Neither of them saw a need for the owners to know of their convenient arrangement whereby Roger used a room for an hour or two if he met a pretty woman in the vicinity.

'Mademoiselle is waiting for you in Room 212,' he said.

Roger nodded and didn't bother to correct him. Marie Messager was waiting for him above, the wife of Martin Messager, the mad bestower of tattooed initials on a smooth female belly. If only she were Mademoiselle Brantome still – that would simplify life enormously for Roger and for her!

The open-cage lift creaked its way slowly upward. Roger stood lost in thought – more precisely an impossible mélange of doubt and hope. Did Marie really want him, as he wanted her – is that why she had returned to the hotel room where he'd first made love to her? Or was this another false dawn?

And then he was walking down the narrow corridor to room 212. He paused outside the door to take a deep breath and square his shoulders before he tapped discreetly. Marie opened the door at once and stood looking at him without a word. She was wearing a cream-coloured silk slip that had embroidery around the top and ended halfway down her thighs. No stockings, no shoes – and her toenails were painted a subtle rose shade.

He stepped forward to take her in his arms and kiss her. She stepped back into the room, keeping a space between him and her – shaking her head sadly and not letting him touch her. He shut the door behind him and leaned back against it, giving her time to make up her mind what she wanted. Her beautiful face seemed troubled – the thin-plucked eyebrows were drawn down in a frown and her mouth drooped a little at the corners.

There was a contradiction here that puzzled Roger. Undressing before he arrived indicated she wanted him to make love to her, but the expression on her face said the opposite.

'*Je t'aime*, Marie,' he said – his words were chosen to compel her to take the initiative.

And so she did – with a dramatic gesture she reached down and took the hem of her slip between finger and thumb and lifted it halfway up her bare belly.

'See what he has done to me!' she exclaimed in a tone almost a sob, almost a denunciation.

The cream silk slip was her only garment. Beneath it her body was completely nude. Before Roger could look for the little MM monogram near her groin – that barbarous mark of her husband's jealousy – his eyes were caught by a new nakedness: her *joujou* was shaved bare, it was as hairless as the palm of her hand.

'Oh,' he sighed, he could hardly believe what he was seeing, to comprehend it was impossible. 'What have you done?'

Marie stood with her slip up to her belly-button and her

feet apart on the thin carpet, a defiant expression on her face now.

'Look at me, Roger,' she said, 'he's turned me into a school-girl again – I look at myself in the mirror and I'm not a woman any more. He has humiliated me past endurance!'

'But why?' Roger stammered. 'Why have you let him do this to you, Marie – why do you put up with these humiliations?'

'He thinks you and I are still seeing each other,' she said. 'I beat my fists against his chest and demand, Why are you doing this to me – why? He laughs at me and says that if I behave as irresponsibly as a child then I must be made like one.'

There was a pleased anguish in her voice, and a certain pride that didn't tally with her expressed indignation and outrage at Messager's attitude towards her. Roger didn't hear it – or chose not to. He stared entranced at her smooth-shaven belly and long bare lips.

He sank down on his heels to look. First at the little tattoo of two initials, then at the bare split mound between her legs. He touched the smooth flesh, he stroked the soft lips – without question he was charmed beyond expression. Since the first time he'd undressed Marie he'd thought her *lapin* was the sexiest he'd ever seen or touched – now that the *lapin* had been skinned and lost all its fur it was impossibly exciting. His male part stood hard inside his little black silk posing-pouch.

Under his fingertips the skin was as smooth as her face – and to his lips too, for he couldn't resist kissing it. Marie let him, standing poised on her high-arched bare feet, her thighs apart. The wet tip of his tongue confirmed what fingers and mouth told him, the bare flesh between her legs was satin-smooth.

'What shall I do, Roger?' she moaned. 'Tell me what to do!'

That was for later, he thought. First there was an urgency to be attended to – he rose to his feet, scooping her in his arms, took three strides and had her on the bed on her back.

'Help me or he'll kill me,' she moaned, her eyes rolling, her arms stretched above her head in appeal – or perhaps submission – her long legs apart, 'he is insane...'

'Yes,' Roger gasped, 'yes, I'll do anything for you, Marie, I adore you.' All the while he was ripping off his clothes.

There they lay, the two of them, naked together on the hotel bed. Marie's stylish slip up about her waist, exposing half her beautiful body for his ardent adoration. His fifteen centimetres of stiff flesh jerked as rhythmically as a metronome on a piano.

He adored her with his fingers and with his lips and with his tongue, all between her spread thighs – totally obsessed by the strange nudity there, the complete and perfect revelation.

'You can see for yourself I've been humiliated and punished,' Marie sobbed, 'he's made me ugly, please don't hate me, Roger.'

'But I love you,' he protested, 'you know I do!'

He lay over her and softly rubbed her little-girl *joujou* with the pink-purple head of his twitching length. Marie was already open and her inner lips were showing. They were slippery-wet – if he pushed inside he would feel their velvet softness. But he couldn't escape his obsession with the new nudity of soft flesh between her thighs. His belly was on hers – he rubbed his stiff shaft against the exposed lips.

'Roger,' she moaned, 'are you really in love with me?'

'To desperation,' he gasped, 'from the first moment I saw you – from the first time I kissed you!'

His voice was shaking, his emotions and actions had raced out of control. He clutched at her bare shoulders and spurted hotly – not in her but over her split mound.

'Oh, oh!' she cried out, her legs jerking up off the bed and gripping him between them.

Her arms were about him, her hands were on his jerking bottom and her nails sank into the cheeks while she rocked him on her belly. He wailed and convulsed in his ecstasy, sliding over the slippery wetness he had spurted on her, gasping out her name.

'But why?' she moaned as her nails raked his bottom. 'Do you hate me after what he's done to me? Don't you want me?'

'I adore you, Marie,' he sighed.

'But you don't want me,' she said.

Roger slid off and lay beside her, propped up on his elbow to look at her. He touched his fingers to the bare-shaven wet lips and then clasped his hand between her legs, covering the tender folds of flesh he'd made so very wet.

'Of course I want you,' he said, 'I want you more than ever – I adore you. I couldn't resist paying my regards to your pretty *joujou*, it is so charming that I was carried away! I shall not let you leave this room till I've convinced you that I am so in love with you that nothing else matters.'

'I am disfigured,' she said, 'first the tattoo, now this. You find me ugly, Roger, there is no need to pretend.'

'*Je t'adore, cherie,*' he murmured and leaned over to kiss her mouth, his hand still clasped between her thighs, 'tell me when your insane husband did this to you. It is over a week since we last saw each other.'

'Three days ago – I went to see a friend and when I came home Martin was waiting. He thinks we are still meeting, you and I – that we are lovers. He accused me of being with you all day and he said I'd let you make love to me.'

The lure of her smooth bareness was irresistible to Roger. He felt the warm wetness in the palm that held it – the wetness of his own spurting. While Marie told him her tale of jealousy and humiliation, he pressed his middle finger slowly in between the warm wet lips and found her secret bud.

Three days ago, he was thinking, *she hasn't exactly rushed to ask for my assistance. Evidently she was with someone, to cause Messager to fly into a rage, but it wasn't me. Another man – no, I doubt that. Anyone else would seem a clumsy amateur after me. We come back to my first theory about my dearest Marie – blonde Michele Legarnier is her lover. That's who she was with.*

The scene was so clear in his mind – it had always been clear in his mind, from the moment he first saw her walking along the Avenue de l'Opera. She was naked on her back on a bed, with her legs spread wide. Blonde Michele Legarnier was lying beside her, exactly as he was lying beside her now, her fingers inside Marie, caressing her bud – exactly as he was doing at this very moment...

This blonde woman with the plump, round *nichons* he'd seen with Marie in the night-club, she'd lie naked between Marie's spread thighs and her tongue would caress Marie and send fast flickers of ecstasy through her. This picture was clear and vivid, the picture of Marie on her back, with her arms stretched out sideways as if crucified – her eyes closed, her body shaking as Michele's tongue lapped over her little bud.

Then that moment when Marie cried out, as her back arched off the bed and she moaned, *Je t'adore* to Michele – and while these thoughts were in Roger's mind, Marie's loins bucked up in quick little spasms – the soft stroking of his fingers had brought on her orgasm. He stared down at her beautiful squirming body, and he asked himself why he was in love with her.

That question never has an answer, of course. It is pointless to ask it, it leads only to confusion. But it reminded Roger of something of importance – to him, at least. There was something he could do for Marie that Michele never could. The realization had an instant effect on him – his drooping part grew stiff and thick.

Marie's eyes opened in sudden surprise when she felt him roll on top of her, his thighs between hers. She was still trembling to the final throes of her orgasm and it was hardly ten minutes since he had spurted over her bareness. Naturally, she couldn't know what thoughts inside his head had revived his desire – and reinvigorated his most cherished part.

'Roger?' she murmured doubtfully – but all doubt disappeared when she felt his long stiff part sliding into her.

He slid in and out strongly, his mind filled with an image of plump-breasted Michele crouched between Marie's open thighs and pushing her tongue into this pretty *joujou* he'd penetrated. The thought made him almost laugh and it sounded like a gasp. There was no possibility that a mere soft tongue could compete with a solid fifteen centimetres of hot and throbbing flesh.

Marie seemed to agree with his conclusion of superiority

even without knowing what he was thinking – or at least her body did because her loins were pulsating up rhythmically against him to meet his thrusts. He slipped his hands under her bottom to lift her and help her time her thrusting to his own.

When she was gasping and responding vigorously he slipped his hand between those taut bare cheeks and pushed them apart. He pressed the tip of his forefinger into the tight little node in between them.

Marie shrieked faintly – she bumped her belly harder against him. Each time she jerked up she felt his hardness slither into her, each time she fell back she made his finger slide a little deeper. Roger was moaning loudly at the excruciating sensations surging through him from the rhythmic palpitations of her body. She was sobbing into his open mouth, her nails were flaying his bare back. He cried out and shook violently in long hard throbs as he spurted deep into her bare-shorn *joujou*.

'Yes, yes!' he cried. Even in ecstasy he managed to suppress the other words in his mind: *You can't do this to her, Michele – I can because I'm a man!*

But if he had said the words out loud Marie wouldn't have heard them – she was wailing and writhing in orgasm and bucking fiercely up at him.

'*Je t'aime*, Marie,' he moaned into her gaping mouth.

'*Je t'aime*, Roger,' she sobbed back.

Because of the circumstances he very nearly believed her. She clung to him hotly, long after her spasms of delight were over. She kissed his mouth a thousand times, she stroked his hair and his face, she laughed and cried both at the same time.

When they were both calm again and lay side by side with arms about each other, she confessed she had misjudged him when she'd said he didn't want her because her husband had made her ugly by his barbaric punishment. Roger insisted that she wasn't ugly at all and if she would be so good as to wait for ten minutes or so he would demonstrate convincingly that he desired her desperately.

As she had raised this subject herself, it seemed to him that it was as good a time as any to ask her a question or two about her denuding at the hands of Monsieur Messager, the insane husband. How had he gone about it? for example. It struck Roger as quite a difficult task, to shave a woman between the legs, unless she co-operated completely. He had seen for himself she had no cuts on her thighs, as might be expected if there had been a struggle.

Marie was reluctant to explain except in very general terms – she protested that the experience was so utterly shaming it was distressing to speak about. She said she had arrived home about nine one evening after visiting a friend to find her husband in a rage of jealousy. There was a violent quarrel, he dragged her into the bedroom and tore off her clothes.

She thought he was going to rape her, she told Roger, just as he had that time at the tattooist's, when the needle-artist had completed his work on her belly and was sent out of the studio. But no, to her amazement and her outrage her husband Martin had scissors and his razor and a tube of shaving cream all ready to use. He flung her down naked on the bed ...

At this point Marie became silent and looked away from Roger. He was agog to hear the rest of the tale – what she had said so far didn't fit very well with what he could remember of the man he'd seen sitting beside Marie in the night-club. Not that he'd paid much attention to him – Roger's main interest had been the woman holding Marie's

245

hand and murmuring to her. Her lover, he was sure of it, ten years older than Marie – a blonde with a fine big pair of breasts.

The two husbands at the table were very similar and nobodies, both of them over forty, well-dressed, smooth-faced. Whichever was Marie's husband made no difference, neither was the type to drag an erring wife to a backstreet tattoo-parlour and have his initials put on her belly as a warning. And not the type to hold her down on her back with one hand while he shaved between her legs. It was all fantasy, Marie was deceiving him.

Who better to enjoy fantasy than Roger Chavelle, professional lover of many women? Partner in bedroom games, clever deviser of sexual entertainments. He sat Marie up with her back against the bedhead and eased her cream-coloured silk slip up over her head. Her breasts were round and not large but perfect and this was the first he'd seen of them today. Or for many a long day.

Marie sat with her legs stretched out flat and well apart. He sat between them and stroked her bare *joujou* very lightly while he asked for the rest of her story of bedroom shame.

'I've already told you,' she said. 'He said he'd make me look like a child because I had been irresponsible. And this is what he did to me.'

'After he'd done this,' said Roger, 'did he hold you down and make love to you by force?'

He could feel himself becoming long and hard again, simply by looking at the soft bare smoothness between Marie's thighs and touching it.

'No,' she said, 'no, he didn't. It was enough for him to make me ugly.'

'But you're not,' Roger told her, 'see the effect you have on me – I am more desperately in love with you than ever.'

Marie grinned and reached out to hold his upright part and massage it gently. The discussion of her shearing was at an end now that more urgent consideration had arisen.

'If I'd guessed this before,' she said, 'perhaps I might have volunteered to be shorn like a lamb. But truly, Roger, you must find it strange and unappealing, a grown woman bare as a little girl?'

'In another woman perhaps, but in you it is so sexy, *cherie*,' he said, 'the proof of that is in your hand, stiff and strong.'

She pulled her knees up and sat with them apart, her bareness fully revealed to his eager eyes.

'Marvellous,' Roger sighed, 'I've adored the front view, let me see from behind. I think my heart is breaking with delight. Turn round, *cherie*.'

She was relieved that Roger had been diverted so simply from his enquiries into what had happened that fateful afternoon between her and her husband. In another moment she was on her hands and knees on the bed, facing away from him. He kissed the taut lean cheeks of that pretty bottom of hers – he pushed her knees apart on the bed so he could get his hand between her thighs.

She smiled secretly to feel his fingertips caressing the lips of her smooth-shaven *joujou*. She heard his sighs of delight and felt how his hand trembled while he touched her. And indeed, he was with the angels in Paradise at that moment. Martin Messager had done a very expert job of removing Marie's curls. If it was Messager who skimmed the sharp razor over her soft flesh and in between her thighs. Roger was certain it was impossible without her full consent.

It was clear to him Marie must have taken her clothes off and lain down on her back with her legs open while Messager did it. There was only one other possible explanation he could think of – that Marie used the razor herself while her husband watched and gloated in anticipation. The instant she'd finished he would have jumped on top of her to affirm his right of possession.

But those complexities aside, the truth was that whoever had used the razor had done it extraordinarily well. Viewed from behind, Marie's split mound was smooth and soft as a nectarine. All the way from her little belly-button to the crease of her bottom – not a single hair had been left on her. She was fully revealed, and the effect on Roger was fiercely aphrodisiac.

He kissed the cheeks of her bottom again and again, he played with the long moist split of her *joujou*, touching and stroking, he moved very close to her on his knees to put an arm about her waist and slide his hand down her belly and between her thighs, to hold her open with two forked fingers.

'Ah yes, Roger,' she said as she felt his stiff shaft sliding up inside her.

The mere act of pushing into those bare, silk-skinned lips was enough to bring Roger to crisis-point. Only the bare purple top of his precious part had entered, his fingers were still hooked into her to prise her open. But even as he penetrated Marie his passion spurted.

'Ah Roger!' she exclaimed. 'It is true – you do love me!'

Twenty minutes later she picked her thin gold wristwatch off the bedside table and said she must leave soon. Naturally Roger wanted her to stay all day and all night, all week and forever. He held her and tried to kiss her into compliance – she settled in his arms with one leg over him so he could feel her bareness against his side.

'I love you, Roger,' she said, 'we'll meet very soon, as soon as I can arrange it, I promise.'

'Don't go,' he murmured, 'leave him and run away with me.'

'Where would you take me?' she asked curiously.

'Marseilles – I've always wanted to see it.'

Whatever she thought of the suggestion, she said nothing. She stroked his face till his eyes closed and he went to asleep. He had, after all, amused Celeste most of the night. And even when Marie had phoned that morning, he had just been subjected to sexual experiment by the inquisitive if flat-chested receptionist. And in the past hour he had made love three times to Marie – it was no wonder he needed to rest and restore his strength.

When he woke up Marie was gone. He was alone on the hotel bed, from the pillow and sheet rose a faint trace of the perfume she wore – Lanvin, he knew that now. Then into his delicious memory of making love to her there came the realization that he'd been asleep for hours – the way the light slanted in the long window suggested it was early evening.

He sat up and checked his watch. It was after six o'clock. He remembered he had an appointment that evening. Madame Lenoir at eight. But this is impossible, he told himself, she would be in for a disappointment, I cannot raise the enthusiasm. But on the other hand, Madame Lenoir was a regular of his, a woman needing special consideration, and she was content to pay well for it. Twice a week – that made her important to him.

The folding doors at the end of the room were open. Marie had showered before leaving without disturbing him. The thin towels lay scattered on the floor, used and wet. He stood for a minute or two under the warm water while he washed – then under a cold jet to wake himself. And in another five minutes he was outside the hotel and ordering a fast meal in a restaurant opposite the Gare St-Lazare.

To entertain Madame Lenoir he required sustenance – even then it was going to be an effort. He had steak tartare and most of a bottle of Beaujolais and felt better for it. At five minutes to eight he was ringing Madame Lenoir's doorbell, with a spray of pink tulips in his hand. His calling-card, so to speak – the gesture that set him apart from competitors.

Francoise Lenoir was invariably delighted to see him. She put her arms round his neck and kissed his cheeks and his lips. She thanked him for the coloured postcard of St Flavia. It was his private joke to mail religious pictures to her when he passed a shop selling them – but she took it seriously.

She was thirty-seven, this Francoise, darkly good-looking, living apart from her husband, well-off. This evening her long hair was tied back and she was wearing a little black dress from a good hand, long-sleeved and dipping to a point between her plump breasts – as usual a gold crucifix dangled deep in the valley between.

After they'd kissed and she'd put the tulips into a vase she had ready for his customary offering, she took him straight into the bedroom. Roger had never liked her bedroom. The walls were papered with costly silk in palest pink, the furniture was from the type of shop that didn't display price-tickets. The carpets on the golden parquet floor were priceless Afghan.

Gold-framed pictures of saints hung on the walls – that

was what Roger found off-putting. And most especially the
large painting of St Barbara over the bed. He knew it was
there because of the legend – Barbara was so beautiful that
her father locked her up to protect her virginity while he
decided who should marry her. It seemed to Roger that
Francoise Lenoir was flattering herself with this implied
comparison. Apart from that, to be pleasuring Francoise and
hear her gasping in incipient orgasm, and to look up at a
picture of a girl in a long robe and golden halo – it was
dismaying, to say the least.

Francoise stripped off her chic little dress and hung it in a
wardrobe. Meanwhile Roger was taking off his jacket and
tie and shoes. She held his hand and pulled him down to sit
with her on the side of the bed – as he'd supposed, she was
in black satin bra and knickers, and the gold cross bounced
between her fleshy *nichons*.

'I've done some wicked things since you were here last,'
said she, rubbing his hand on her thigh well above her
stocking-top, 'I try not to give in to temptation, but I'm
very weak-willed.'

Roger nodded gravely while he stroked her plump thigh
between stocking-top and knickers. He understood her
odd desires – that's why she was a twice-a-week regular
client.

'You must tell me about it,' he said very sympathetically,
'I would like to help you, Francoise. What have you
done?'

She informed him she held him responsible – his visits to
her were so eagerly awaited and fondly remembered that
she'd fallen into a habit of fantasizing about him between
visits.

'Ah, I understand,' he murmured, his fingers gliding over
the black satin that covered her *lapin*, 'you slip your hand

between your legs and caress this darling *joujou* and think about me.'

'Every day,' she said breathlessly, looking down to watch him slide her knickers down to reveal her patch of dark curls.

She was so keen to explain the details of her misdeeds to him that she stood up and took her knickers off. And her bra – when she sat down by him again her fleshy pink body was naked except for her dark stockings and a black lace suspender-belt.

'I must insist you explain more fully,' Roger said, his hands on her full breasts to stroke them.

They were two good handfuls, a delight to feel. Francoise was sighing lightly as his hands travelled down her belly, stroking the warm soft flesh. Her thighs were open for his hand, he felt her mound and pressed a finger between the long plump lips. Her hand crept between her legs, her finger joined his in caressing her *joujou*.

'I do it like this,' she breathed, staring into his face with adoration in her dark eyes, 'I think of you making love to me.'

Her finger pressed against his as they stroked her wet little bud with a slow and delicate touch.

She gasped, 'Oh yes, Roger, you always make me do it...'

Her body shuddered in long spasms, she moaned and squirmed as the two fingers together triggered her orgasm. Then his finger was touching her – and her finger was in his mouth. She slipped it between his lips and Roger tasted her excitement. She pushed her finger deep into his mouth while his fingertip caressed her slippery bud and prolonged her orgasmic convulsions.

The inconvenient truth was that his often-used part was

still limp in his underwear. Francoise hadn't put her hand on him and felt him, not yet. But the moment would undoubtedly arrive when she wanted to feel his strength and handle it before he slid it inside her.

This was very awkward for Roger – his usual strength was mere feebleness. Francoise would be grossly insulted to discover the part for which she paid a handsome fee was small and useless at present. He was thinking furiously what to do to avert disaster and disgrace.

Francoise wanted a little rest after her pleasure and curled up on the bed – there was a problematic moment when she put her head in his lap; if she felt his softness under her cheek there was no obvious way to explain it. But Roger arranged himself so that her cheek was resting on his thigh while she talked to him of her little misdeeds when she was on her own thinking of him. Gradually an idea came to him.

'I'm happy you've told me this,' he said, as enthusiastically as he could manage, 'I feel that I am involved in your pleasure even when I am not with you.'

'Oh you are, you are,' she sighed – and her hand was slipping towards the join of his thighs. He halted this dangerous advance by taking her hand and raising it to his mouth to kiss her warm palm. It was imperative she didn't touch him or see his shame.

'You must make an act of contrition,' he told her cheerfully, 'that's the proper religious thing to do.'

'Yes, Roger!' she agreed at once, knowing what he meant.

She jumped off the bed and went down on her knees beside it – elbows on the pale yellow satin coverlet and her body bent in a prayerful attitude. Roger knelt behind, still dressed in shirt and trousers, and opened the lips

253

of her dark-haired split with his two thumbs. She sighed and laughed together when he tickled her pink little bud.

He'd pleasured her often before in this kneeling position at the bedside – she seemed to enjoy it particularly. It reminded her of childhood prayers at bedtime, she said. Whether she actually prayed to any of her favourite saints while she was skewered on his fifteen centimetres of throbbing flesh he could never determine. Religious fervour could lead to very curious practices.

He had two fingers inside her warm slipperiness, stroking her slowly. She was too involved with her sensations, her eyes were shut and she couldn't tell that his proud part was drooping its head and his trousers were zipped up to conceal it.

'You'll make me do it again,' she moaned, 'I want you to make me do it, Roger – I want to feel you inside me.'

'So you shall,' he said, with a conviction he didn't feel, 'I am going to turn you inside-out with sensation until you scream with delight – say your prayers, *cherie*.'

On his knees behind Francoise's plump bare bottom, fingering her wet *joujou*, sliding two stiff fingers in and out of her, it was impossible not to be reminded that only hours ago he'd been doing this to beautiful Marie, the woman he was in love with.

One difference – he hadn't needed to use his fingers to slide into Marie, his cherished part had been desperate to get inside her! So much so that he'd jetted his desire before he was even into her more than two centimetres.

Apart from his eagerness and his strength then, there was the other enormous difference – in between her slender thighs Marie was sleekly smooth and hairless. This *lapin* he was playing with now, Francoise's, had a fur coat of thick dark curls. And after his delicious interlude with Marie in the hotel room, it seemed to him bizarre to see curls between a woman's thighs.

On the other hand, it was very pleasant, what he was doing to Francoise. So much so that, sexually replete though he was, his dangler stiffened and rose slowly. He pulled his shirt off and dropped his trousers to his knees and pressed himself against her bottom. He flicked his shaft up and down quickly with his hand, to establish its firmness, then steered it into Francoise's wet and open *joujou*.

'Ah yes – right in!' she gasped as he penetrated her slowly.

He reached under her and took hold of her plump soft breasts. He was hoping his hardness would last long enough to get her to orgasm and he rode her fast.

'Oh my god, yes!' she exclaimed after only a minute or two – and to Roger's relief she reached a climax and shook violently.

'*Ah oui, cherie, oui,*' Roger responded, jabbing into her fast to make her think he was spurting. She moaned and shook and was easily deceived.

Later on, after they'd rested, things became more complicated for Roger. Francoise had acquired a scourge from some religious source or other. At least, she called it a scourge and told him it was used by penitents on Good Friday and other holy days. On themselves, she said, to punish themselves for their bad deeds.

It was about as long as a fore-arm and made of three strands of thin black imitation leather. By now Roger was naked, Francoise had insisted. His precious part hung limply between his thighs but that was understandable after

255

he'd pleasured her – she'd expect to see it standing upright
again soon.

'An act of contrition is not enough,' she said cheerfully, 'I
must be punished, Roger.'

He thought she would kneel at the bedside again, but she
went down on her knees in front of him and threw her arms
around his thighs.

'Punish me, Roger,' she sighed, and she took his limp
part in her mouth.

He slid his feet apart on the parquet and surrendered to
warm thrills rippling through him from her lapping tongue.
He stared down at the length of throbbing flesh jutting up
from his belly into her mouth and he smiled at her dark
head bobbing up and down.

He raised his arm and brought the whip down over her
shoulder to lash her bottom. His left hand clasped the back
of her neck, holding her face close to him. Her body shook
as he whipped the plump cheeks of her rump, she moaned
and sucked his shaft as if it were a lollipop.

She'd made him go hard again – and that amazed him.
Her mouth was coaxing his proud male part to grow thicker
and longer, she slipped a hand between his legs to take hold
of his pompoms and tug at them. He jerked his hips to slide
his thick shaft in and out of the wet mouth swallowing it,
and her finger was in the crease of his bottom – pressing,
probing.

'*Ah Dieu*,' he gasped. She was sucking at him so
determinedly that his legs wobbled under him and the old
familiar sensations ran through his belly. *This is impossible*,
he said to himself, *I don't believe it!*

He slashed feebly with the toy whip while his belly went
into spasms. Between the cheeks of his bottom a finger slid
into the little knot of muscle. His eyes were closed, in his

mind it was beautiful Marie kneeling before him, sucking at his stiff part, and Marie's finger pushing up inside him to the knuckle...

He wailed as he spurted into her mouth – but it was Francoise who'd done it to him. She looked up into his face and grinned.

Surrendering

After his sexual exertions with Celeste and Marie and Francoise Lenoir – three of them within twenty-four hours – Roger took two days off to recover. Mostly he stayed in his apartment and read magazines or listened to music. He ate hearty meals four times a day and he slept a lot.

Nadine phoned him twice to ask him to take her to dinner. But it wasn't food she wanted – it was someone to listen to all her grievances against men. And to entertain her in bed afterwards. Roger explained he wasn't well. He'd caught a summer influenza, he said. At once she offered to rush round by taxi to cook him nourishing broth and tend his fevered brow – and that too would end up with them in bed. He told her he was very infectious, knowing that she was too vain to risk red eyes and a running nose.

Celeste phoned and got the same tale. She giggled and said it was from sleeping naked after you-know-what. She promised she'd cancel his threesome with Madame Dubois and her friend Monique, scheduled for the next day – if he was sure he wouldn't be well enough.

'I fear I might disappoint the dear ladies,' Roger said.

The truth was he had no desire to play games with the pair of them that week.

Celeste said she'd make his excuses to Madame Drouet. She did this so effectively that later on that day a bouquet of flowers arrived for him with a card saying, *Be well, cheri*. It was signed by Gilberte in person.

In the intervals when he wasn't reading or sleeping or eating he thought about Marie. He was in love with her. It seemed that she in some way loved him. But there was no trust between them, she told him absurd stories about her husband and his jealousy. Roger even doubted if she was married.

At first he had believed what she told him. But when he came to know her better he had believed only some of what he was told. Now he believed nothing she told him. But he was still in love with her – that was the imbecility of his situation.

When he felt strong and ready again, he did what he'd thought of doing since the chance meeting in the night-club – he went to talk to Marie's blonde friend Michele. He knew her name because Marie had told him when she was explaining how she'd got the tattoo of two entwined Ms on her belly. His theory was one M stood for Marie, the other for Michele.

He guessed she lived not far from Marie. He knew Marie lived in the Parc Monceau area because he'd pursued her in a taxi there. From the Paris telephone directory it was easy enough to locate the address of a Monsieur and Madame Legarnier. And here he was at the apartment door, introducing himself to blonde Michele.

'I've heard a lot about you,' she said, 'you'd better come in and tell me why you're here.'

It was an elegant apartment, as he'd expected it to be. Marie and her friend Michele were used to living well, Roger knew. He sat on a sleek modern armchair in black and chrome, Michele sat on a similar chair facing him. It was almost eleven in the morning. She was wearing an expensive white shirt with pale blue stripes, tucked into dove-grey slacks.

In terms of fashion Roger saw the slacks as not a good choice – Michele was well-fleshed and her rump was very beautiful, but a skirt would have made it less round and prominent. Most women try to conceal a large bottom. Roger asked himself if there was a particular reason for her to wear trousers – perhaps the same reason Marie often wore tailored suits.

Perhaps it was because they both liked to play at being a man pleasuring a woman – that was his conclusion.

Marie and Michele were lovers – he was more than ever sure of it. Michele was ten years older than Marie. She had a fine, big pair of breasts filling her white shirt. He guessed that it was Marie who took the active part more often, and Michele who more often lay on her back. But who could say?

'Marie has told you of me,' he said with a smile, projecting all his very considerable charm at her.

'Non-stop,' she said dryly, 'you seem to be our main topic of conversation. Why are you here, Monsieur Chavelle?'

The truthful answer was to discover the whole truth. But it's not that simple, to ask intimate questions of a stranger, and he was still trying to decide the best approach.

'I am in love with her,' he said finally, 'I adore her. And I believe that she is in love with me.'

'Of course,' Michele Legarnier said casually, 'what of it?'

'She is married to a lunatic, or so I believe – he treats her atrociously. She needs me. But I'm sure you know this already.'

'Ah – it is dangerous to think you understand the

concerns of other people better than they do. Marie and I have been friends a long time – but I wouldn't presume to tell her how to arrange her life.'

'Perhaps,' Roger persisted, 'but the time comes when a friend has a duty to be frank. You have seen her tattoo, I imagine.'

'That little tattoo,' said Michele, as she smiled and crossed her legs, 'oh yes, I've seen it. I thought it very pretty.'

'And you know why her husband had it inflicted on her? He is a monster of cruelty, this Messager.'

'That depends on your point of view,' Michele told him. 'I've always found Martin interesting. Don't scowl at me – I know she adores you, Roger, but if she wants to stay with Martin, that's the end of it.'

'No!' he declared indignantly, 'I refuse to accept that.'

Michele stared at him thoughtfully. She had a long gold chain around her neck and her fingers were playing idly with it. She sighed and her breasts rolled a little under her shirt.

'Darling Marie has a habit of getting details wrong,' she said carefully. 'It is not always necessary to take her explanations at face value – if I were you I wouldn't pay too much attention to the circumstances in which she acquired her little tattoo.'

'Ah,' Roger exclaimed, 'I was right about you and her!'

He stared at Michele, visualizing her naked on her back, with her legs stretched apart, and Marie touching her tongue to the softness between those sturdy thighs. Marie making Michele gasp in orgasm and arch her back off the bed.

'What do you mean?' Michele demanded. But she knew, her face turned pink.

'You are lovers, you and she,' Roger said, 'I guessed it from the beginning – the initials on her belly stand for Michele and Marie. It's nothing to do with Martin Messager.'

Michele glared at him.

'That's what you think, is it?' she said.

'And another thing,' said Roger, not caring if he annoyed her or not, 'if I took your slacks down I'd find the same MM tattoo on your belly. Admit it!'

She stood up quickly – Roger thought she intended to slap his face in outrage. But a moment later he was gasping in amazement as she undid her stylish dove-grey slacks and dropped them down her thighs. Down came her knickers, her thumbs were hooked into the waistband, pushing them over her hips – Roger saw her belly and, down between her thighs, her blondish fur. It appeared not to grow up her belly at all.

'Do you see a tattoo on me?' she demanded. 'Look hard – have I an MM? Are you convinced Marie and I are lovers?'

Roger saw no MM tattoo, or any other tattoo, but he was still certain they were lovers. He had not failed to notice Michele's little knickers as she slid them down, the same subtle orchid-pink and the identical design as Marie had worn the morning she had come to his apartment to say goodbye.

She was wearing her steel-grey two-piece costume that day, he recalled it clearly. She stood inside the door to tell him that it was the last time they'd ever meet – it sounded like a death sentence, impossible to comprehend. In the urgency of desire he had put his hand up her skirt. He had wanted to make love to her, lying down or standing up – but she had refused.

He'd forced Marie back to the wall and pressed close to her – his desperate part out and stiff. He had tried to push into her but her knickers prevented him and his hot passion spurted onto the flimsy pink silk.

She'd taken them off then, the entire front soaked through, and given them to him. He had them still, washed and ironed, scented with the Lanvin perfume he'd bought to remind him of her. And now here was her dear friend Michele wearing the exact same type of orchid pink underwear. The case was proved.

But there was no tattoo on Michele's belly.

'A thousand pardons,' Roger was puzzled, 'I was certain.'

'You're easily persuaded,' Michele said with a grin. 'I never knew till now how Marie gets away with her fairy-tales.'

'What! You mean you *are* lovers, after all?'

'Suppose I have a tattoo like hers, it may not be in the same place, hasn't that occurred to you? Evidently not, you've only inspected my belly for it. What if it's on my backside?'

'Is it?' he asked instantly.

Truth to tell, the sight of her blondish fur and smooth belly was having the usual effect on him. He was fully restored after his two days off and his trousers were bulging out in front. He looked up boldly into Michele's eyes in challenge.

She turned about – not an easy or graceful manoeuvre with her slacks and knickers halfway down her thighs, more of a shuffle. But there she was, facing away from him, showing her bare round bottom. *Oh la la* he murmured, and well he might – for Michele's bottom was perfection, beautifully moon-like in shape.

There was no tattoo he could see – to be sure he went

down on his knees behind her and scrutinized her plumply oval cheeks at close range. He felt it necessary to run his hand slowly across those twin expanses of satin flesh. Even that wasn't enough to convince him of her guiltlessness, he leaned forward and kissed her smooth cheeks with eager lips.

'Well – am I tattooed?' she asked, her voice sounding amused.

'It seems I must apologize again,' Roger admitted.

'How easy you are to trick!' she said. 'I didn't say I had a tattoo on my bottom, I said *suppose*. And since we are supposing together, I might have a little MM tattoo between my legs where only a lover would ever see it – have you considered that?'

'Why are you determined to torment me?' he sighed, his kisses hot on her bare bottom. 'I know that you are Marie's lover – so show me the tattoo, it is useless to hide it.'

Michele shuffled about once more, this time within the circle of his arms, until his face was against her bare belly. He gave a long sigh, half-delight, half-frustration, and then kissed it repeatedly. He slipped his hand between her thighs and tried to open them to search for a tattoo – if that was still his target – but slacks and knickers prevented them from parting more than a few centimetres.

'I must know,' he said breathlessly.

She stood still while he peeled her dove-grey slacks and pale pink knickers down her legs and slid them over her feet. Before he could resume his ardent inspection she sat down again on the armchair behind her and spread her sturdy thighs.

'If you must know, then you must know,' she said with a grin.

Roger fell to his knees and examined her minutely. First with his eyes and with his fingers and at last with his lips and his tongue. Not content with just her thighs, he gave her *lapin* the the same intimate treatment. Now that her legs were spread wide he could see that she trimmed the curls from her belly and only kept those between her legs, to adorn her plump lips.

Marie came into his mind – she was shaved completely bare. No hair at all between her legs or on her belly, smooth flesh, all as bald as the palm of her own hand. Michele's *joujou* was half shaved – both women were trimmed, it must mean something, Roger thought. It proved they were lovers, whatever Michele might say to the contrary, it must prove it.

Yet while he inspected her with his fingers and tongue he was compelled to admit to himself that, for one who preferred other women in bed, Michele seemed to enjoy being caressed by a man.

She made little whimpering noises, she opened her legs wider and gasped, *Have you found my tattoo? Look closer.* She drew her knees up and set her heels on the edge of her chair, her thighs spread wide. And after a minute or two of gasping and trembling to his caresses, she jerked violently in orgasm.

Instantly he unzipped his trousers and had his fifteen centimetres of hard flesh in his hand.

'Oh,' she exclaimed as he slid it into her, 'oh Roger!'

She was moaning, her orgasm was over, her shudders of ecstasy slowing, but the feel of his solid length sliding into her and filling her revived her desire at once – Roger felt the nervous little contractions of her wet *joujou* gripping him.

He slid his hands up her back, inside her shirt, and

unhooked her bra. He had her big bare breasts in his hands, pulling them and rolling them, hearing her sighs and moans as he stared into her eyes. Her mouth was open; he felt the warmth of her breath on his face and on his mouth as she held his shoulders and pulled him in close to her body and kissed him.

It was not a question of a second orgasm for Michele, that he understood as he stared into her eyes; by penetrating her he'd extended her first – it was surging through her shaking body in wave after wave of ecstatic sensation. She was babbling as she pushed her belly at him, her raised knees gripped him between them like a wrestler's deathlock.

Roger was exhilarated by the belief that he was asserting his virility on Marie's lover – as he asserted it when he made love to Marie in the hotel. While he was doing it to Marie the image in his mind was Michele on her back with Marie between her open legs, her tongue in these lips he was penetrating.

And now Michele was on her back for him, he was crowing inside his head as he jabbed in and out: *feel me inside you, stiff and strong. I have something that neither you nor Marie possesses, something long and thick to slide into your belly – I am a man, cherie, I can do this to you and Marie.*

Be that as it may, the little contractions of Michele's belly drew him into her slippery depths, and the sensation was so intense that his mouth stretched in a silent moan. He knew that he was incredibly strong and hard – he was so deep inside her that his sweating belly was glued to hers and her blondish curls tangled in his profuse dark brown curls. The crisis came like the thump of a fist and he spurted his hot desire into her.

When they were both calm again he started to ease out of her and move away. Michele lifted her legs and threw them over his shoulders to hold him belly-to-belly. Her face was serene, she was a most attractive woman, he thought. She might prefer women in bed, but she certainly enjoyed being pleasured by me.

Have I been wrong about her and Marie? he wondered. *There's no tattoo that I can find on her body.*

As he watched, the tip of her tongue showed between her parted lips. She stretched her arms up and gave a yawn of content. She lifted her white shirt to her armpits and bared her round heavy breasts. The long gold chain around her neck looped down almost to her belly-button and glinted dully against her smooth flesh. And below, the oval of blondish curls framed long wet lips.

'You say you love Marie,' she said casually, 'but that didn't stop you jumping on her best friend. You took me by surprise, I was off-guard and unable to resist – you don't imagine I wanted that to happen.'

'Yes,' Roger said firmly, 'I'm sure you did.'

'You're right,' she said, grinning, 'I've heard so much about you from Marie and how superb you are at making love that I had to find out for myself.'

'And were you disappointed?' he asked, looking down from her face to her full breasts and their prominent red buds. And down her plump and perspiring belly – down between her sturdy thighs to her blondish oval of curls and the open wet lips there.

'My god, no, it was marvellous. At a time like this words are inadequate,' she said, her eyebrows arching in amusement.

'Tell me what I need to know about Marie,' he said.

'Perhaps,' she said, and she slid her legs off his shoulders and pushed him away. His wet and softening part slid out of her and flopped downward. Without another word she took his hand to lead him to her bedroom. All she had on was her shirt, while he was still fully dressed, his trousers open and his limp dangler on show.

'You're a good-looking man,' she said, sitting on the side of the bed to watch with inquisitive eyes while he took his clothes off and posed briefly for her, as if he was being photographed.

'Ah, you are a model,' she said, 'Marie told me – but I can't remember seeing you in magazine advertisements.'

Roger did not wish to discuss his profession with Michele. He smiled his charming smile at her and sat down naked beside her. He slipped his hand between her thighs, his fingertips brushed over the blondish curls and over soft loose lips. She took off her shirt and she was as naked as he – her heavy round breasts waiting to be felt and stroked. He ducked his head and set his mouth to the breast nearest him, his tongue licked at the bud.

She kept her gold chain on as she stretched out on her back, and it lay between her breasts and on her belly.

'Tell me what I want to know,' Roger said, his fingers playing between her open thighs, the ball of his thumb sliding over her secret bud and making her tremble and gasp.

'First tell me what I want to know,' she said.

'Of course, *cherie*,' he replied, '*je t'adore*, Michele, you are beautiful and exciting and enchanting – but you know that.'

'Yes,' she murmured, 'but it is always good to hear it said.'

He kissed her while he stroked her, he slid on top of her and put his belly on hers, he reached down with both hands

269

to pull her legs up and bend her knees until she was wide open for him. One push and he was inside her, sliding in and out in a strong and compelling rhythm, his hands kneading her soft breasts.

In the sitting-room, on the armchair, he had done it to her for pleasure. But now, on the bed, he was acting professionally. Not for money but for information. She knew things he wanted to know about Marie. So he used his skills to put her in the right frame of mind to reward him.

When he decided he'd done enough for his purpose, he finished her with short fast strokes – she moaned as her back lifted off the bed in frantic spasms.

She happily told him about Marie, when she'd recovered. Roger lay beside her, listening carefully and weighing up what he was told. He learnt that Marie was a runaway at sixteen and that Martin Messager found her at the Gare Montparnasse one night – she was penniless and hungry.

Messager then was nearly thirty – well-to-do and un-attached – and he found Marie irresistible. He took her to his apartment.

'For his pleasure, you understand,' said Michele, her hand on Roger's thigh as she lay facing him, 'but she caught his fancy, there was something about her that held his interest after he'd done all he wanted. He didn't push her out of the door next day with a few francs in her hand, as he had with girls in the past – he asked her to stay.'

'And she has stayed for seven years?' Roger asked.

'Eight years – she is twenty-four now. Martin married her when she was eighteen and I met her then. He and I are distant cousins.'

'Where did she come from?'

'She has always refused to speak about her life before

Martin found her at the railway station. Even to me, and I am her best friend now.'

'This is a strange story you are telling me,' Roger said with a lift of his eyebrows, 'and Messager is a very strange man. He may have fallen in love with Marie then, but now it's turned to jealousy and obsession. You've seen the tattoo – do you know he shaved her between the legs as a punishment?'

Roger was hoping Michele would let something slip – by chance or not – to confirm that she and Marie were lovers and who trimmed themselves or perhaps trimmed each other. But Michele laughed and stroked his thigh.

'Martin is a strange man, I agree,' she said, 'we were lovers before he picked Marie up, but that was the end of it. Nowadays we are still friends; I think I know him as well as anyone. But something you don't know is that Marie is as strange as he is.'

'What do you mean?'

'He is still obsessed with her, after all this time – and she is obsessed with him. He rescued her and married her and so she believes she belongs to him, that she is his property. When she fell in love with another man she was racked by guilt – she did things to herself to prove to Martin that she's his. Her little tattoo – it will surprise you to learn that she begged me to go with her when she had it done. As her friend I couldn't refuse, I sat and watched her lie on a table with her knickers off, and a bald man with a moustache used his electric needle on her.'

'You were there? She told me that her husband dragged her to the tattooist's shop and watched the process. And forced her to submit to him on the table afterwards. What am I to believe?'

'Believe whatever you please,' Michele said with a grin,

'the letters on her belly are M and M. Martin Messager's initials.'

'But she came back to me after that,' Roger protested, 'in my apartment, she showed me what had been done to her.'

'She is in love with you, though she is obsessed with Martin. If you cannot accept that she is a very strange person at heart you'll drive yourself mad trying to make sense of what she does and says.'

'Why does she dress in suits and cut her hair like a man – is it because Messager prefers her to look like a boy?'

Michele smiled at his credulity.

'She does it because she wants to do it. She tells Martin she does it to make herself unattractive to other men. That was not the effect it had on you, was it? If he had his way she'd wear dresses with a neckline down to her belly-button and a hem-line halfway up her thighs. And no knickers.'

'But why?' Roger asked.

'Who can say? We are not discussing ordinary people. Perhaps it pleases Martin to have other men drool when they see Marie – and she cold-shoulders all of them for him, although he is much older. A psychological game, I think, but how do I know what is going on in his head or in her head.'

'Shaving between her legs,' said Roger in growing dismay, 'he didn't make her do that?'

'It was her own idea – she showed herself like that to Martin one evening and asked him to forgive her for loving another man now she'd punished herself in this way. He always forgives her, he rolls her on the bed to prove it. Each is as obsessed as the other.'

'What am I to do?' Roger asked. 'I'm crazy about her.'

'You have two choices,' Michele told him. 'Break off

with her and never see her again – that's one choice. Or stay as you are and enjoy the strangest love-affair you will have in your life. She'll meet you and love you and go away again and tell you the most imaginative stories about Martin and what he makes her do. All of which you can ignore – make the most of what you have.'

'Tell me one more thing,' Roger was struggling to take in all he had heard, 'are you lovers, you and Marie?'

'You still don't understand her,' Michele said, 'which is not surprising – I have been her dearest friend for years and don't understand her. Martin has lived with her since she was sixteen – he doesn't. But what does that matter? Understanding is the cause of unhappiness and the enemy of love.'

'You haven't answered my question, Michele.'

'You think we are rivals, you and I, competing for Marie? It is absurd, your question – Marie belongs to Martin.'

'Answer the question.'

Michele smiled seraphically at him and bounced her breasts on her hands.

'Answer it yourself,' she said.

After his conversation with Michele Roger didn't know what to think. He brooded all the rest of the day and lay sleepless for most of the night, trying to decide what to do about Marie. She fascinated him, he adored her, he mistrusted her. On reflection he saw it was not a question of trust or mistrust any more. That was when he half-believed what she told him. Now he had no need to believe her about anything, only to be wary.

Only two choices, Michele had said, leave her or love her. He wasn't sure he could do either. He considered phoning Edmond to arrange a meeting and ask his advice.

But he didn't, because he thought Edmond might very well laugh at him.

In the end the matter was resolved for him. Marie phoned him. She said she must see him, she was leaving now to get a taxi to his apartment. And she put the phone down before he had time to say yes or no.

The tiny apartment was a mess. The divan-bed was unmade, the sheets creased and hanging half-off, two empty wine bottles and a used glass stood on the coffee-table, half-read magazines lay scattered open on the floor. And as for the tiny kitchen!

It was ten to ten in the morning when Marie phoned. Where she lived there were always taxis waiting. From the Parc Monceau to the Place Denfert-Rochereau wasn't going to take all that long, not even through the mid-morning traffic. He dropped the phone and jumped into action to make the apartment presentable.

He was still at it when she arrived. He opened the door – she was in a dress today, not a suit. Perhaps it was originally designed to be demure, it was a sleeveless little summer dress from a good couturier. It was in shot silk, dark in colour, black or red, as the light fell. Broad straps on the shoulders, close at the waist, a swirling skirt. But dress or suit, her dark glossy hair was still parted on the right and brushed back like a boy.

However demure the original thought had been, second thoughts had caused certain modifications to the dress. Between the wide shoulder straps the neckline plunged down between her breasts. And while *les grands couturiers* decreed that hemlines were well below the knee, Marie's was at knee-level.

Roger remembered Michele's words on how Martin Messager would dress Marie, if given the chance.

Neckline down to her belly-button, hem halfway up her thighs, no knickers, that's what Michele had said. An exaggeration, but it had to be said that the dress Marie was wearing was on those lines. *What new obsession is this?* Roger wondered as he opened the door wide for her to come in, *she must be dressed like this to please her husband — and then she comes to see me!*

All the same, her breasts were beautiful and her legs beneath the shimmering black-red skirt were a delight. Whether she wore any knickers remained to be seen — if not, that would surely be an obsession too many!

He closed the door and kissed her tenderly and adoringly. She put her hands on his shoulders and closed her eyes. Her hat was in the way — a broad-brimmed straw coolie-hat, dyed to the same colour as her dress. Roger wanted to take it off but was afraid he might damage it.

'Am I beautiful, Roger?' she breathed, her expensive perfume drifting up from between her breasts.

'Beyond words,' he murmured, 'and I adore you.'

Marie eased herself out of his embrace with a smile, off came her hat and she skimmed it across the room.

'Help me out of my dress,' she murmured, turning away to show him the zip at the back. His hands were on her breasts while he kissed the back of her neck, she rubbed her bottom against him. He undid the zip, she lowered the dress and stepped out of it.

She had no bra, but Roger was pleased to see she was wearing knickers. It encouraged him, it gave him reason to believe that she was not dressed for Martin Messager's pleasure. He needed a little encouragement, Roger, after hearing Michele on the topic of Marie's devious marital relations with Messager.

But on second thoughts, could this be a part of those

devious relations? Had she dressed like this to persuade Messager that though other men found her desirable, she was his alone? Only to disprove it by coming to a lover? No, Roger told himself, it is too complicated – if I start to ask questions like that I shall drive myself mad, exactly as Michele warned me. If I love and adore Marie, I must accept her as she is.

On the other hand, there was a tale about a king long ago, it was surely a fable, not a true event – Roger couldn't remember his name. He had a young wife in his harem so beautiful that he wanted other men to see her – then they would envy him and know how important he was to have such a wife.

He told the captain of his guard to hide behind a door in the palace. The beautiful young wife was sent for – the tyrant told her to strip naked for him to admire her. She did what he said, otherwise he might have her head cut off with a sword. But she was no fool and she guessed someone was hiding behind the door.

The outcome was as one might expect. The captain of the guard fell in love with the beautiful naked girl. They found a way of meeting – she let him experience the other delights that the fool of a king thought his alone.

Worse soon followed. The captain was young and strong and the king was middle-aged and weary. A palace revolution removed the king from his throne and his head from his body. The captain of the guard took possession of the kingdom and the young widow.

Has beautiful Marie cast her husband and me for those roles, Roger asked himself, or can Messager be repeating the fable in blind ignorance and pride?

He helped Marie to take off her stockings and her black satin knickers. He took off his own clothes and they lay on his divan facing each other. She was so close to him that the buds of her perfect breasts rubbed against him. Her hand lay on his thighs and caressed him.

'Michele told me you went to see her,' she murmured, 'did she tell you all my poor secrets? Do you hate me now?'

'She gave away no secrets,' he said, with complete disregard for the truth. 'I asked her if she thought you loved me and she said she was certain of it.'

'Michele was right,' said Marie, her fingertips trailing over the stiff part standing out from between Roger's thighs.

The divan was longside to the wall. Roger arranged cushions, which were also pillows when their covers came off, behind her. She was propped on her side by them, her back against the wall. His left arm supported her while his right hand played over her breasts – he felt her fingers clench around his throbbing shaft while she pressed her mouth to his. He slid his tongue into her mouth, to lick her tongue.

When the long kiss ended at last she moved down his body till she could take his hard-swollen part into her mouth, her tongue darting over the unhooded purple head. He could feel her glossy hair against his belly. Then her beautiful body was full-length to his again, their mouths joined, her clasping hand pumped up and down.

'That day I told you I could never have a lover,' she sighed, 'I was wrong – you will always be my lover.'

Roger wasn't at all sure which day she meant – there had been many confusing days with her. But he welcomed her announcement, whether it was reliable or not. He slipped his hand between her thighs and felt the delicious nakedness of her smooth flesh. He sighed as she parted her knees, opening herself to him, showing him her bare mound and long soft lips.

And her little tattoo, red and blue, MM entwined, on the soft flesh of her belly, almost in her groin. Roger stroked it with his fingertips, it fascinated him, this tiny work of art on her pale skin. Not only its existence, but the tangled explanation.

She'd told him her husband had insisted it was put there. But Michele Legarnier had a version which Roger thought more likely to be true. Or half-true. And perhaps Marie told her husband it was his initials, that MM stood for Martin Messager – a sign of his dominion over her body.

But that was a fantasy, a convenient myth, a deception – told to deceive Messager. Roger was more than ever certain it stood for Marie and Michele – he was convinced the two women had been lovers for years. Since Marie was sixteen, that was his guess, since shortly after Messager took her into his home and life. Michele was displaced in his affections by Marie and she compensated by taking Messager's new girl as her own lover – and he never knew he was sharing Marie.

That was Roger's version of the past: Michele and Marie were lovers, even though when he'd made love to Michele, she'd sighed and moaned in orgasm to the thrust of his long, hard shaft. Even though she denied it, and Marie also would surely deny it if he asked her. It was better not to ask. Happiness lay in accepting the version of love Marie offered him.

*He pressed his belly close to hers, her hand guided his stiff shaft in. He clasped the cheeks of her bottom as he pushed into her, her arms were about his neck, her eyes gazed into his.

'*Je t'aime*, Roger,' she whispered, her lips brushing over his cheek, her breath warm and sweet.

Inside his head he was thinking, I believe you do, Marie – but in your own strange way. Ours will be the most bizarre *affaire*, an undeclared *ménage-a-quatre*.

There are four of us involved – you, me, Michele and Messager. After I have loved you to a standstill you will go back to your husband and ask him to forgive you. And he'll throw you on your back on the bed and forgive you that way.

Then you will go and tell Michele – all that Messager did to you and all that I did to you. You will assure her you love me and adore your husband as well – then you and Michele will make love to each other, hands between each other's legs, your soft tongues caressing each other's secret little buds. And the next day you will be here with me and I shall love you until you sob in ecstasy in my arms.

Roger's palms were stroking her satin bottom, pressing her to him while he thrust slowly in and out of her wet *joujou*.

'*Je t'aime*, Marie,' he sighed and he meant it – but he smiled at his own words.

Headline Delta Erotic Survey

In order to provide the kind of books you like to read — and to
qualify for a free erotic novel of the Editor's choice — we
would appreciate it if you would complete the following
survey and send your answers, together with any further
comments, to:

> Headline Book Publishing
> FREEPOST (WD 4984)
> London
> NW1 0YR

1. Are you male or female?
2. Age? Under 20 / 20 to 30 / 30 to 40 / 40 to 50 /
   50 to 60 / 60 to 70 / over
3. At what age did you leave full-time education?
4. Where do you live? (Main geographical area)
5. Are you a regular erotic book buyer / a regular book
   buyer in general / both?
6. How much approximately do you spend a year on erotic
   books / on books in general?
7. How did you come by this book?
7a. If you bought it, did you purchase from:
   a national bookchain / a high street store / a newsagent /
   a motorway station / an airport / a railway station /
   other . . .
8. Do you find erotic books easy / hard to come by?
8a. Do you find Headline Delta erotic books easy / hard
   to come by?
9. Which are the best / worst erotic books you have ever
   read?
9a. Which are the best / worst Headline Delta erotic books
   you have ever read?
10. Within the erotic genre there are many periods,
   subjects and literary styles. Which of the following
   do you prefer:
10a. (period) historical / Victorian / C20th /contemporary /
   future?
10b. (subject) nuns / whores & whorehouses /
   Continental frolics / s&m / vampires / modern realism /
   escapist fantasy / science fiction?

10c. (styles) hardboiled / humorous / hardcore / ironic / romantic / realistic?

10d. Are there any other ingredients that particularly appeal to you?

11. We try to create a cover appearance that is suitable for each title. Do you consider them to be successful?

12. Would you prefer them to be less explicit / more explicit?

13. We would be interested to hear of your other reading habits. What other types of books do you read?

14. Who are your favourite authors?

15. Which newspapers do you read?

16. Which magazines?

17 Do you have any other comments or suggestions to make?

If you would like to receive a free erotic novel of the Editor's choice (available only to UK residents), together with an up-to-date listing of Headline Delta titles, please supply your name and address. Please allow 28 days for delivery.

Name   ....

Address   ....

....

....

A selection of Erotica from Headline

BLUE HEAVENS	Nick Bancroft	£4.99	☐
MAID	Dagmar Brand	£4.99	☐
EROS IN AUTUMN	Anonymous	£4.99	☐
EROTICON THRILLS	Anonymous	£4.99	☐
IN THE GROOVE	Lesley Asquith	£4.99	☐
THE CALL OF THE FLESH	Faye Rossignol	£4.99	☐
SWEET VIBRATIONS	Jeff Charles	£4.99	☐
UNDER THE WHIP	Nick Aymes	£4.99	☐
RETURN TO THE CASTING COUCH	Becky Bell	£4.99	☐
MAIDS IN HEAVEN	Samantha Austen	£4.99	☐
CLOSE UP	Felice Ash	£4.99	☐
TOUCH ME, FEEL ME	Rosanna Challis	£4.99	☐

All Headline books are available at your local bookshop or newsagent, or can be ordered direct from the publisher. Just tick the titles you want and fill in the form below. Prices and availability subject to change without notice.

Headline Book Publishing, Cash Sales Department, Bookpoint, 39 Milton Park, Abingdon, OXON, OX14 4TD, UK. If you have a credit card you may order by telephone – 01235 400400.

Please enclose a cheque or postal order made payable to Bookpoint Ltd to the value of the cover price and allow the following for postage and packing:

UK & BFPO: £1.00 for the first book, 50p for the second book and 30p for each additional book ordered up to a maximum charge of £3.00.

OVERSEAS & EIRE: £2.00 for the first book, £1.00 for the second book and 50p for each additional book.

Name ....

Address ....

....

....

If you would prefer to pay by credit card, please complete:
Please debit my Visa/Access/Diner's Card/American Express (delete as applicable) card no:

Signature .... Expiry Date ....